A DOOR INTO EVERMOOR

A DOOR INTO EVERMOOR

The Unbound Realm
Book 1

KENT WAYNE

King's Entertainment Press LLC

First paperback edition May 2024

Published by Kings Entertainment Press LLC

ISBN 978-1-959476-04-7 (paperback)

www.dirtyscifibuddha.com

Prologue

"You think outside the box."

"You're wise beyond your years."

"You're an old soul."

I've heard these phrases time and again, uttered with knowing looks and sly grins, as if they were amazing consolation prizes for not fitting in. Ironically, I have cookie-cutter parents, a cookie-cutter diploma, and a cookie-cutter acceptance letter from San Francisco State University. People say I'm special because I've written a few stories (which I never finished, surprise surprise), I have a big vocabulary, and I occasionally make a profound observation.

To top it all off, my name is Jon Dough. Yep—like what they call an unidentified body.

I thought I was destined to toil in an office, doomed to monotony and enslaved by routine. I thought I would fade with the passing of years, reminiscing wistfully about what might have been.

But then I entered a parallel dimension, complete with dragons, dog-warriors, and evil sorcerers. Crazy, right? A nameless kid from San Francisco, whisked away into an epic fantasy world. One day I'm sitting in English 101, the next day I'm exploring an arcane empire.

I met strange and wondrous people and creatures. Rennarean Arteris, Arganti Knifelock, the Watchers of Erendor...I could go on, but you get the point.

It all started when I opened a door.
A door into Evermoor.

1

I rode a surge of purpose when the pandemic began, but bit by bit, things went back to normal. Peoples' attitudes, specifically. *Gotta keep grinding. Why, you ask? No one knows, but 'round and 'round it goes.*

During my first semester at SFSU, the mother of all questions reared its ugly-ass head:

What's it all *for?*

I never found meaning in pop culture-fads—in Kylie's tweets or the hottest backside trending on Insta. I like older stuff, but not just because it's off-beat or vintage. When I watch weird movies from decades past, I feel a sense of possibility and budding potential; their courage to be strange calls to my heart.

Anachronisms are my thing, which makes me one of them, I guess.

I know, I know—I'm a cliché. The crotchety old guy cursing at the new-fangled youngsters. (And yes—being nineteen, I know I'm technically a teenager.)

As a first-world kid from a well-off family, I'm painfully aware that I've been dealt a good hand. I'm right on track for a college degree, a job with benefits, and a 401k. But I can't shake the feeling that I'm destined for something more. Something different and strange, drawn from the stuff of dreams and fantasy.

I know happiness is subjective (miserable rich folks versus off-the-grid hermits who love their life) but it doesn't change the fact that I loathe the idea of rotting in an office, raising 2.5 kids, and assimilating into a world of corporate doublespeak. I suspect a lot of people feel the same way as me; when I talk about ditching the 9-5, I'm usually met with hearty agreement. *Yes—YES! Chained to a desk for forty hours a week? Kill me now!* (it's more by the way, if you add in commutes, a boss who measures your worth by how late you stay, and the fact that each day is actually 8-5, once you account for the unpaid lunch).

But when I try and elaborate, I earn a rueful chuckle or a blank stare. Half the time, I elicit some form of vague irritation. *Give it a rest, will you? I wasn't being serious.* Often accompanied by a helping of side-eye.

I feel like an alien, doomed to live in a human body. And I say as much to anyone who will listen. Every so often, their eyes widen with fear and surprise, and I know I've spoken to their truest selves.

————

I leave Arts and Humanities, taking the same route I always take. Cut through the quad, past the food carts, and into the street where I've parallel parked.

I-280 is a couple blocks up. A half hour later, I pull into the lot of an Armed Forces Recruiting Center. I head inside, poke through a stand of glossy brochures, then pay a visit to recruiters from Army, Air Force, and Navy. (The Marine Corps office is dark and unoccupied.)

None of them resonate. Despite their promises of lusty groupies and the chance to become a *Call of Duty* badass, I remain unmoved. I can instinctively sense the pointless ennui; the meat-grinder system the recruiters endured, all so they could convince their younger selves (me, in this instance) to embark on a distorted version of the hero's journey.

After the last one hands me their card, I step into the main hall-way. As I turn to leave, a casual voice stops me in my tracks.

"Hey."

I turn around. Standing before me is the sharpest-dressed man I've ever seen. Blue pants, khaki short-sleeve, and a stack of ribbons that starts at his left breast pocket and nearly touches his meaty shoulder. His plastic nametag (it'd be chintzy on anything other than a Marine uniform) reads ATRIYA.

"Gunnery Sergeant Chris Atriya." He walks up. We shake hands. "Looking to join?"

I study him carefully, thrown by his attitude. He's interested in me—me as a person, not as a number.

"Thinking about it."

"Don't." A rueful grin. "You're not cut out for this."

"*That's* your pitch?" I ask incredulously.

"Usually, we say it in a *bet-you're-not-tough-enough* kind of way, but I'm over all that." He taps the ribbons atop his chest. "I've lived some dog years, if you couldn't already tell by my stack of legos. So believe me when I say this isn't for you."

My gut twists, my heart cracks. Not because I want to shoot or fly or live on a ship—I was hoping for a glimmer of higher purpose. An escape from the tedium that stretches before me.

"C'mere." He opens the door into a darkened recruiting office. The lights click on, and he steps behind a three-panel screen. "Gimme a sec." Minutes later, he steps out in a sweatshirt and jeans. With his low-faded hair, he could easily pass as a beefy college student.

He offers his hand (again). I shake it.

"Chris Atriya," he says, as if he hasn't already said it.

"Jon Dough. Good to meet you."

He angles behind a desk and takes a seat, gesturing for me to do the same. As I lower into the chair, he leans back and steeples his fingers.

"I've worked in this office for over a year. I haven't recruited a single prospect."

"What?" My brow wrinkles in confusion.

"Not a single one," he affirms. "My boss lets me do whatever I want. Says I've got an 'impressive record.' " He makes quote marks with his fingers. "Fine by me. Chest-thumping, war-cries...it gets real old, real fast. And that's the stuff that recruiters gotta peddle."

"So if you were anyone else—"

"They'd work my ass off." He laughs. "Make no mistake—the Corps will get its pound of flesh. I'm an anomaly: the dirty secret of the whole 'warrior' thing." His gaze turns distant. "It's all good. Soon enough, I'll be right back at it. Not here, though—not in recruiting." His eyes refocus.

"Uh, not to be rude, but why are we talking if you're not trying to recr—"

"Bear with me." He regards me again, and I notice that his pupils are a strange shade of gray. Rich and deep, but only if you look directly into them. "What would you think if you were destined for greatness? What if I said it was your natural state?"

I scoff without meaning to. "I'd say you were crazy. I go to school, write half-finished stories, and ruminate deeply on meaningless philosophy."

"I see things, Jon. Hidden things." A flash of light glints off his eyes. "And I can see that everything you've done—every thought you've had and dream you've pondered—has set you up for massive change."

I'm taken by a shiver, but I cover it up with a nervous chuckle. "You friends with Doctor Strange or something? Let me know how to find that monastery; it looks pretty dope. Look, Sergeant—"

"Chris."

"Chris. I think you've confused me with somebody else." (Crap —don't forget he's a gun-toting war-guy. Better apologize before he gets angry.) "And sorry about the Doctor Strange remark, I didn't mean to—"

He waves dismissively. "If we can't take a joke, we're truly lost." He leans forward, pinning me down with those strange gray eyes. "I have an offer for you. If you want to sign it, feel free to do so. If not, we'll go our separate ways and leave it at that."

He opens a drawer, withdraws a single sheet of paper, and lays it carefully onto the desk. The front is marked by two bold words:

SOMETHING DIFFERENT.

Below the words are a pair of signature lines.

"What do you say?" He places a pen in front of my hand.

I pick up the sheet and flip it over, making sure there's nothing written on the back. "Is this a joke?"

He shakes his head. "It's everything you've been asking for."

"What?" I can't keep the ridicule out of my voice. "What are you talking abo—"

"Doesn't matter." I lay the page down. He taps it twice with his right index finger. "Sign it or don't. Sorry, but you don't get details —that's where people trip themselves up. They try and wait for all the info so they can stay inside their personal comfort zones. Which is pretty ironic, because they're setting themselves up for long-term discomfort."

"That's dickish," I argue. "You're withholding information using a philosophical sleight of—"

"I don't get details either. And trust me: even if I did, you wouldn't want to know—they'd turn everything you see into a dusty shadow."

"I don't get it." (This guy is *nuts.*) "You've seen combat, right?"

"More than I care for."

I open my mouth, but nothing comes out. I'm trying to think of a polite way to recommend psychiatric help.

He sees right through it. "Don't worry—I'm stable." Now he's amused. "The question is: are you? You'll graduate college and get a job, but have you given any thought to what comes next? Do you think you'll live a fulfilling life?"

My brain grinds to an absolute halt. You ever listen to someone, really listen, and your *entire being* responds to their words? He's not addressing my surface persona, trained to navigate societal norms. He's engaging with something a hell of a lot deeper—something beyond words or language. It doesn't have a name. I don't think it wants one.

Nevertheless, it needs to be heard.

I pick up the pen. My mind is a storm of conflicting emotions. My hand, however, is steady and sure.

I sign the paper.

He plucks the pen from my frozen fingers, then scrawls his name on the line next to mine.

"That was easy, huh?" He slaps the desk and gets to his feet. "Take it easy, Jon." He shrugs into a jacket.

I blurt, "Wait, that's it? I just signed a two-word contract." The logical part of me—the one that worries about GPAs, scholarships, and getting enough hours as a part-time dog walker—has taken back over.

"You took a step toward what you wanted. Most of the time, that's all you can do. Doesn't matter if it makes any sense, because a deeper part of you knows the angles—it sees beyond the visible connections." He puts his hands in his pockets and gives me an exasperated look. "Come on, you think you'd be happy with the 9-5? Living for the weekend, an extended vacation once a year, fretting and fussing over your white-picket life? There's more to you, Jon. You know it in your heart. You know it in your soul."

Chills. Again. "What next?" I manage.

"For you?" He holds the door open for me. "Things will get weird, but that's not a bad thing. Trust me, working at a job would have driven you insane."

"*Okaaay...*" I'm not quite sure of how to respond. But still, I want to know more. "Wanna grab lunch? I'm caught up on school, so—"

"Nah. I got me a date," he pauses and smiles, "who would kick my ass if I stood her up."

"She sounds pretty gnarly." I walk through the door. He locks up behind me.

"You have no idea." We stroll out the entrance and into the lot. "We share the same name: 'Chris.' She spells it with a 'y' instead of an 'i.' "

Chrys. I try it out in my mind. "Huh. It's easier to think of her as a woman, now that you told me that."

"Yep." We head for his car, which is parked next to mine. "When I was younger, it would have been weird if a woman was named Chrys, 'y' or not. Funny how things change, huh?"

I feel obliged to agree. "Yeah. Funny."

I get in my car and drive off the lot. A second later, it starts to pour—fat, heavy drops that clack against the glass. Typically, the rain would add drear onto my normal state of blah.

But this time, for some reason, I don't mind.

I don't mind at all.

2

Dad comes from generic anglo. Mom hails from Korean immigrants. (My mother's genes are definitely stronger—I could easily pass for a full-blooded Asian.) A month after my eighth birthday, they filed for divorce. Two years later, Mom re-married to a coder named Gary. Gary, like my biological dad, is generic anglo.

If I sound kind of blah, I apologize. I'm kind of blah about everything, I guess.

Life was supposed to be a thrilling adventure, filled with meaning and crystalline purpose. But instead of adventure, I got a confusing slog where you "win" by piecing together an eventual retirement. Time freedom after seventy-odd years of toil and sacrifice? No thanks.

Am I lucky I think this way? I'm not sure—my peers seem genuinely psyched about the white-picket life.

I couldn't care less.

Still, I suppose I should be grateful for my parents' support. They pay for tuition, my one-bed apartment, and food for my dog: Gribbles.

Mom's Americanized, but some old-school Korean came to the fore when I told her I wanted an elderly rescue. She wanted a doodle or a Frenchie—something fashionable. At the time, I couldn't have explained why I insisted on Gribbles, but now I recognize it as the same urge that made me sign that contract.

SOMETHING DIFFERENT.

Gribbles isn't fashionable, not by any stretch. His right eye is blind and milky, his left ear is ragged and torn. If I had to guess, I'd say he's a ridgeback-daschund mix. His body is wide and squat—not as ungainly as a pure-bred daschund's, but not as graceful as a true ridgeback's. He likes to snooze on my lap (sometimes my nose or my mouth), and he's hopelessly addicted to food and toys (big surprise, I know). When he scarfs down kibble, it sounds like he's saying *gribble gribble gribble,* hence his name.

Speak of the devil. As I open the door, Gribbles waddles up, tail wagging.

"Hey goofus." I hunker down and scratch his sides. "Miss me?"

His wagging intensifies—his back paws lift off the floor, thumping the ground in alternating time.

"Yeah." I scratch his ears, chuckling at his enthusiasm. "Yeah, you did."

Gribbles is the best thing that ever happened to me. Sure, I have family and friends, but my dog loves me *unconditionally.* And to experience unconditional love in a conditional world...well, it gives me hope for something greater. Something greater than money and likes and Twitter verification badges.

"Want a treat?"

Predictably, the 'T-word' flips a switch in his brain—he circles in place with manic excitement.

"Easy, nerd. Same menu, different day."

I walk in the kitchen, open the fridge, and grab some Nommie McGobberYoms out from a ziploc. These are cookies made by my neighborhood pet store: ZigZag Zoomies. (if you're unfamiliar with all things Dog, "zoomies" is slang for Frenetic Random Activity Periods, or when a dog sprints back and forth for no apparent reason). ZigZag's products rock every label in the history of food:

free trade, organic, wild caught...I'm a true San Franciscan, and it shows in my groceries.

None of that matters—not to me, anyway. During sophomore year, I became briefly obsessed with names and titles. But as the world turned and the years passed, I cared increasingly less about pigeonhole labels, and even less for the tribes they spawned. Tribes seem to make everything worse—join up with one so you can fight with another.

When the virus hit, I fostered the hope that people would come together (they did, for a bit) but people are people—soon enough, we grew back into our collective indifference. I guess I'm a symptom of it. I am in no way interested in stupid square hats or fancy diplomas. I don't get psyched about paid time off or a sweet corner office. It all feels like a cheap facade—an excuse to rejoice in empty status symbols.

Gribbles is the only one I know who seems truly content; he honestly enjoys his fur-bound life. Sometimes I wonder—is he wise or ignorant? If I could limit my perception to his little doggy brain, would I choose to do so, if it meant being happy?

He finishes eating, then runs back over and paws my knee, brimming with *please-gimme-eatos* urgency *(eatos* is dog-speak for food, in my mind).

Back to the kitchen. This time, I pull out a rawhide from a plastic jar, earning a loud, tortured whine. I roll my eyes in mock-annoyance.

"Tell me how you really feel."

I hand it over and he heads for the balcony, poking through the pet-gate attachment I fitted to the sliding glass door. (That's how I know if he really likes his treat—if he goes outside to eat it by himself.) Gotta say, one of the greatest joys in life is giving your dog a—

I freeze in place. My mouth drops open.

The open pet-gate, instead of displaying foggy San Francisco, flashes with a man's blindfolded face: thin, tight-lipped, and grim. Glowing runes shine from his blindfold, alternating between searing violet, midnight blue, and a black so dark it has a light of its own.

As the view pans down, I glimpse a curved knife in his armored hand. In the stormy backdrop, there's a craggy fortress atop a mesa.

And then he's gone.

————

I run to the pet-gate, my face slack with disbelief. This little plastic square is a magic portal into another world. I can't believe—

Wait. I close my eyes, hands out as if to say *hold on, calm down.*

It wasn't real.

Then: *You're not well. See a doctor.*

I'm struck by dread as I consider my fate. Pitying looks. Prescription meds.

Judgment.

No. I clench my jaw. *I'm not crazy.*

I poke my head through to the outside balcony. Gribbles—splayed on his belly, chewing his rawhide with singular tenacity—warns me off with a trailing growl: *Leeme 'lone. Dis bone is MINE.*

Relief crashes through me. No chasms, knives, or blindfolded Night Elves. The world is normal and sane, as it should be. Gribbles on the balcony, eating his treat. People down below, doing whatever.

The world is normal and sane.

As it should be.

3

Over the next few weeks, I see a lot more of Dragon World. That's my name for it, because all the scenes are from a fantasy realm. (And in case you're wondering, yes—there are dragons in Dragon World.)

Any door can serve as a portal. Car door, bathroom door, double door, revolving door... (those are the worst. They alternate between Normal World and Dragon World in epileptic flashes). It's always short and always vivid—like a fleeting trailer for an upcoming blockbuster. But unlike a preview for the latest *Avengers,* Dragon World isn't exciting or awesome; it's downright scary. Magic is cool when you see it in a movie or read about it in a book, not when it's making you question your sanity.

Initially, all I see are armored soldiers. They walk around in full-body plate—jagged and austere, impossibly white. A couple days in, I see them fighting with forest people who dress like Aragorn.

After a week, I start catching glimpses of the guy with the blindfold. He wears pitch-black armor, made from lightweight sections defined by elegant gold tracery. Stormtroopers and Foresters fight like regular people, but Blindfold fights like a Marvel superhero. He can twist and flip, kick and spin, and throw combos that take out multiple opponents.

He also knows magic. Every so often, he'll zap his attackers with colored energy. Sometimes it's smooth, sometimes it's ragged, but it's always surrounded by glowing runes. He's a cross between Daredevil, Batman, and a 50th-level wizard.

That's just the tip of the fantasy-world iceberg.

I see pirates sailing turbulent seas, raiding ships or fleeing serpents. I see dragons breathing lightning at gargoyle hordes, dotting the sky with their smoking corpses. I see palace interiors filled with lords and warriors.

Three weeks in, I start seeing peasants who line up for bureaucrats: small, measly men who write stuff down in hidebound notebooks. Stormtrooper bodyguards dawdle behind them, fiddling with weapons or picking at their armor.

Occasionally, a peasant won't have enough to pay their tribute. The bureaucrat-recorder will throw a fit while the unfortunate commoner hangs their head. After a lengthy scolding, the recorder signals for the nearest Pain Wizard. (I'm pretty sure they're called something else, but Dragon World doesn't come with captions or audio.) Pain Wizards dress in ebony robes. Some of it's cloth, but the rest is an ever-shifting mass of pitch-black smoke. The only visible skin is their jaws and noses. The rest is eclipsed by a shadowy hood.

The Wizard will twist and clutch the air, causing black veins to erupt across the peasant. It looks straight-up torturous—whoever's getting punished will scream and howl. Everyone else just stands and stares.

At first I'm shaken by their seeming indifference, but later I realize that on-the-spot punishment is seen as a blessing. The real torture happens out of sight. If the peasant is shackled and taken away, the entire community begs and pleads.

I see this every time I open a door. Wizards. Soldiers. Creatures.

It's not getting better. I think I'm losing it.

———

Atriya. That's where it started. I'm gonna track him down and figure this out. If necessary, I will threaten his life. I do not care if he's a gun-toting war guy.

I slide in my car (as I open the door, I glimpse a grimy Forester riding a silvery lizard) and strap into my seat. Hop on 280, take the exit, and park in the lot of the Armed Forces Recruiting Center. I get out (this time I remember to close my eyes) and rush inside.

"Atriya!" I forget to close my eyes as I yank on the door. I see a line of monks hiking a mesa, topped by a fifty-foot man made entirely of stone. He's sitting on the summit sound asleep, chin propped onto a bent-wristed hand.

"WHERE'S ATRIYA?"

"Whoa." One of the Marines stands up from his desk. "Calm down. He doesn't work here. Not anymore."

"What? But he was...he was just...where is he?" I'm abruptly aware of my sweat-soaked hair, my beet-red cheeks and my coffee-stained shirt.

The Marine gives me a hard stare. A *keep-your-hands-where-I-can-see-them* stare. "Gone. Retired."

"What?" I'm repeating myself, I know, but I'm too disoriented to care or apologize.

"Come in," he says gruffly.

As I step in the office, the other Marines regard me warily. Can't blame them—it's been a couple of days since I last showered. Haven't changed clothes in at least three.

"You got a place to stay?" The Marine crosses his brawny arms.

"Uh...yeah." I run a hand through my hair, willing my heart to slow the hell down. "Yeah. An apartment."

"Hungry?"

"No." I look sideways, suddenly ashamed by my ragtag appearance. "I have plenty of food. Money, too."

"You sure?" His tone isn't gentle, but there's genuine concern. "If you need some help, I can make a call."

"No, I'm fine." I shake my head. "Atriya used to work here, right?"

"Yeah." He gives me a suspicious once-over. *Why do you care?*

"I, uh...we're friends."

His eyes grow a notch more suspicious—*he's pulling a scam he wants attention he's lost his mind*—then he relaxes and gives a non-committal shrug. *He's a skinny teenager. High-strung, not crazy.*

"He didn't like it here, but he always did whatever he was told. Name's Hardwick. Gunny Hardwick." He extends a hand.

I reach out and shake it. "Jon. He told me his boss left him alone. Because he'd done some hard time."

"He told you that, huh?" Hardwick chuckles, loosening up. "Yeah, when I say he 'did whatever he was told,' I mean he stayed home or went to the gym. The guy earned it." He shakes his head in quiet respect.

"What do you mean?"

"C'mere." Hardwick beckons me into a walled-off room. He clicks on the lights, sits behind the one and only desk, and opens a knee-high cabinet. Out comes a wooden box, roughly the size of a standard laptop.

"This is a shadow box."

Its contents are shielded by a glass display cover. Inside, mounted on a sleek pad of black velvet, are rows upon rows of ribbons and medals.

"We made it for him." As Hardwick studies it, I can tell that a big part of him has gone somewhere else. There's deep emotion behind his eyes—a bit of sadness and a whole lot of stuff I can only guess at.

"Here." He slides it toward me.

I stare at the box, captivated by its sense of weight and history. "All these ribbons..." I murmur.

"He left it behind. He was supposed to take it." A rueful smile.

My breath catches. Hardwick's talking, but I'm not listening. Under the ribbons, centered beneath a Marine emblem, is a small black plate with six gold words.

THERE ARE OTHER WORLDS THAN THESE.

"What...what..." I can't speak. I'm blown away.

"Huh?" Hardwick follows my gaze, then relaxes in his seat. "Oh. Weird, right? Most guys want a unit motto. Not Atriya. That quote was all he insisted on. Who am I to judge?" He shrugs. "You don't say no to Chris Atriya."

THERE ARE OTHER WORLDS THAN THESE.

With a conscious effort, I look away from the box. "Do you have his number?"

"Nope. He got a new one after he left. He wanted to cut all ties; didn't even want a damn retirement ceremony. I got him to compromise—on his last day, we took him out for beer and pizza, but he made it crystal clear that he didn't want to discuss his service. All he wanted was to hang out and chat. Said he was gonna live in peace and pursue his hobbies. Guitar, jiu-jitsu, carpentry...it was always something new. Before he left, he was learning how to dance. Can you believe that? Dancing." Hardwick chuckles. "He wanted to dance like Techno Viking."

I force a laugh, trying to hide my unease. "Sounds about right. I mean, I didn't—"

"How'd you guys meet?"

"It was a couple weeks ago. I walked in and—"

"A couple weeks? He hasn't been here in over a year."

———

My mouth opens and closes, trying to form words. *A year? A YEAR?*

"Something wrong?"

"Uh, no." I rub my neck and cough awkwardly. "I meant to say a couple years ago. Years, not weeks."

"Right." The atmosphere shifts—our weird bonding moment has come and gone. He stands up and clears his throat. "If there's anything else..."

"Nope. Thanks for your time."

I make my body stand and turn. I force my feet to start walking. I close my eyes as I open the door.

THERE ARE OTHER WORLDS THAN THESE.

I break into a trot as I leave the office.

THERE ARE OTHER WORLDS THAN THESE.

I get in the car and start the engine.

THERE ARE OTHER WORLDS THAN THESE.

I drive off the lot and onto the road.

THERE ARE OTHER WORLDS THAN THESE.

I have to pull over because of the visions. It's not just the doors... Now it's the windows.

4

The glass erupts with fantastic images. Elves. Sorcerers. Lizard-people.

I park at the curb and take off running. Up ahead, a homeless Black man kneels on the grass, scribbling on newspaper with a worn-down Sharpie. As I sprint toward him the paper shifts, allowing me to see what he's written in the margins:

THERE ARE OTHER WORLDS THAN THESE.

I hear myself screaming, feel myself running. I make it a dozen yards before I trip and fall, glimpsing a whirl of trees and sky. Cold water invades my ears, turning everything blurry before the world goes dark.

————

"Easy, buddy."

A dreadlocked head looms above me, silhouetted by the glare of the afternoon sun.

"What...what happened?" I sit up slowly. First on my elbows, then on my hands.

"You fell in the water. Hit your head." The Black man nods at a pond behind me. "Had to pull you out so you didn't drown."

I take a moment to study my surroundings. Chirping birds, towering trees...

"Golden Gate Park. I'm in Golden Gate Park."

"That you are." My transient savior gives me a smile.

I rise to my feet, brushing sediment off my waterlogged sleeves. "Sorry…I didn't mean to cause you any trouble."

"No trouble," he assures. "Name's Al."

"Jon." I duck my head, chagrined. "This isn't how I usually—"

Al laughs, loud and hearty. "No worries. Everyone thinks I'm Looney Tunes crazy." He waves dismissively. "I get it."

Curiosity bubbles to the fore. "The newspaper. You wrote—"

" 'There are other worlds than these?' " Al grins. "Got it from a book. Cool quote, huh?"

"I've seen it before." A circuit trips inside my brain; before I can stop myself, I blurt, "I've never talked with a homeless person. I'm not really sure of what I shou—"

He holds up a hand, cutting me off. "We all have a home. I—like most of my wanderer brethren—am simply taking a leave of absence." He gives me a once-over. "Speaking of homes, where's yours? You look a little ragged, but you're no wanderer. Not yet, anyway."

"I live over by San Francisco State." My brow furrows. "What do you mean by 'not yet?' "

He flashes a smile. "You'll find out. Take it from me: Alijyar SyCajister."

Everything blurs. By the shift in the backdrop, I can tell I've experienced missing time.

"What did you say?" I clutch my head, fighting off vertigo. Alijyar. A-LEE-jee-are. I know that name. (why do I know it?)

"I said you'll find your way home, sure as my name's Al Smith." His smile gives way to mild concern. "You okay?"

"I'm fine." I say it roughly; I want to change the subject.

"You said you live by the college, right?"

My brusqueness turns to muted embarrassment. "Yeah, but I left my car at the edge of the park, and I need to get it before I head home. I'm not trying to hide where I live, it's just…" (this is true—I don't know why, but I would invite this guy over without hesitation) "I think I'm sick. It's why I had to pull over and...and..."

Whoa—head rush. I press a hand against my temple.

"Take a little break?" That knowing smile. "I understand. The real world's tough. Hell, the 'real world' isn't even real, but if you say that outside of physics or philosophy, people think you've lost your mind. Who's crazy though, when you stop and think about it?" He cackles gleefully. "Come on—let's go find your car." He starts heading west.

I fall in beside him. "What did you do, Al? Before you wrote quotes on discarded newspaper."

Al launches into a long, complicated tale. Pre-virus, he worked with techies, designing an app that could quantify and maximize someone's fulfillment. After gaining a rough idea of their goals and priorities, it helped them organize and schedule their day.

"Sounds awesome. Where can I get it?"

Al sighs. "You can't. We had to abandon it. When the virus hit, our investors bailed. No one cares about spiritual blight, not when they're worried about money or health."

"Your app is important," I argue. "A lot of people hate their life." We cross the street and head down the sidewalk.

A grin and a shrug. "I thought I could peddle fulfillment like it was food or medicine, but that's not how it works. When someone's ready, they'll find a way to level up. Whether it's through an app or a book or even a song, it doesn't matter—everyone gets their heart's desire."

"That's insane," I scoff. " 'Everyone gets their heart's desire?' So we choose injustice? We choose a life of horror and failure? I can't accept that. I won't."

He nods knowingly. "That would be ridiculous, wouldn't it? Since too many people get less than they deserve, and too many people get far too much. But it's only ridiculous if our fleshy bodies define our existence—if we live a single life and that's it."

"What? How does that—"

"Or maybe it's random, like you're implying. Maybe we're born into arbitrary circumstances. The thing is, a universe with any true randomness is unconscionably cruel, because it will sometimes reward atrocity and evil." He lifts a hand, directing my attention further up the street. "That badly parked automobile wouldn't happen to be yours, would it?"

My Hyundai Accent is right where I left it. I'm pleased and surprised. In San Francisco, if you leave your bike out for longer than fifteen minutes, a street entrepreneur will strip it to the frame. Cars are trickier, but still—I'm glad it wasn't stolen, especially since I left the keys in the ignition.

I turn back to Al, determined to stand my philosophical ground. "So you're saying we reincarnate? And that we choose our next life?"

"What do you think?" He looks me in the eye. "Do you believe in a world where you're given a choice? Or are you simply a cog in a random machine, at the mercy of forces that would just as soon kill you as see you succeed?"

"There are certain things you can't control. Sorry Al, but that's just how it is." I shake my head, sealing the argument. "Thanks for the help but I gotta go—gotta feed the dog." I dig in my wallet and hand him some bills. "Here. I'll swing by later and bring you a meal."

As he pockets the money, he gives me the kindest smile I've ever seen. It should creep me out (I mean I barely know the guy) but it surprisingly has the opposite effect: warmth and surety flood my brain.

"When times get tough, remember this: you may lose your way, but you're never off the path."

"Uh...thanks," I mutter. "Take care." I open the door (remembering to close my eyes) and slide into my car.

He taps the roof with the flat of his palm. "There are other worlds than these, Jon." I pick up speed, watching him shrink in the rearview mirror.

"There are other worlds than these!" He spins around, arms out, laughing aloud at the cloud-dotted sky.

Despite my reservations, a gut-deep part of me is right there with him, cheering up at the gray-smeared blue. I'm taken by a rush of absolute certainty—a tangible sense of adventure and passion. For a brief moment I try and deny it, but I know in my heart that Alijyar's right: there are other worlds than these.

I'd bet my life on it.

———

During the ride, the visions start up. Unlike before, I find them comforting.

I'm drenched in views of lush blue forest, speckled with clumps of fairy-tale fauna. Then it's snakelike creatures with glittering fins, weaving through the waves of a twilit ocean. Stone giants crossing a dry lakebed, rife with a web of dusty cracks. Elves and pixies *(Elves —like in the movies!)* relaxing inside a sylvan kingdom. An aerial metropolis, jutting from the side of a cloud-ringed cliff.

I see countless oddities, wonders and marvels. Some I have words for, others I don't.

A nameless part of me is calling out, yearning to connect with this deluge of novelty.

———

I head for the bathroom, peeling off clothes and letting them puddle behind me. When I step in the shower, scenery envelops the frosted glass walls, engulfing my soul in magic and dream.

I was never doomed to a sterile office. That was a lie, a fleeting nightmare. As Dragon World blooms across the panes, I realize there is more to life than I ever imagined.

I turn the faucet, watching images appear in the falling water. They drip and stream off the crown of my head, brim and spill from my cupped fingers. Melodic song swirls up my spine, igniting my cells and flooding my brain. Creation and movement blending together, stretching every iota of my swollen perception.

Dragons. Elves. Monsters. Spirits.

It all flows through my baptized hands.

———

I'm dry and dressed, driving my car through a slashing downpour. I don't remember how I got here. My mind feels hazy...like it's stuffed with gauze or heavy cotton. That isn't the case with my hands or my feet—they move on their own, steering and braking without my guidance.

Strangely enough, I'm not afraid.

Rain pelts down, coating the glass in Dragon World visuals. As I lower the windows and let it in, Gribbles spins in the passenger seat, barking and whining with manic intensity.

We come to a stop at Lafayette Park: a grassy slope capped by a circle of trees.

I have to go up there. I can't say why.

———

Gribbles follows me up the hill, yipping and barking at the top of his lungs. Thanks to the rain, I'm blitzed by an ocean of fantastic sights.

Dragon World.

That name was created by my surface mind, reflexively trying to contain and categorize. Now it's different—I'm deep in the grip of my entire being, free and trapped at the same time.

There are other worlds than these.

Lightning rips across the sky. For a blazing instant, I see the trees as they truly are; as giant knights made of stone, hands stacked on downturned swords. One of them, however, remains a tree—the one in the center of this ancient assemblage.

I stride toward it without intending to.

The bark on the tree begins to move, writhing and squirming like a nest of snakes. My belly ripples with jittery nerves.

Is something coming out?

Then it transforms into an ornate door, replacing my fear with knowing resolve.

No—nothing's coming out. I'm going in.

I approach the portal, drawn by the weight of its mythical promise. A false part of me wants to flee, but it's washed away in the slashing rain.

Not Dragon World, I realize. *That's not what it's called.*

I open the door.

And I walk into Evermoor.

5

"Down!"

Someone shoves me, sending me tumbling across the grass. At the same time, a blade slices past, tickling my scalp with a flare of wind.

"Move!" The guy who shoved me (from my upside-down perspective, I glimpse a flowing green cloak and a leathery vest) parries a slash and counters a thrust. He throws a wheel-kick, misses, then uses his momentum to power into an aerial twist, scoring several cuts on his second attacker.

His opponents (they're wearing blindfolds with glowing runes, just like Blindfold Guy) turn and flee. Green Cloak Guy lands in a crouch, runs a cloth across his sword, then slides it neatly into a scabbard.

"Name?" He walks over and extends a hand. I grab hold and pull myself up.

"Jon." I brush twigs and grass off my clothes. If I had to guess, I'd say we're about the same age. He pulls his hood back, confirming my suspicions: early twenties, Middle Eastern (I think). If not for his worn eyes and haggard expression, he would easily be handsome.

"You hail from afar. Where?"

"Uh..." I look around and it suddenly hits me:

I'm not in San Francisco.

"Is this Dragon World?" I whisper.

Before I can register he's drawn a knife, he's got one pressed against my throat. "Answer me." He grabs the back of my head with his other hand, making sure I can't escape. "Where are you from?"

"Earth. Bay Area." With each syllable, the blade cuts a little deeper into my neck.

He stares hard, then abruptly lets go. I stumble back and dab my throat, gaping at my bloody fingers.

"You're no threat. That much is clear." He flicks his knife into a chest-sheath. There are five others like it in a diagonal line, going from his right shoulder to his left hip. "May light find you in dark places." He brushes past me and starts walking.

"Wait!" I hurry up beside him. "Where are we?"

"Two faires east of Jynewind Township." Without slowing, he gives me a once-over. "I've never heard of 'Earth.' Or 'Bay Area,' for that matter."

"It's...it's..."

I'm in another dimension. My mouth drops open.

"It's what?" His expression darkens. "Hasten your tongue."

"It's a different world."

He stops and squares up with me. I'm acutely aware of the distant birds, chirping faintly in the wooded backdrop.

Finally, he says, "Another plane?"

"Uh...yeah. I think."

He puts his hands on his hips and bows his head. "That would explain why you appeared out of nowhere, along with your odd clothes and strange speech. 'The Traveler will hail from an adjacent cosm. He will depart and return before he reaches the Unbound Realm.' "

"What are you talking about?"

"No. It cannot be." He regards me with utter disbelief. "What do you wield? Do you know arcanix? Primal magic? Velic sorcery?"

I raise my palms in a *slow-the-hell-down* gesture. "Velvet what? Arctic *who?* The only things I've wielded are forks and butter knives, unless we're talking about World of Warcraft, where I traded Thunderfury for a—"

"Have a care." He stalks forward, leveling a finger. "I am not in the mood for jests or riddles."

I lurch back, raising my hands a couple inches higher. "Whoa, dude—*whoa!* I'm telling you the truth!"

He stops a foot away, raking my face with a wire-tight gaze. I try not to shrink.

It seems to suffice. He backs off and adopts a thinking man's posture—left arm across his ribs, left hand cupping his right elbow while staircasing his right hand's fingers over his mouth.

"In the *Turning of Evermoor,* it is written that an extraplanar migrant—the Prophesied Traveler—will vanquish Lyderea, reach the Unbound Realm, and set things a-right. But it can't be you. You cannot fight, you cannot cast, you just—" He looks me up and down, as if he can't believe I even exist. "You are not the one described in the tome."

"Wait—Evermoor? What's that?" My memory stirs; I've forgotten something important.

"Evermoor." He spreads his arms. "What we call this gods-cursed world."

My brain affirms it—like a key clicking into a well-oiled lock. *Evermoor.* The name that arose when I entered the portal.

"So a prophecy predicted I would come to your world? What am I supposed to—"

He resumes walking. "Clearly, it is referring to another."

"Hey!" I follow in his steps. "How do you know I'm not the Traveler? What if I reach the Unbound Realm?"

He pivots on his heel and storms toward me. "Countless heroes have tried and failed! High Taire Duelists, Fair Folk Bladeshadow, wizards and sorcerers of every lineage! And *you—"* he jabs a finger into my sternum, *"are not them!"*

"You don't know that," I hiss, smacking his hand away from my chest. "You have no idea who I am. You have no idea what I'm capable of."

He crosses his arms. "Who are you, then? And what are you capable of?"

"I...I..." My expression falters.

I'm Jon Dough. A basic college kid who writes unfinished stories. I have a part-time job and a stable future.

That's it. That's me.

But what about the visions? All the D&D stuff I dismissed as imaginary...it's real. It's right here in front of me. Am I here by design? Or is all this random?

He interrupts my reverie with, "You're shaken. While you recover, you may journey with me."

"I...okay." I don't know what to say. Up is down and black is white. I'm just along for the dimension-hopping ride.

"What's your name?" I ask as we start down the road.

"Ren of the Barrens. Ren will do."

I feel an insistent nagging at the edges of my brain. I've forgotten something else...what could it be?

Then it hits me.

"Gribbles!" I look wildly around. *"Where's Gribbles?"*

Ren halts, clearly irritated. "I know of no one named 'Gribbles.' "

"My dog!" I rub my temples, at a complete loss as to what to do. "He came here with me!"

"Your dog?" Ren laughs, incredulous. "How is your *dog* a matter of concern?"

I grab his shoulders in sheer desperation. To his credit, he doesn't snap my arm, break my face, or whatever else he's been trained to do. *"He's my best friend! We have to find him!"*

"Jon." He delicately removes my hands from his shoulders. "We have an old saying here on Evermoor: 'Be dust upon your breath.' "

"What?" My frustration spills over into my tone. "What does that even *mean?*"

"It means a greater part of you chose your conditions. And though a smaller part of you may not like them, the best course of action is to embrace the present and let things unfold in a spirit of readiness."

I force myself to take a breath. "So the greater part of me is the one that breathes, and the smaller part of me is just the dust."

"Exactly." He gives a nod. "We'll keen our minds, clear our senses, and stay alert for any signs of his presence. Gribbles is his name?"

"Yeah." I take another breath. Still forced, but not as much. "Yeah. Gribbles."

"We'll call it out if we suspect he's near. Otherwise, let's keep to ourselves. Best to avoid unwanted attention."

A complicated emotion—a little like faith and a lot like resignation—washes through me. "Yeah...okay. That's all we can do, right?"

"Indeed." He turns away and resumes walking.

Be dust upon your breath.

Huh.

———

"Where are we going?"

"Hafferly Crossing."

I wait for a bit, hoping he'll offer more information.

Nope. So I prompt him with, "Is that a city or—"

"A trader's outpost. While we are there, watch your step and mind your tongue. Let it wag without a care, and a blade will cut it from your mouth."

Great. We're headed for a medieval version of the Star Wars cantina, only I don't have a lightsaber and Ben Kenobi's nowhere in sight.

"So I should stick by you, right?" I chuckle nervously. "In case we get hassled."

He draws a knife and holds it out. "Here."

I tentatively accept it with both hands. "Thanks. Uh...I don't know how to use this."

"Learn."

"Right." I clear my throat. "Can I at least have a sheath?"

He undoes some buckles and a couple of ties, then pulls off the just-vacated sheath and flips it toward me. Much to my relief, I'm able to rig it onto one of my belt loops.

"So..." I slide the knife into the sheath, tugging and turning it to make sure it's secure. "Those guys you were fighting...you know, with the—" I make a vague gesture around my eyes. "The blindfolds?"

"Nightkeepers," he says. "Agents of the Protectorate's clandestine service."

"Oh. What exactly does this clandest—"

"They infiltrate gatherings and execute rebels."

"But they're blind, right? I mean they would have to be. Seeing as how they cover their—"

Ren scoffs. "Far from it. Their cloth wrap is highly enchanted—it augments their sight, strength, and martial skills. It also enhances their arcane perception, allowing them to perceive subtler energies."

"I see." (not really, though). "But what if they have to go undercover? I can't imagine a blindfold would help them blend in."

He looks annoyed and perplexed. " 'Undercover?' "

"Sorry—it means to gain your enemy's trust by pretending to be someone else."

"Right." He grunts an affirmative. "They don't always wear it. When it's not on their face, it can change their features to a moderate degree." He laughs harshly. "The Nightkeeper motto is 'We keep the night at bay.' But given their allegiance to the White Veiled Queen, many joke that it's 'We keep the night in place.' "

Magic blindfolds. Magic blindfolds that bless you with nunchuk skills and also double as superspy impostor masks. I want to know more, but he might shut down if I start geeking out. So I decide to go with a simpler question. "What's a 'White Veiled Queen?' "

Ren throws me another look. Not irritated, this time, but full-on angry. *"Are you trying to—"* Then he cuts himself short and takes a breath. "Apologies. You were born and raised on a different world—there is no reason you would know our history."

I'm a little proud that I didn't flinch (even though I wanted to). "No worries."

His voice drops into a hateful growl. "The White Veiled Queen, otherwise known as Lyderea Fairdyle, is our sovereign tyrant. She has imposed her will on over half of Evermoor."

"Are we in her kingdom? Or...is it 'queendom?' Not really sure if—"

"We are." Ren picks up the pace. "The Eldritch Protectorate comprises nine-tenths of Evermoor's surface."

"So when you say over half..."

"I mean nearly all. Yes."

"Has it always been this way?"

"No."

"When did it change?"

"Over twenty years ago, during the Fracture. Before Lyderea, our world was ruled by many leaders, each beholden to their own community."

"The Fracture? What's that?"

"A time of great upheaval. Rife with chaos, war, and low-shadow treachery. It marks the end of the Decline and the beginning of the Shadow Age."

"How did this happen? I mean, did everyone go crazy, or—"

"For several millennia, the folk of Evermoor lived in peace. That changed a hundred years back, when a wizard named Velys Skyseer constructed a network of intricate magics. It allowed for instant communication, and in some cases, immediate transport of material goods. It was known to all as the Velic Tessellate."

"Instant communication? How is that bad?" I cock my head, puzzled.

"It isn't. Not inherently, anyway. But as the Tessellate expanded and grew in power, it spawned a glut of ease and luxury. Subsequently, logic and consensus fell by the wayside, and folk lapsed into anger and vitriol. Few—if any—reaped the consequence of their words and actions."

"Sounds familiar. On my world, we're spoiled by technology instead of magic."

His hooded face turns toward me. "Aye?"

"Yep. It's definitely helped, but it's got its downsides. I mean, we haven't collapsed our civilization—"

"Consider yourself lucky."

"—but we easily could if we kept on quibbling. When the virus hit, it only served to highlight our weaknesses. One of our biggest was the inability to get along with each other."

"What is a 'virus?' "

"Oh, um...disease or plague might be a better way to put it."

"Are you ill?" He tenses slightly.

"I was, but it passed. Some died. Most got better."

He relaxes and nods. "We stayed healthy in life and limb, but the majority grew increasingly irrational. Our bickering took form as a transmissible curse: the Crimson Reft. It appeared without warning and corrupted the Tessellate, repurposing it into a vector for hate."

"What does it do? If it infects you or whatever." We've been walking up the road on a steady incline. Now it smooths into level ground.

"It taints your aura, amplifying your anger to a destructive degree. The prevailing theory is that it originated from a buildup of Primal energies."

"Primal? You said that earlier, but I'm not sure if it means what I think."

"Primal Magic is an intentional channeling of pure emotion. It is easily the most powerful of all magics, as it is extremely wild, extremely dangerous. Only masters are able to shape it."

"Did one of these Primal guys mess with the Tessellate?"

"No." He shakes his head. "That was the first possibility our mages ruled out, as there were too many points of arcane entry. They think a breakdown in dialogue was the underlying cause—our collective malice grew and festered, until it ultimately developed into the Reft. The Fracture was simply the physical tipping point. In the span of a week, diplomacy vanished and conflict reigned. Bonds and treaties were thrown to the wind."

"Why is it Crimson?"

"The first symptom is a deep reddening around the eyes. After a month, it begins to affect a person's behavior. Depending on their temperament, they become anything from angry to murderous."

"Did your wizards find a cure?"

"No. After Lyderea seized the Tessellate, she cut off access to its internecine web, allowing the Reft to fade away on its own. Eventually, most regained their original demeanor. There are a few, however, who remained brutish."

"Did people go to war?"

"Aye. Humans, Fair Folk, Wildlyre..."

" 'Wildlyre?' "

"A catch-all term for creatures, entities, and spirits. Non-humans."

(Magical creatures? *What?*) I resist the urge to blitz him with questions. "There must have been some who didn't get it. I mean, if it's anything like a virus—"

He gives a nod. "By and large, monks remained unaffected."

"What about you?"

"It happened shortly before I was born. As a child, I witnessed the last of the Crimson Wars, followed by Lyderea's rise to power." His gaze turns distant. "Many thought she would bring back the Bright Age."

I think of the Stormtroopers punishing the peasantry. "I'm guessing she didn't."

"No. She entranced the masses with her fiery speech, channeling their fear into anger and zealotry. It was part of her plan—she was plotting to conquer all who opposed her. She wouldn't have been able to wreak such havoc if..."

He clenches his jaw and shakes his head, as if his words are causing him tangible pain. "We cast our ballots in desperation—appointed Lyderea Interim Seneschal. She refused to step down and made herself Queen."

"Holy crap," I whisper. "You elected her."

He nods tightly.

We walk in silence for a couple of minutes. Then I say, "With the virus, it was mostly physical. Philosophy-wise, you could say it was a flesh-and-blood metaphor for what we had been doing to each other all along."

"And that would be?"

"The same thing as you: we couldn't stop bickering. People said anything and everything without having to explain their logic or reasoning, and it drove us further and further apart. Ironically, what started in our minds ended in our bodies: when the virus hit, we had to distance from each other to keep it in check. We found cures and preventatives, but—"

"I wish it were so on this cursed world," Ren hisses. "The Reft is gone, but we have accepted brutality as the new norm."

(My writer-brain approves of the way he says "cursed." Cur-sehd. Sounds way better.) "I think I know what you're talking about. For the last few weeks, I've had visions of Evermoor. The Stormtroopers were—"

"The what?"

I clear my throat, embarrassed. "I didn't know what they were called, so I made up a name for them. The soldiers with the uh—" I stammer for a moment. "They always wear armor...do you call it plate mail? It looks smooth and white. Like impossibly white."

He faces away and spits in disgust. "Iaetrix Knights:"

"Oh, okay. What do these Iaetrix—"

"Lyderea's foot soldiers. Low-level thugs by and large, but some are formidable. A few are dangerous."

"They were collecting taxes. They seemed—"

Ren interrupts with a harsh bark of laughter. "Taxes? *Taxes?* They may call it that, aye, but taxes are meant to spread opportunity and access. No, if you have any bit of sense you'll call it what it is: a tribute. Lyderea and her cronies are addicted to luxury—there is ne'er enough gold or gimmickry to satisfy their greed." He turns his head and spits again.

"That makes you...what—a rebel or something?"

Beneath his hood, his eyes grow cold. "I do what is necessary."

"Uh, right. Didn't mean to pry. On a related note, I've also seen people fighting the Knights. They wear dirty gear and stick to the woods."

"The Birthright Alliance, or just the Alliance, for short. They claim to be a movement. In reality, they are a loose confederation of insurgent warlords, beholden to a rogue named Ardos Rygar. A cruel man, but also capable."

"He wants to overthrow the Queen?"

Ren nods. "And claim rule for himself."

"Hmm." I let the silence grow, then clear my throat.

"Yes?"

"Earlier you mentioned the Prophesied Traveler. Who is that exactly?" I raise my hands in capitulation. "I know, I know—it's not me."

Ren grunts in affirmation. "Some believe he is a real person, while others think he is simply a metaphor. There are differing opinions on what he will do, but everyone agrees on two things: he will come from a plane not our own, and he will be in possession of Laiddinic powers."

"Laiddinic?"

"The story of Laiddin Altaenic is the oldest tale in all of Evermoor. It tells of a boy who stumbles upon a magic lamp. One that—"

"Contains a genie!" I blurt excitedly. "Who grants three wishes, right?"

Ren looks miffed. "A what? No, the lamp grants wishes, but not just three—an unlimited number. At first Altaenic thinks it's three, until he uses the last wish to wish for more wishes. Eventually, he discovers the lamp was left by his future self, who has already gained access to unlimited wishes, and is, in essence, a god."

"Huh." I scratch my head. "Interesting. So what are 'Laiddinic powers?'"

"They trump all magic, but not because they are higher up on the arcane hierarchy. They're..." he struggles for a second. "They form the hierarchy, but at the same time, they are apart from it."

"That doesn't make sense."

"I know." He shrugs in defeat. *The Turning of Evermoor* is filled with riddles and paradox. Even now, scribes pore over its dusty breadth, trying to wring meaning from its scrawl. A waste of time, if you ask me."

"And the Unbound Realm?"

"From what I understand, it is the final destination. Not death—for death is the beginning of another life—but a definitive endpoint for all of existence. Supposedly, the one who finds it will gain the ability to control reality."

I study the sunlit blue, then turn back to Ren. "You said a bunch of people have tried to find it. Why didn't they?"

"It switches locations at random intervals. And according to the *Turning,* it can only be found by one who has been there."

"That's absurd. Why seek godhood if you already have it?"

He shrugs again. "It is outside my purview."

Up ahead, the horizon gives way to a walled-off town. The road ends at a thirty-foot high, iron-banded gate, bordered by towers on either side.

"Hafferly Crossing," he mutters. "You will never find a more wretched hive of scum and villainy."

"Wait—what?" I laugh involuntarily. "You watch *Star Wars?*"

Ren looks puzzled. "Why would a star go to war? I am merely speaking of what I know to be true."

"Oh, okay. It's just...you said a line from a famous story. Famous on my world, anyway."

"Hmm." He's silent for a moment. Then: "Perhaps we are connected in a subtle fashion. It is not my area of expertise—I was never any good at arcane philosophy."

(Arcane philosophy. *Cool.*) "So. Hafferly Crossing. Anything I should know before we arrive?"

"Stay alert. Eyes open, knife close."

"Sure," I manage, trying to keep the tremor out of my voice. "Eyes open, knife close."

Jon, what the *hell* have you gotten yourself into?

6

"Announce yourself!" the tower guard calls.

"Ren of the Barrens!"

"You!" The guard points at me. "Name and purpose!"

"His name is Jon," Ren answers. "He is under my protection."

The guard confers with someone out of sight, then faces us again. "Ren of the Barrens, I would ask you a question!"

"Ask it in haste, guardsman! I would fill my belly and rest my feet!"

"Your last dalliance—how in the gods did she stand your odor?"

"Speak not of your mother, Eckles, lest she flog us both for your careless tongue!"

The guard laughs and cycles a hand, signaling the others to open the gate. "Let them in, let them in."

Giant chains clink and clank. As the doors swing wide, I notice big wooden bands—each dotted with uniform craters—run lengthwise across their interiors.

I'm puzzled at first, then I spot some logs beneath the tower. Ah, okay—if the gate were to ever come under siege, they could prop the logs against the bands and keep the doors from buckling inward. The depressions in the bands act as cradles for the logs (to keep them from sliding or slipping out of place) while stone braces dot the deck, ready to buttress the logs from the ground.

Ren walks forward and abruptly halts. I try to keep going, but he grabs my shoulder and pulls me back.

"Wait."

A man and a woman emerge from a shack, built into the foundation of the right guard tower. "Should have let him through," the man grumbles. "Would've liked to see him jump and twitch."

"He doesn't have wards," Ren explains. "His guts would have spilled from his mouth and nose."

"All for the best. I'm not in the mood to clean up innards."

Wait—what? *Innards?*

The man faces his partner and blows into his palm, releasing a mote of shimmering haze. His partner lets it alight onto her hand, then squishes it in her clenched fist, causing tendrils of light to squirt through her fingers.

A rune-laden wall blinks into existence, illuminating the air between us and the gatekeepers, then slowly fades and disappears.

"You're free to enter," the woman declares. "Barring emergencies, the main gate is always open. These side gates are not—we cut off access from dusk 'til dawn."

Ren nods and strides forward. As I follow behind, the gatekeeper (wizard, I now realize) shakes her head in disgust and bafflement.

"What's the matter with you? Trying to enter without any wards..."

She raises a finger like she's about to scold me, then crosses her arms and shakes her head again.

"Damn tourist."

————

We proceed onto a main avenue, bordered by a jumble of shops and booths. The people and creatures are rough and loud, heckling and bartering for wares and services.

Time to address my endangered innards. "Ren, after we entered..."

"Yes?" He shoulders past a man and what I think is an Ogre.

"That was magic, wasn't it? When the man and the woman deactivated the uh...light-wall." (I want to say forcefield, but I'm pretty sure that's not what it's called.)

"Magic. Yes. What of it?" He's irritated. Apparently, I just asked a stupid question.

"It's...I've never seen it before. I was just making sure."

"Right," he mutters.

(I think he's being nice. If I were anyone else, I probably would have earned the Evermoor version of a Captain Obvious joke.)

"Was it Velic magic, or—"

We emerge from a crush of merchants and traders. There's clusters of people milling around, but no longer standing shoulder to shoulder.

Ren locks eyes with me. "Your knife—you have it on you, aye?"

I do a quick check. "Yeah. Why wouldn't I?"

"I forgot to tell you: watch out for pickpockets."

"Oh."

I think for a bit, trying to figure out how to guide the conversation back to magic, but he does it for me. "Aside from Lyderea and her Protectorate sorcerers, no one uses Velic spells. For the most part, the only magic you'll see is lower hedge magic. Or in the case of those gate-side mages, some intermediary arcanix, which is the same thing, only stronger. A bit more advanced than charms and readings, but nothing special."

Nothing special. *Riiiiight.* "Got it. One of them said that I needed a ward, or I would die horribly when I cross the forcefie— the barrier, I mean. Do you uh...do you have any wards I could borrow?"

"No. Mine are immaterial." He waves his hand in a vague circle. "As you can see."

"What do you mean, 'as you can see?' "

"What do you mean 'what do you mean?' " he snaps. "They're right here." He makes the same gesture, only faster and angrier.

"You said *subtler energies* a little while back. Were you talking about your wards? Are they invisible?"

"*No.*" (Grumpy McGrumperson is *definitely* grumpy). "These aren't subtle. They're right there for all to—" His eyes widen in shock. "Your sight...it isn't quickened."

Now I'm confused. "As far as I know, my sight is just as fast as—"

He cuts me off with an open hand. "You haven't been opened to the orphic sphere."

"The orphic—"

"Another name for the arcane realm." His expression turns doubtful. "How did you manage to survive on your own?"

"It's not that bad." I shrug. "No one on Earth has 'quickened sight.' Well, maybe a few, but people dismiss them as crazy or fake. They're deified, sometimes, but more often than not, we burn them alive or nail them to sticks."

"With unquickened senses, curses and hexes would be slow to take root. But at the same time..." he shakes his head. "Never mind. Until we reach safer harbor, I see I will have to act as your personal guardian."

"I'm not a baby," I argue. "You don't have to—"

"Do you know how to use that?" He points at the knife hanging off my jeans.

"I...touché." I rub the back of my neck. "Okay, I'll follow your lead. What's the plan?"

"I told you: I need to trade for goods and supplies. Stay close, because I have no desire to—"

"I mean after that. What'll you do with me?"

He blows through his lips—a resentful sigh if I had to describe it. "I shall leave you in Naversé. A smaller city with calmer folk."

"Wait—you're dropping me off in another city?" Sudden panic takes hold in my chest.

"Is that a problem?"

"I just—" I grab my hair with both hands. *I'm not supposed to be here, okay?*

"I know. Which is why I will leave you in Naversé Township." He cocks his head, mildly puzzled.

"No, that's not what I—" I clutch the air and groan in frustration. "Look, I am in *way* over my head! You can't just leave me in...in...

"Naversé."

"Whatever!" I throw my hands up. "You can't just abandon me, Ren! For Christ's sakes, I walked through a door in a *goddamn tree! And now I'm living in DUNGEONS AND DRAGONS!*"

Everyone stops. And stares.

"Come hither," Ren hisses. He grabs my neck, herding me into a nook between a couple of trading tents. "This is *not* the place to act unwise." He squeezes hard, causing a yelp of pain to fly from my mouth. Man, he is *strong*.

But that doesn't mean he's right. I reach for my knife, intending to show him I'm deadly serious. His other hand drops, trapping my wrist before I can draw.

"What are you doing?" he asks incredulously.

"Let...*go.*" I bare my teeth in a pained grimace. "Or I swear I'll cut you."

His eyes search mine. Then he lets me go with a rough shove. "You have spirit," he says grudgingly. "Test it with care, or your lifeless boots will face the sky."

"Is that your way of saying that someone will kill me?"

"Yes."

(Fantasy-speak. *Cool.*) "I wear sneakers," I counter, "not boots." (Lame, I know, but it's all I can think of.) "We met for a reason,

Ren. If you're gonna leave me in a random city, you might as well kill me here and now."

"Naversé is safe. You're being overdrama—"

"How do you know I'm not the Traveler? It might seem unlikely—"

"Unimaginably so."

"—but until you can definitively rule it out, there's still a chance I might be the one."

He falls silent. Then: "I'll think about it. Fair?"

I answer with a nod. "Fair."

"Come." He brushes past me. "Supplies and a meal, and then we're gone."

And just like that, I'm back to being a nervous kid. "Uh, not trying to nag, but could I get one of those ward thingies? To keep my guts from flying out?"

He closes his eyes and lets out a sigh. "Yes. We'll get you a ward."

"Thanks." *Whew.*

Not gonna lie—I like my guts inside my body.

———

For the next two hours, Ren barters with humans and Wildlyre, changing his dialogue to match the vendors'. At times he sounds perfectly normal—a slapdash mix of casual and formal—but just as often he sounds like a different person altogether. During one exchange, he throws around gutter-slang patois that completely changes his carriage and bearing. It's like he's suddenly become a rhythmic sleazebag, conversing mostly in winks and nudges.

Over the course of his barter, I realize his cowboy man-purse is a magical storehouse. He packs it with loads of meat and bread, but it never changes size; it always appears exactly the same. I never would have guessed he would need this much stuff.

After his seventh trade, he says, "Let's get you a ward."

We head to a stand, tended by a six-foot lizard-man in an armless vest. Hanging from the ceiling are dozens of amulets.

"Basic protection," Ren says. "Nothing lavish."

Lizard Guy scans his inventory, then picks out a bronze disc embossed with a pair of boots. "Traveler's ward. Made in Tarcony." He holds it out by its hide neck-strap.

Ren drapes the strap over his fingers, appraising the disc with a critical eye. "The artisan?"

"A witch named Parsily. Best one around for a hundred faires."

"Never heard of her." Ren grunts. "But it'll do. What do you take?"

"No coin from Karos or Chime Shadow. Also—nothing from Fair Folk."

"That's a first. Fair Folk goods are desired by all."

"Not anymore. If Lyderea's Knights find anything Fair, they'll take it for themselves and throw you in gaol."

Ren's expression twists in surprise. "What? Why?"

Lizard Guy shakes his head, as if to say, *Unbelievable.* "A pact was struck between the Alaewyn Fair Folk and the Birthright Alliance. Supposedly, it was just an agreement to trade wares, but Lyderea was angry nevertheless. That much is rumor, but this much is fact: the Queen has banned Fair Folk merchandise."

Ren's voice tightens with anger. "Alaewyn lands are a thousand faire distant; we have nothing to do with them. And the Fair Folk are not a singular people, they are a vast collection of disparate—"

Lizard Guy gives him a tired look. "It is none of my business. None of yours, either."

For a moment, Ren looks like he's about to retort, then he takes a breath and settles down. "Speak your cost."

They go on autopilot, trading offers and counteroffers in a quick, efficient monotone. A minute later, they arrive at a price.

"May light find you in dark places." Ren hands over a trio of coins.

"Aye, wanderer. May it ease your eyes and guide your feet."

And then we're off. Ren hands me the ward.

"Thanks." As I slip it around my neck, I say, "What uh..." I'm not sure how to ask about Lizard Guy's race. "He's Wildlyre, right?"

"Yes." Ren keeps walking, toward a tavern called Gantry's Fire.

"What kind of...of..." (How do you say *race* in a world that has lizard-people?)

"His designate? He's Sauric. Of the Saura."

"Oh. Okay." I snap my fingers, struck by a sudden epiphany. "You know, I just realized you speak English. Where did you learn how to—"

Ren scoffs. Not in disgust, but more of a WTF scoff. "What is 'English?' I speak Scopic and so do you. I'm also fluent in Ilianesti, Lyrdic, and Enkonese."

"Wow. Impressive."

"Not in the least. Nearly everyone here speaks three or more languages."

"Has that always been the case?"

"At the end of the Decline, most only spoke a single tongue, but that was a time of aberrance and chaos."

"The Decline...when is that, exactly?"

"The last hundred years preceding the Fracture. Now mind your speech and shorten your aura. We'll talk more after food and drink."

As we walk through the door of Gantry's Fire, I find myself grinning. I might be stuck in another dimension, but it's a hell of a lot better than what I was facing on Earth—slow assimilation into an uncaring machine, driven by convoluted laws and humdrum standards.

That damned contract changed everything. **SOMETHING DIFFERENT.**

Now, as I enter a tavern filled with rogues and wanderers and God knows what, a surge of purpose rushes through me—like a springtime breeze laden with promise.

You were right, Atriya. You were right about all of it.

There are other worlds than these.

And I wouldn't have it any other way.

7

Ren stops at the counter and nods at the barkeep—a brawny man with a handlebar mustache. "Meat and bread." Ren dances his hand back and forth, indicating him and me in the same gesture. "A table as well."

The barkeep jerks his head at a booth in the corner. "There's your table. Ale?"

"No. Thank you."

We both turn and head for the booth. As I take my seat, I gape at a dozen or so dog-people on the other end of the tavern (the smallest one has to be six and a half feet tall). Some could pass as straight-up werewolves, while others resemble athletic dog breeds. Shepherds, Malinois, boxers...They're dressed like humans but everything's bigger—bigger cloaks, bigger weapons, bigger armor.

"Whoa," I whisper. "Who are they?"

"Children of Fenrus. They call themselves Wolven. *Attend me.*" Ren snarls it with unexpected force, surprising me into an involuntary flinch. "Do not draw ire with your careless stare. Keep your eyes to yourself, lest someone cut them from your head."

"Right. Sorry." I look down at the table, embarrassed by my interdimensional tourist moment.

"Good." He crosses his arms and lowers his chin. With his hood drooped forward, he almost looks like he's taking a snooze. Despite that, I get the sense he's fully alert.

After nearly a minute of uncomfortable silence, I venture, "Your uh...purse."

"Carry."

"Right—carry. You pack it with items, but it never changes size. I've never seen anything like it. Outside of a video game, that is."

"It's bound with a catch-fold charm and a tangle-me-never. The first enchantment boosts its storage. The second ensures it stays out of my way."

"How much stuff can it hold?"

"Several months of supplies and equipment. No weapons, armor, or heavy apparatus. Other spells will allow for such, but they cost a fair bit more than I'm willing to pay."

"So you could store a house in there, theoretically speaking."

"Yes. An entire castle, given the right sorcery."

"Wow." I shake my head, at a loss for words.

His face shifts beneath his hood, allowing me a glimpse of his shadowed eyes. "You said you've seen something like it in a...virulent game, was it?"

"Video game."

"What is that? A 'video game?' "

"A game where you press buttons to make things happen. Your actions show up on a glowing screen. It's electronic, though, not magic."

"What is 'electronic?' "

"It means powered by lightning."

He lowers his chin. "Seems pointless."

"We can't all fight or cast magic spells," I counter. "Some of us have to—"

"Sounds like a personal problem."

Before I can reply, the barkeep arrives with our meals. "Bread. Meat."

"Our thanks." Ren hands him a coin. The barkeep takes it and walks away.

I study my food with a dubious eye. It's some kind of rodent, if I had to guess. Organs glisten from its split-open center.

"Why do you tarry?" Ren cracks a bone and sucks out the marrow. "This could be our only hot meal for the next few months."

"I...yeah." No use explaining that I like to eat at the Whole Foods hot bar. I doubt this place has chile lime rice.

So I draw my knife and dig in. The meat is burnt and the bread is stale, but hey—better than nothing, right? As I chew the organs, I feel a tiny flash of pride—a lot of Earthlings would lose their minds if they had to maow down on a fantasy-world critter.

Ren pauses, holding a chunk of bread by his lips. "Why are you smiling?"

"Well, it's just that..." I almost tell him, but I decide against it. I'm guessing that grody meat is a complete nonissue to a guy like Ren. He's probably eaten a 30th level mindflayer.

So instead I say, "I didn't realize I was this hungry."

"Right." He resumes eating.

(Mental note: keep celebratory grin to idiot self, especially when it's over something as small as Evermoor cuisine.)

I use the bread to soak up the juice, then jam it all into my mouth. A second later, Ren does the same. I feel another flash of pride—I was a step ahead; I guessed the right thing to do without being told. I can't cast magic or fight with swords, but—

The door bangs open. The room goes silent.

Standing in the entrance is a white-armored knight.

———

"Eyes down," Ren whispers.

A dozen knights filter in, boots clacking on the wooden deck. "Stay where you are," one of them orders. "Or we'll knock the teeth from your cursed mouths."

Their leader halts in the middle of the tavern, hooking his gauntleted thumbs into his crimson belt-sash. "My name is High Justicer Thane. Address me as such, or I will shatter your fingers and rip them off." He lets that sink in, then continues speaking. "If you haven't already heard, Fair Folk goods are now illegal. This is your one and only chance at amnesty—declare your contraband and you shall be pardoned."

No one says a word.

"I see." Thane strides forward, lowering his head as if he's deep in thought. "So everyone here is an honest trader."

He halts again.

"Search them." His voice rises with frigid authority. "If they have anything Fair—anything so much as a residual spell—take them outside and slit their throats." He sweeps the room with a hard stare. "On your feet. All of you."

"Ren," I whisper. "Are you carrying any Fair Fo—"

"Yes."

"So what do we—"

"Follow my lead."

I'm about to tell him I've only heard that in eighties adventure movies, when a shadow falls across our table.

"Up. Now."

We rise from the booth and face the Knight. Sweat springs out across my body, gathering and pooling in my pits and my crotch. I don't want to die. I thought I was ready, but that was before I discovered parallel dimensions and magic blindfolds.

"Turn around."

We both turn around.

"Hands on the wall."

We do as he says.

Gauntleted fingers pat me down. He finishes with me and steps behind Ren. I try and relax, but I can't stop my teeth from grinding together. *Follow my lead.* In my mind, I feel out the motion of drawing my knife. Could I actually stab another human bei—

"Catch-fold enchantment, eh?" The Knight calls, "Garn!"

Knight Garn hurries over, armor clanking in time with his steps. "Yes, Justicer Roke?"

"You've taken a course in minor arcanix, aye?"

"Yes, Justicer Roke."

"Did those frail-bodied mages teach you Elkor's Eye?"

"Yes, Justicer Roke."

Roke points at Ren. "This one has a catch-fold enchantment. Search his bag for anything Fair."

"Aye, Justicer Roke." Red-glowing runes appear by his temples. He opens Ren's carry and peers inside.

"A lot of supplies, but..." Garn's helmeted brow furrows in concentration. "I'm not sure, but I think there's a—"

"Don't you touch him!" someone snarls. *"You have no RIGHT!"*

Roke slaps Garn on his armor-plated shoulder. "Draw steel and watch my flank—quickly, *quickly!*"

As they hurry over to the other end of the tavern, Ren and I turn and look. The Knights are all brandishing swords, standing in a loose semicircle around the Wolven. The canine warriors have their backs to the wall.

Thane swivels from side to side, pointing his sword at anyone and everyone. *"Stay where you are!"* he screams. *"Or I'll mount your heads atop the gate!"*

A Knight reaches for a Wolven's carry, but its mastiff owner shoves him back, causing him to stumble onto his butt. Several blades flick up and out, forcing the Wolven to halt in his tracks.

"Hold!" Another Wolven extends his arms. "We have no quarrel! Hear me, all of you—*we have no quarrel!*"

The Knight who was shoved gets to his feet. "They're trafficking contraband, High Justicer. I found a loaf of Elven bread."

Thane gives the dog-men a malicious smile. "Fair Folk wares, eh?"

The Wolven leader—the one who's been trying to keep the peace—says, "Just a few crumbs of leftover food, caught in the folds of my aide's carry. There's no need to punish my kin."

"On the contrary," Thane sneers. "There is *every* need. If we failed to honor the Queen's edicts, madness and chaos would swamp these lands."

The Wolven leader lowers his voice—despite his predicament, he manages to sound earnest and dignified. "Please. This isn't necessary."

Thane looks to either side, meeting the eyes of his Iaetrix Knights. "Cut their throats. Do it quickly."

And then all hell breaks loose.

8

The Wolven leader yells, *"No weapons! No weapons!"* right as his warriors steamroll the Knights. A handful of patrons join in the brawl, but most of them break for the unguarded entrance.

Before they can flee, a booted foot kicks the door inward—it's followed by a stream of oncoming Knights.

"GET ON YOUR BELLIES! GET ON YOUR BELLIES!"

No one listens; everyone keeps cursing and shoving. The Wolven are in a full-on frenzy, throwing white-armored Knights into walls, tables, and chairs.

"On my heels!" Ren ducks a slash from a panicked Knight, then hooks his neck and sweeps his legs, clearing the way for us to tumble outside and take off running. *"On my heels!"* he screams. *"Close on my heels, Jon!"*

"I'm—" I trip and stumble into an enormous Wolven. It snarls angrily and swats me away. *"—TRYING!"*

Calls erupt from outraged Knights: *"Bar the gate! Bar the gate!"* The thirty-foot portal looms high in the distance.

"Eckles!" Ren waves his arms, catching the tower guard's eye. *"Look here, you tub of guts!"*

"Sorry Ren! I'm bound by coin!" Eckles wraps his hands around a lever.

"Stay that lockbolt!" Ren bellows. (I'm guessing by "lockbolt" he means the vertical beam off to the right, held in place by

a latch-bound chain—basically a deadbolt that goes all the way across.) *"You still owe me from our last game of cards! Cry off and I forgive your debt!"*

Eckles wavers, torn between duty and greed. Then he shouts, "Fine! But now we're even!"

Ren glances to either side. *"Wolven—get us through that cursed gate! I'll dispel the Verilliac barrier!"*

The Wolven leader barks an affirmative. *"Done!"*

Ren blows into his half-fingered glove, summoning a pure blue swirl into his palm. He chops his steps, cocks his arm, then snaps forward in a full-body throw. The orb stops short of the massive gate, collapsing into a ripple that makes the forcefield fully visible—a glyph-limned wall that fluxes and peaks, then rapidly fades and disappears.

"Forward, brothers! And woe to any who stand in our way!" The Wolven leader drops to all fours, doubling his speed in less than a second. His fellow Wolven follow behind, pounding the earth with their giant paws.

"Now wait just a second!" Eckles screams. "We'll crank it open for you if you *wait just a—"*

A trio of Wolven slam the gate—cr-cr-*CRACK*—rebounding off it like hairy wrecking balls. At first I think their efforts are in vain, then I see daylight between the doors. No more than a couple inches wide, but still—my heart races with desperate hope.

Three more Wolven smash the gate, drawing a gunshot *bang* from the solid wood. Eckles curses and begs them to stop, but his pleas fall on deaf ears; the last six Wolven rush forward, a shaggy mass of muscle and fur.

With a thunderous clap, the doors swing wide.

Eckles hollers, *"You owe me, Ren, you low-shadow grifter! YOU OWE ME!"*

———

We forge ahead for a hundred yards, then Ren yanks me sharply left—off the road and into the woods. Eventually, we come to a stop in a forest clearing. We're accompanied by traders and a dozen Wolven, the same ones from the tavern brawl.

"Well." A man with a Zorro-style mustache crosses his arms (whoa, he's got two sabers hanging from his waist). "That was fun."

His buddy—a pretty-boy rogue with a quiver on his back and a cutlass on his hip—laughs merrily. "I welcome the exercise. Keeps the blood flowing."

Ren gives him a suspicious glance. "Right. If that's all, my companion and I will take our leave. Come on, Jon."

Pretty Boy asks, "Where are you headed?"

"Naversé." Ren starts walking.

"What a coincidence!" Zorro and Pretty Boy fall in beside us. "We share the same heading!" Pretty Boy calls, "Do any of you have business in Naversé Township?"

The traders shake their heads, but one of the Wolven extends a hand. "Slow your stride—we might have interest." As they approach, they debate quietly but heatedly. Apparently, some of them would rather go it alone.

Ren halts and turns around. "I have no need for a High Taire duelist." He scrutinizes Zorro, then the Wolven. "Or a pack of Fenric warriors." His gaze tracks left and settles on Pretty Boy. "Lastly, I have no use for a low-shadow pickpocket."

Pretty Boy looks astonished and affronted. "What are you—"

Ren hands me my knife. "He took it from you while I was speaking."

I'm hit by a flash of cognitive dissonance. Wait, how did—

Oh—right. Pickpocket.

"I'm not just a pickpocket!" the man exclaims. "I'm a professional thief! And a damn good one at that!"

"I'm fine with parting ways," one of the Wolven growls (he appears to be a giant husky; one eye is blue and the other is green). "I do not care for smelly humans."

"Good. Everyone's happy." Ren turns to leave.

"Wait." The Wolven leader peers at my face. There's something familiar about him. I can't quite place it, but...

"Jon?"

My mouth drops open.

"Gribbles?"

Holy crap. I just found my dog.

And he's a seven-foot tall, canine warrior.

9

A were-shepherd snarls, "He is Warrior Rex to our kith and kin. Refer to him as your Majesty or I swear I'll—"

Gribbles waves him away. "Cry off, Ripfang. I wish to palaver with these Human wanderers." He stares pointedly at the thief and the Duelist. "But neither you nor you. The two before me and no one else."

The thief shrugs, while the Duelist acknowledges him with a dip of his head. Ripfang walks away, muttering something-something-something about nasty little Humans.

Gribbles guides us over to a secluded tree, then examines my face with wondering eyes. "I can't believe...come here." He envelops me in a hug. I instinctively return it. (Whoa—there's a giant battle-axe slung across his back.)

"I thought I lost you," I say tightly. "What *are* you? Besides my dog, I mean."

He breaks the hug and gives me a massive grin. "Gyrax Aclasian, Fenric heir to the Wolven Clans. And just so you know: the others will take offense if you refer to me as 'yours.'"

"Sorry. It's just that—"

"Don't worry. A part of me remains your loyal dog."

"Did you just get here?" I cock my head, puzzled. "It doesn't seem like it."

"Blame the interdimensional portal; they're unreliable when it comes to space-time. You appear to have just arrived, whereas I have lived here for three and a half months."

"Good to know. So are you king or doggo? I'm a little confused."

"Both. I was assigned to guard you by Alijyar SyCajister, otherwise known as the Vagabond King. He sent me to Earth, where I adopted the form you are most familiar with."

Ren gives a slight bow. "Apologies, your Majesty. I did not realize who you were."

Gyrax scoffs. "Fie on your titles." Then he studies Ren with a piercing gaze. "Perhaps *I* should apologize. I did not know you were—"

Ren stiffens. "Ren of the Barrens and naught else. I do not wish to attract attention."

My dog-turned-warrior nods in response. "As you wish." He turns back to me. "Where is your cloak? You stick out like a sore thumb."

"What?" I suddenly realize that everyone here—and nearly everyone I've seen up until now—has been wearing some form of hooded cloak. "Oh, um...like you said, I just got here. I'm not really sure where I can get a—"

"The fault is mine," Ren apologizes. "I thought he was but a stranded child. I was going to take him to Naver—" His eyes widen. "Hold...you were assigned to guard him by a Sentry of Evermoor..." His lips part in astonishment. "Does that mean..."

"He is the Prophesied Traveler," Gyrax affirms. "The one who will reach the Unbound Realm."

"He is completely incapable of swordplay or magic." Ren shakes his head in disbelief. "If there was ever a worse candidate—"

"Take it up with Circle SyCajister."

"With all due respect, your Maj—Gyrax, I mean. They're Primal Mages, not oracles. Jon is not the Traveler. I am all but sure of it."

I'm inclined to agree. I'm enjoying my role as fantasy-world tourist, but *heroic savior* sounds a little grandiose. The only reason I argued for the possibility was because Ren wanted to ditch me in Naversé. Now that Gyrax is here, that isn't a concern—I can follow him instead of Ren.

"Ren's right. I'm not the guy you're—"

Gyrax lifts a hand, cutting me off. "It isn't of consequence. Not yet anyway. Take things moment by moment, step by step. Everything else will fall into place."

"Uh, okay." I nod cautiously. "Moment by moment, step by step. I can handle that...I think."

Ren gives me a doubtful look. "Mayhap it's better if I stay by your side. At least until I grasp why you are here." He dips his head at Gyrax. "Would you care to share travels? Our crossing seems fated."

"I would be honored to join you, Rennare—" He stops himself and says, "Ren of the Barrens, I mean."

Gyrax beckons to the Wolven, who are hunkered beneath a distant tree. They stride over and form a loose circle around their king.

"Warriors." He scans their faces with a steady eye. "Go on without me. Relay my missive to Sendric Kyanjer."

"My liege," a pitbull protests, "we were chosen to protect you during your journey!"

"Aye, as I was chosen to protect life and light. The fates call, and we must heed their summons."

They don't seem enthused, but none of them protest. As they turn to leave, Gyrax gestures to the shepherd who threatened me. "A moment, Ripfang." Gyrax bows his neck and slips off his necklace: a hide-bound medallion depicting a snarling wolf's head. "Take it," he holds it out to his canine lieutenant.

Ripfang accepts it with a shallow bow. "I shall guard this with my life."

"You will *not.*" Gyrax growls. "Cross into the Clear for a worthy cause, not for the sake of a meaningless trinket."

Ripfang acquiesces with a sullen, "Aye."

Gyrax doesn't like it—he steps closer, looming over his recalcitrant subordinate. As his shadow darkens Ripfang's face, it becomes strikingly clear that my dog-turned-king is a hell of a lot bigger.

"Swear it," Gyrax rumbles. "I would hear it from your lips, packmate."

Ripfang gulps. "I swear it, Rex. I will place my life above your cachet."

"And the lives of my warriors, as well."

"This I swear," Ripfang says.

"Good." Gyrax appraises him. "I value loyalty, but it must be pointed in the right direction, lest it rot and curdle into blind dogma."

"Cry off, will you?" Ripfang mutters. "Don't let your title go to your head."

Gyrax laughs, loud and hearty. "Well said." He jerks his chin at the other Wolven. "Go. They need your guidance."

Ripfang salutes with a fist on his heart, then about-faces and heads for the pack. After a brief word, they leave the clearing.

The pickpocket, who has been edging closer during the exchange, asks, "Do my ears deceive me? Are you truly royalty?"

Gyrax responds with a faint smile. "All I can offer is debt and promises. Save your graft for richer folk."

The thief chuckles. "I have more than enough coin for food and shelter. Nevertheless, it is good to have a royal owe me a favor." He waves to his friend, who's busy fighting an imaginary enemy. "Isn't that right, Elier?"

No response.

The thief shrugs. "I speak for the Duelist. As steel is sure and water is wet."

Gyrax nudges Ren. "Two seek to join our party."

Ren is silent for a long moment. Then, "Let them join, if they so wish. But just so you know, the thief is incompetent. He poses little threat to your coin or carry."

The thief steps forward, wagging a finger. "Careful how you speak, wanderer! I stand unmatched in my criminal skills!"

Ren's eyes glint with amusement. "Perhaps we should inform our fellow travelers." He surveys the traders, most of whom are leaving the clearing.

The thief pats the air, suddenly nervous. "No need, no need. You're a sharp one, aye?" He peeks over his shoulder, making sure the traders haven't heard. "I'm glad we're friends, sure as my name is Lucky Hap."

"Right." Ren examines the Duelist, who sheaths his swords as he saunters over. "Elier, is it?"

"Aye. Elier Finn, at your service."

"I somewhat doubt that," Ren says dryly.

Elier laughs. "You say true, wanderer. I have sworn allegiance to both my sabers, while my companion Lucknar believes first and foremost in a bulging purse. Often at the expense of a trader's wealth, I might add."

The thief grins and pats his carry. All of a sudden, Ren's threat to tell the traders about Lucky's profession makes a lot more sense.

"You stole from *all* of them?" I ask incredulously.

"Nearly." He looks quickly at Gyrax. "But I am not without scruples—there are certain lines I do not cross."

"Out of prudence, not fidelity," Gyrax counters. "Nevertheless, I appreciate your restraint."

"You are royalty, milord—my larcenous fingers are not without shame." He glances at Ren. "When do we leave?"

Ren shades his eyes and studies the sky. "We have an entire clearing to ourselves. Let us enjoy a good night's rest."

———

A short while later we're sitting by a fire, dining on bread and smoked duck. Ren lends me a spare bedroll, which I put to use as an improvised seat-cushion.

"Not bad." I appraise my loaf with a critical eye. "Lots of butter in it."

"Makes everything better," Lucky agrees.

"Duck's good too," I say. "Got some spice to it."

"Try eating it for months on end," Ren mutters.

"Full belly's a happy belly." Elier flashes a cheeky smile. "Just like a bedroll—two bodies are better than one."

Gyrax reaches in his carry and pulls out a cloak. At first it appears jet-black, but upon closer inspection, the fabric ripples with midnight blue. "Here." He holds it out to me.

"Thanks." I stand up and let it unravel. "Why does everyone wear a cloak?"

"How do you not know?" Elier raises an eyebrow.

"He was raised in seclusion," Gyrax states, saving me the trouble of having to lie. "During the Wars, his family fled to the Belukhai Hills. He has lived as a hermit for most of his life."

The Duelist grunts in acknowledgment. "Explains your odd choice of clothes and your strange manner of speech."

"You were about to tell me why everyone wears a cloak?" I ask, eager to divert the topic of conversation.

"The custom arose from Reft-stricken folk," Gyrax says as I hunt for the neck-hole. "They were deeply ashamed of their reddened eyes, and tried to hide them with hooded cloaks. After the curse spread throughout all of Evermoor, everyone began wearing them." The Wolven shrugs. "Now they're a part of our day-to-day life."

"Very practical," Lucky remarks. "Lots of pockets, lots of items."

"Lots to steal," Gyrax says amusedly, "for an enterprising pick-pocket."

"Thief!" Lucky exclaims. "And there is more to thievery than picking pockets—I am an artist, milord!"

"I stand corrected." Gyrax watches as I throw the cloak around my shoulders. "Here." He fiddles with a black opal broach sewn into the corner. "Squeeze the broach against the other side—" he presses it against the fabric, "—and the fabric will bind around your neck." The broach flickers with purple light. "If anyone tries to choke or entangle you, the cloak will sense it and detach on its own."

"Wow." I study the broach with wondering eyes. "Thanks."

"None needed."

Elier and Lucky produce some pipes, stuff them with a blend of crumpled leaves, then announce they're going for a short walk. Gyrax and I wish them well, but Ren doesn't; he continues staring into the fire.

Fine by me—it gives me a chance to learn more about Gyrax.

"You were born on Evermoor, right?"

"I came of age during the Wars." His face grows still; there's deep sadness beneath his words. "I left my kingdom in the hands of a steward, so I could heed Alijyar and seek you out."

"I met him in Golden Gate Park. He was disguised as a homeless man."

A thoughtful nod. "There are numerous wizards in San Francisco. Interplanar travel is hard on their minds—it often drives them to addiction and madness. They account for many of your city's displaced folk."

"Whoa..." I straighten up, taken aback. "So all those homeless...some of them are wizards?" I shake my head. "That's cool and sad at the same time."

"It can happen to the best of them." Gyrax holds up his bread, studies it briefly, then snaps it down in a single bite. "But not to Alijyar. The Vagabond King is a wizard amongst wizards."

"Man, who would've thought..." I shake my head again. "A powerful sorcerer, disguised as a homeless guy."

"And who would have thought you could end up in Evermoor?" Gyrax grins.

"Or that my elderly dog was Wolven royalty?" I look Gyrax up and down.

"Truth is often stranger than fiction."

"I don't get it. Back when you were Gribbles—"

His face tightens with annoyance. "I'm still Gribbles, Jon."

"My mistake." I try and hide my smile, but I'm only partially successful. My lifelong friend is still with me—he's just a whole lot more than I ever imagined.

"Back on Earth, I should say. Back on Earth, your daily routine consisted of making me laugh and inspiring me with kindness. But here on Evermoor, you're a beast-mode dog-warrior, super courageous and hella wise. What gives?"

"Jon." He lays a giant hand on my shoulder. "On your world, laughter *is* courage. Kindness *is* wisdom."

I feel my eyes welling, feel a lump growing large inside my throat.

Because that was the truest thing I've ever heard.

"Right," I manage in a slightly choked voice. "Well...I'm gonna snooze. Big day tomorrow, you know?" (I have no idea if it is or not, but if I end up crying, I don't want Ren to know or see.)

He squeezes my shoulder and turns away.

"Sleep well, Jon."

10

The next morning, I pack up the bedroll Ren loaned me, then slip it back into his carry. He gives me a chunk of bread and duck, which I maow down in quick, wolfish bites. After taking a minute to do the same, he walks over to Elier and Lucky, ready to kick them both awake.

Gyrax stops him with a raised hand. "Let them sleep. In the meantime, we can teach Jon how to use his dagger."

Ren leans against a tree and crosses his arms. "As you wish."

For the next two hours, Gyrax trains me in basic knifework—rudimentary defense paired with attacks. Apparently, there's too little distance and too much risk to not do both at the same time. Much to my surprise, the moves start to click. I'm no John Wick, but I can at least sense a bit of the rhythm—the gain and cost of each movement, and how they open or close off new opportunities.

"Good." Elier sits up in his bedroll, hugging his knees. "You're talented."

"Thanks." I wipe sweat off my brow with the back of my wrist. "It almost feels natural. Like I'm riding a bike or something."

" 'Bike?' " Lucky yawns loudly.

"A wheeled machine," Gyrax explains. "He means to say that it feels familiar."

I'm puzzled by his knowledge, but then I remember he's spent several years as an Earthling dog. Of course he knows what a bike is.

Ren approaches Lucky. "Out of your bed and onto the road."

Lucky squints up at him. "Breakfast?"

"We've already had it." Ren grabs his elbow and hauls him up (thank God he's wearing underwear). "Dine on the road or take your leave. I do not care for slow-footed thieves."

"All right, all right," Lucky grumbles. He rubs his eye as if he's clearing it of gunk, but it's actually a distraction; his other hand reaches for Ren's carry.

Ren intercepts it, bending it neatly into a compromised twist. Lucky faces away and drops to his knees.

"Innocent mistake!" he wheezes. "Force of habit!"

"The next time it happens," Ren warns, "I'll snap your bones and leave you to rot. Understand?"

"Aye!" Lucky gives a vigorous nod.

Ren cranks harder, adding a few more ounces of excruciating pressure. "Didn't hear you," he says in a deceptively soft voice.

"You have my word!" Veins jump out across his forehead. "Grace, Ren! Bloody gryphons on a witch's eyesore, *I plead your grace!*"

Ren lets go with a forceful shove. The thief takes a moment to regain his bearings, then studies Ren with newfound respect.

"Who taught you how to fight?"

"Careless idiots who tried to rob me." Ren starts walking. "Onto the road, Lucknar."

"You're no fun," Lucky mutters.

————

During our trek, Gyrax and I break away from the others so he can field my questions out of earshot (Lucky and Elier don't need to know I'm an Earthling). Unsurprisingly, talking with Gyrax is a fantasy geek's dream.

Almost everyone here can cast magic. It's usually bordered by glowing runes, which serve as a form of arcane signature. The runes can be thought of as the spell's code, while the spell itself is the actual computer program. Throughout Gyrax's spiel, he weaves in terms like *meridians* and *loci*. Apparently, our auric bodies have channels and reservoirs (meridians and loci) that function like veins and organs, only in a magical sense. He goes on to say that Lyderea and her minions have exclusive access to the Velic Tessellate, which means they possess an enormous advantage. They don't have to rely on the magic in their auras—they have a surplus of power at their beck and call.

Eventually, the conversation turns to our Earthling life. He's quick to bring up Nommie McGobberYoms.

"I enjoyed their cookies, but the freeze-dried bison—by the *gods* it was tasty!" He smacks his lips and bugs his eyes, surprising me into a full-throated laugh.

Lucky draws abreast, attracted by the noise. "What do you speak of?"

Gyrax smiles. "None of your concern."

A nonchalant shrug. "As you will."

Gyrax falls back and appraises Elier. "What about you, Duelist? What captures your interest?"

Elier responds with a rakish grin. "A worthy opponent. I know enough magic to hold my own, but my first love is—and always will be—for my cavalry sabers."

As they're conversing, I peek at Ren. He hasn't joined in but there's a certain attentiveness to him. It doesn't show in his face or posture—it's a slight *offness* if I had to describe it.

After Gyrax and Elier finish their convo, Lucky regales us with tales of his exploits. He's stolen from lords and taxmen, seduced married noblewomen (and sometimes their daughters), and worked as part of a team-run burglary, like a fantasy-world version of *Ocean's Eleven*.

"But you still pick pockets," I interject. "Why?"

"It's the very first skill I learned as a thief. As such, I consider it forthright and honest—it works to keep me grounded and sharp."

Elier snorts. " 'Forthright and honest?' It's kind of the opposite, don't you think?"

Lucky wags a chiding finger. "Now, now, consider our history: a kingdom-wide curse, unchecked war, Lyderea's rise...we're justified in doing anything and everything to balance the scales."

"The scales are balanced by way of the blade. I have never lacked for coin or shelter—there is always a need for a good Duelist."

"And is that how you think the world should be?" Gyrax asks. He isn't judging; he's genuinely curious.

"That's how it is."

"Perhaps." Lucky flips a dagger, letting it whirl and twirl before snatching its hilt. "But I do not believe the world is transactional—I believe that abundance abounds."

"In others' purses," Ren mutters.

"Which is why I love my unwitting marks!" Lucky chortles. "If not for their coin, I would be forced to beg for crumbs and scraps!"

"Maybe there's a better way," Gyrax ventures. "Waiting on the other side of our imagination."

Elier scoffs. "Open your eyes, Wolven, before someone cuts them from your skull. Dreamers live short, painful lives."

"Then I cede my doom, for I refuse to set my dreams aside. As for my eyes..." Gyrax shrugs. "What my eyes can't see, my nose will smell. What my nose can't smell, my ears will hear."

Lucky says excitedly, "You speak of faith, Master Wolven! I am of the same mind as you—if not for faith, I would never snatch a wayward coin, as fear would strike me dumb and clumsy."

Ren turns and spits in disgust. "So because of your 'faith,' you steal from the needy, lining your carry with their blood and sweat."

"And they would do the same, given the chance." Lucky flips his dagger, tries to catch it, but almost grabs it by the blade. "Whoop!"

He bends over and retrieves his knife. "See?" He grins up at Ren. "My faith protects me."

Ren falls silent. His contempt for Lucky is a palpable thing.

"I agree in part, but I believe your view is incomplete," Gyrax offers.

Lucky resumes flipping his dagger. "To each their own, eh? Time will prove who is right: Elier and his blades, your dreams and fancies, or..." he trails off and looks at Ren.

Ren turns and spits again.

Lucky laughs and sheaths his knife. "Well, there you go." He catches my attention with a jerk of his chin. "Jon. While we're thinning our soles on this damnable road, allow me to teach you a bit of my craft."

I'm shocked into laughter. "I'm not a thief, Lucky!"

"Everyone steals. Time, aid, companionship...someone pays and someone profits."

"Some give freely," I counter. "Ever think of that?"

"Not since I was a child in Lydenfeld Castle, with tailors to clothe me and cooks to feed me."

"What?" Now I'm confused. "You're royalty?"

"Daiken Yetshaw, at your service." Lucky dips into a sweeping bow. "I prefer to refrain from my given name, as it might attract unwanted scrutiny."

"The son of a lord?" Gyrax asks, puzzled. "So why would you—"

"My kin are known far and wide as sailor-merchants, but known farther and wider as treacherous scum. My brothers and sisters are no exception—shortly after my tenth birthday, I was accused of treason and stripped of lineage."

"Your *tenth birthday?*" I gape at him.

"Aye," Lucky affirms. "I was cast from my house as a luckless child. Ironic, isn't it?"

"So your family took what was rightfully yours, and now you do the same to others." Ren scoffs. "Predictable."

Lucky's face tightens with anger—the first time he's expressed anything besides cheer or mischief—but then his merriment returns. "If I am, it is only the work of a greater hand. Call it fate, call it fortune, call it whatever you plea—"

"Wrong has been done," Ren snaps. "But that is no excuse to leech off others."

Lucky straightens up, mock offended. "I am merely a lesson from the world at large!"

I raise an eyebrow. "Interesting way to put it."

"But true, no?" Lucky's grin is charming as hell. It's also predatory. "I relieve my prey of their naivete, and they pass on the lesson by doing the same to others. The disillusionment goes 'round and 'round, and that is how the world is kept spinning."

Gyrax shakes his head. "You're wrong, Lucky. As the sky is blue and the night is long."

"Prove it, Wolven. Grace me with coin from your royal largesse."

"That I shall do," Gyrax replies. "But first I must parlay with Ardos Rygar."

"The Birthright Alliance?" Lucky tilts his head. "They aren't known for their kindness or amity."

"We have agreed to meet at Tyr Noctin, when Ilae the Moon eclipses the sun. Until then, I have cast my lot with Ren and Jon."

"When Ilae the Moon eclipses the sun..." Lucky chews his lips. Then he exclaims, "That's ten months distant! Why so long?"

Gyrax contemplates the road. "I can only guess. But knowing Ardos, he is forging a pact that will work to his favor."

"Makes sense. But why would you follow Ren and Jo—"

"My reasons are my own."

Lucky and Elier exchange a glance. Unspoken communication flows between them.

Lucky turns back to Gyrax. "We shall watch your back and assist with camp. Not as soldiers, but as roadside companions. However, you must pay us six hundred regals and cover our costs. Also, give us an advance of half our fee."

"How about collateral instead?" Gyrax reaches in his carry and produces a multicolored, unhewn rock. Most of its surface is rough and craggy, but the clearer parts glimmer and shine.

"A dimfire gem?" Lucky's eyes widen with greed. "Give it here!"

Gyrax parts with the stone. "Forgo your advance. In return, I will pay you a thousand regals after meeting with Ardos, upon which I will ask that you return the gem."

"Fair," Elier agrees. "More than fair."

Lucky holds the rock close, inspecting its facets with a piggish gaze. It's a little unnerving—he looks a lot like Gollum and a bit like Joker.

After an awkward silence (for us, not him), he nods with vigor. "As you say, Master Wolven."

Elier asks Ren, "Now that's settled, what is your business in Naversé Township? We follow the Wolven and the Wolven follows you, so..."

"It was twofold, originally," Ren says. "I was going to leave him—" he gives me a nod, "—with someone better suited to care for his needs, but that is no longer the case. Now I go there to soothe a friend. When last we met he was severely ill; I fear he is approaching the Eventide Clear."

(Eventide Clear...wow. So much cooler than heaven or hell.)

"You're a better man than I," Lucky remarks. "If death came a-knocking, no one I know would ask for my presence. I've charmed too many wives, lightened too many carries."

"And if you lighten my friend's, I'll lighten your body of your thieving spirit. The man I seek is not to be touched. Do you understand me, highwayman? *Do. Not. Touch him.*" Ren steps in front of Lucky, gripping his sword and assuming a draw-stance.

Lucky raises his hands in a conciliatory gesture. "Easy, Ren. While you palaver with your friend, Elier and I will wait outside."

For a long moment, Ren is silent. Then he starts down the path, cueing the rest of us to follow. After a couple minutes, he eyes me and Gyrax. "You two may accompany me during my visit. You both reek of fate and destiny."

I throw him a sideways look. "You say that like it's bad."

"It often is," Ren says grimly. "Fate and destiny grind many to dust. And in so doing, they create men like him." He regards Lucky with clear disgust.

The thief shrugs with upturned hands: *What can you do?*

Gyrax leans in and whispers, "Learn from him, Jon. Take him up on his offer."

"What? Why? I'm not gonna steal!" I'm a little shocked. A little offended, too.

"His skills hold value. It is only theft because he makes it so."

"Yeah...I guess. For some it's survival, I would imagine."

"For you it's protection," Ren growls, "from low-shadow thieves who would beggar the world."

"That's right!" Lucky declares. "Always watch out for those low-shadow thieves!" He claps me on the shoulder. "What say you, Jon?"

"I..." I look at Gyrax, who gives me a nod. "I...okay."

"That's the spirit!" Lucky snaps his fingers, producing a coin from seemingly out of nowhere. "Now listen close—thievery centers around desire and focus. Everyone shares the same desires: safety, security, companionship...To ply my trade, you must understand how a desire becomes focus, then coax that desire toward a focus of your choosing. In the beginning, it is about baser perceptions—what the eye sees, what the ear hears, so on and so forth. But with time and experience, theft becomes so much more: a mental tandem of give-and-take, where your mark doesn't miss anything until they've given you everything..."

Thus begins my intro to stealing.

11

Lucky's instruction covers more than technique; it's an insight into how he views the world. He's handsome and charming, but I'm pretty sure he's a clinical sociopath.

As he drills me on the basics (assessing a mark, sleight of hand, and pickup artist-style seduction, believe it or not) he throws in anecdotes about past robberies. They boil down to this: he takes from anyone and everyone. Doesn't matter if it's a lord or a pauper—he's an equal opportunist in the worst way possible.

"You learn quickly," he says after showing me how to hide something by slipping it in my shoe. (Useful, apparently, when a Knight tackles you and wants to see what's in your hands). "That one took me over a week."

"Thanks, man."

Everyone stares, then bursts into laughter.

"What?" I ask, mildly irritated. "Why is that funny?"

"I'm sorry." Gyrax wipes a tear from his eye. "It's just that—"

"Of course I'm a *man!*" Lucky exclaims. "Why declare it? Why does it matter?"

Gyrax throws him a good-natured wave: *Don't worry about it.* " 'Tis a common expression amongst his kin."

Elier shakes his head in seeming befuddlement. "Forgive me, but I have no desire to visit your home. You and your folk seem a tad bit strange."

I almost retort that Evermoor is filled with dragons and wizards, when I remember that all of that is seen as perfectly normal here.

Which is followed by an epiphany: when you put it in context, my life on Earth was definitely weird. I was ready to accept forty-plus years of 9-5 drudgery, knowing full well that it would slowly but steadily kill my soul.

"You're not wrong," I allow. "But we all have issues."

"Aye." Ren looks pointedly at Lucky. "Some of us hide behind past misfortunes—use them as an excuse to prey on the weak."

"Not just the weak!" Lucky cries. "I take from any and all!"

"Your integrity is impressive," Gyrax remarks dryly.

"Exactly!" Lucky gestures at him. "Gyrax understands!"

Ren spits in disgust and continues walking.

————

Over the next three weeks, the trees give way to hills and prairie. We have rabbit for dinner every night, thanks to Lucky and his collapsible short bow. Elier dusts it with salt and pepper, then Gyrax fries it in seasoned lard. It tastes amazing—as good as anything I ate on Earth.

If we want to bathe or do our laundry, one of the others will conjure a pond, concealed beneath a snarl of tree-roots. Way better (and cooler) than a bathtub or shower.

I have three spare sets of Evermoor clothes, courtesy of Ren and his well-stocked carry. No boots, but I'm fine with sneakers. He also gives me socks and undies, which fit better than anything I wore back home. Apparently, they have minor enchantments that wick away moisture and keep my funk from spiraling out of control.

Before I know it, I've spent two months traveling the road. I continue training in knifework and thievery, and even start learning how to shoot Lucky's bow. I get to mess with weapons, eat good food, and listen to mind-bending stories under a starry night sky.

(Which, according to Gyrax, has *four moons*. Most of the time, you can only see one or two, but still—*four moons.)*

Life. Is. *Awesome.*

I know, I know—I should be concerned about my family and friends, but whenever I think about them, inexplicable surety arises in my mind. I know they're okay, I know they're not worried, and I know at the deepest level of their conscious beings, they understand and accept that I'm where I'm supposed to be.

I'd call it clairvoyance, but it doesn't come with visions. Despite that, the vibe I get is undeniable—I can somehow intuit that events are coinciding to account for my absence. Don't ask me how, because I would have no idea where to begin.

I just *know*. I know it mind, body, and soul.

Which allows me to enjoy my D&D trip. People would pay good money for this, but I get to do it free of charge. *And* I get to do it with a bunch of guys that could double as *Lord of the Rings* extras.

If I had to guess, I'd say I'm a third level fighter/thief.

(Well, probably first level, but it's fun to pretend.)

————

For the past four days, the road has been rough and untrod. As we get closer to Naversé, it begins to smooth out.

Only now, after several months on a parallel world, does it occur to me to ask about my encounter with Atriya. (I suspect it's because my crossing wasn't smooth—I still feel scrambled from time to time). So I wait until the others are talking, then sidle up next to Gyrax.

"Hey," I whisper. "I never told you how I got here. There was this Marine recruiter named Chris Atriya—"

He holds up a paw. "Say no more. You were bought to our world by an Eternal Archetype."

"I'm guessing that's important? Sounds important."

"Not in the way that you..." Gyrax scratches his head. "A better word for it would be influential. He's got his fingers in a lot of pies."

"You don't say." I half-scoff, half-chuckle. "In my case, he decided to stick his fingers in the *transport-an-Earth-boy-into-a-fantasy-world-adventure* pie."

"It's what you asked for at the deepest level of your causal being. Usually, he comes in the form of a dream or an impulse."

I'm about to ask what a "causal being" is, but Elier jumps in with, "Ho, Jon. What do you speak of?"

"Food and games," I answer. (I'm a little proud of how smoothly I lie. Lucky's lessons are starting to take). I turn to Ren and ask, "Who's this friend of yours again?"

"Terrelly Jindow," he replies. "Not just a friend, but a mentor as well."

"He trained you?"

"He did."

"So he taught you to be a sour churl?" Lucky grouses. "Joy."

"He taught me to catch a low-shadow thief," Ren counters. "As far as my temper, it comes from the legions of thieves that have crossed my path. I've had to gut more than a few."

"I see." Lucky smiles. "Then it's a good thing I'm promised coin, else I'd foul your boots with my rancid innards."

Ren snorts, which is par for the course, but this time he sounds genuinely amused.

"Bless my ears." Elier cocks his head in surprise. "Is that mirth I hear, Master Ren?"

Ren falls quiet, then grudgingly cedes, "Our world is mired in darkness and hate. Light is needed, from time to time."

"Ha!" Lucky crows. "Mark the date and the time, for I have just drawn cheer from Wretched Ren! Who would have thought?"

"And who would have thought that Lyderea Fairdyle would make herself Queen?" Ren stops in his tracks and points angrily at Lucky.

"Here you stand, much like her, using laughter and chaff to excuse your crimes. All the while, you steal from the poor, absolving your theft with a jest and a smirk. I regret my cheer, for you do not deserve a grin or a smile—*you are a weight around our collective necks!*"

Lucky looks stricken. Gyrax and Elier seem taken aback.

After a hanging silence, Lucky quietly states, "I am nothing like her."

"No," Ren sneers. "She is far more competent. Stay the course, Lucky—she might take you on as her trusted second. You two are a perfect match: you steal from the needy, while she creates the need that turns them destitu—"

Lucky screams and tackles Ren. They transform into a blur of fists and cloaks.

Gyrax hooks Ren's arms and drags him off. Elier kneels on Lucky and pins him down. The thief flails and kicks, then thrusts a shaking finger at Ren's face.

"You know *nothing* about me, Ren! *NOTHING!*"

Ren yells, "I know *enough!* You and your ilk would raze the world, laughing merrily all the while! If you would burn us down to ash and cinder, then do it quickly, damn you! I would rather be char than a smoldering ember!"

Lucky curses and thrashes, but Elier manages to hold him down. Finally, the thief mutters, "Cry off, Elier. I don't want to fight."

Elier gets to his feet and tries to brush off Lucky's jerkin. "Are you—"

Lucky swats him away. "Hands. *Off.*"

The Duelist backs away, palms raised. "As you wish."

Ren grumbles, "My temper has cooled. Let me up, Wolven."

Gyrax releases him. We all take a cautious step back. Ren and Lucky exchange dagger-eyed death-stares.

They both speak at the same time: "I'm—"

Lucky dips his chin and raises a hand. "You first."

"It is in our interest to maintain the peace," Ren says stiffly. "At least while traveling side by side."

"Agreed."

Gyrax studies them, trying to determine if they're being sincere. When he decides that they are, he says, "Grips, gentlemen—I'd see them now."

For a split-second they both hesitate, then reach out and grab each other's forearms. An Evermoor version of an Earthling handshake.

"I plead thy grace," Lucky says stiltedly.

"No need, Kai Yetshaw. I plead yours." Ren's reply isn't as stilted, but it's pretty close.

"All is forgiven. And don't call me Yetshaw—it has been a day and an age since I went by that name."

"As you wish."

They both step away. We resume walking.

" 'Kai?' " I mutter. I've heard it before, but I haven't paid attention up until now.

"An honorific," Gyrax explains. "*Kai* is the masculine. *Sha* is the feminine."

"Oh. Okay." Nice—now I know that instead of shaking hands, you squeeze forearms. And instead of *sir* or *ma'am,* it's *kai* and *sha.*

I throw him a grin. "Think I leveled up. Or at least gained a perk."

Gyrax chuckles. "You and your games. I can still picture you staring at the screen, clicking away at that damned controller."

"Questing through Fallout while you lounged on the sofa. Good times."

"But you didn't realize it—not then." He ruffles my hair. "Now you do."

I'm a little thrown by the reversal of roles (I'm used to petting him, not the other way around) but only for a moment. Gribbles/Gyrax is way cooler than I ever imagined. If not for him, I'd be stuck with Grumpy McGrumperson (my nickname for Ren) and some shady mercenaries. (Which is what Elier and Lucky are, when you get right down to it).

For the next five days, Ren and Lucky stop communicating. It isn't quite a girlfriend freeze-out, but it feels strikingly similar. Thankfully, Elier and Gyrax fill the silence by talking (mostly about duels, since that's what Elier's interested in). I'm happy to just shut up and listen.

Elier grew up in Khairach Taire, one of four nation-states that end with the suffix "Taire." The term is a derivative of the word *Tairya,* which loosely translates to "honor contest." Each Taire—Khairach Taire, Withywick Taire, Genwick Taire and Relting Taire—is a combat society. Together, they form a confederation of libertarian enclaves, committed to producing the deadliest duelists in all of Evermoor. Everyone starts as an Apprentice Duelist, which is their way of calling someone a rookie. After documented approval from a master tutor, they're awarded the title of Journeyman Duelist.

Elier Finn is one rank higher: he's a High Taire Duelist, which is earned after a hundred and fifty duels, all witnessed by an Arbiter Duelist (the highest rank attainable, and also the closest thing the Taires have to a government official). He's won all but one match (it ended in a draw) against a woman named Idinia Skyfold. Due to her weapons—bladed forearm braces and a double-edged short sword—her style favored grappling and entangling. Elier, who uses a pair of cavalry sabers, was unable to keep her from closing the distance.

"Typically, I control my opponent through range and rhythm," he says. "Two sabers quicken my tempo: one-two, one-two—" he moves his hands in alternating slashes, "as well as allowing me to attack and defend simultaneously."

"How did Idinia hold you off?" I ask.

He shakes his head in grudging admiration. "She is utterly masterful at controlling the gap. Even better at in-pocket fighting."

" 'In-pocket?' "

"Extremely close range," Gyrax explains.

Elier nods. "She dominated our match with position and footwork. Once we were locked, she pressed the advantage with her short sword and vambraces. I was saved by luck: her blade snapped during our exchange. It was the unlikeliest of accidents—Idinia knows how to choose her weapons, and cares for them all as if they were family. Since she could no longer express the extent of her skill, I proposed we call off our duel, to which the Arbiter agreed. On any other day, she would have split me open from stem to stern."

I clear my throat, impressed and intimidated. "She sounds...intense."

Elier gives me a puzzled look. "Why wouldn't she be?"

Ren (for the first time in several days) decides to speak up. "Some seek peace, Duelist. Not everyone wishes for conflict."

"But conflict is life."

"It doesn't have to be."

"And yet it is."

"I tell you again, Duelist: it doesn't have to be."

(Irresistible force, meet immovable object.)

Elier gives a noncommittal shrug. "Time will prove which of us is right."

Lucky breaks his silence with, "I am of the same mind as Ren; conflict is unnecessary. I get by fine on faith and fortu—" He glances at Ren's darkening expression and amends it to: "I get by fine without picking fights."

Ren opens his mouth to reply, but an ear-piercing screech cuts him off. Everyone halts and straightens in place.

Three more screeches rip through my brain; a hell of a lot closer, and a hell of a lot *louder*.

Ren breaks right. *"Head for the cairns!"*

We take off running toward a massive ring of standing rocks, roughly a hundred yards distant. They're the only cover for miles around; we're caught in an ocean of rolling prairie.

Shadows flicker across the ground. I glance up and spot a V of silhouettes, made hazy and indistinct by the afternoon sun.

"RUN!" Elier shoves me in the back. *"STOP GAWKING, JON!"*

I do as he says. I'm not sure what's up there, but I trust it's legit.

After a seeming eternity, we reach the rocks and hunker behind them. Lucky opens his bow and nocks an arrow. Ren straightens a finger against his lips, urging us all to keep quiet.

Leathery wings beat the air, then an angry *whoosh* fills my ears. Feverish swelter rolls across us, blanketing my face in torrid warmth. The heat is everywhere, searing my lungs, stinging my skin, filling every nook and cranny with perspiration. I can't believe I made it to Evermoor, only to get cooked behind a giant ro—

"Tsst."

Ren points at his eyes with his index and middle fingers, then flicks them up at our airborne pursuers. He wants me to look.

No way. No *way.* I shake my head from side to side.

Ren pokes out, takes a good long look, then ducks behind cover and turns his hands up.

See? Nothing to worry about.

The rest of us peek around the edges of our rocks. My lips part in utter amazement.

Tree-high flames are eating the prairie. Fortunately, the super-wide road is acting like a firebreak and keeping the inferno from advancing toward us. Up above the red-lit char, six flying lizards —each one about a dozen feet long—are circling and swooping. They're all mounted by armored knights.

One curls inward and blows concentrated fire out from its mouth. When the flames hit the ground, they unfurl into a mess of enormous billows, lashing the plains with displaced air.

"Whoa," I whisper. "Are those...dragons?"

"No," Gyrax whispers backs, "Wyverns. Smaller, weaker, and far less intelligent. Dragons are ten times as large and they don't breathe fire."

"But they're related, right? I mean, not that I've seen a dragon before, but..."

"They are," he says at normal volume, confident that the wyverns aren't targeting us. "During the Wars, Lyderea stole a clutch of red dragon eggs and magically stunted them, causing the hatchlings to mature into wyverns. They became a different species altogether—inbreeding and sorcery have taken their toll."

"What about the riders?"

"Rainfire Knights. Trained to dismantle defensive spells, exposing their prey to fire and talon. That's why the Alliance sticks to the forest. It isn't cover—although with the proper enchantment it can function as such—but it does provide a degree of concealment."

"Why are they burning an empty prairie?"

Ren wipes his brow with the back of his wrist. "They're sending a warning, if I had to guess. Naversé must have angered its Justicers."

The wyverns fly in a wide loop, one behind the other. After three revolutions, the leader breaks off and the rest of them follow. Moments later, they disappear from view.

Whew.

Lucky mumbles something magical, causing his bow to collapse into a small baton. Elier takes a weighted breath.

"I thought they were going to roast us alive."

"I'm halfway there," Lucky groans. "My skin feels cracked, like overworked leather."

"Back on the road." Ren steps out from behind his rock.

Gyrax offers a paw and hauls me up. "What are real dragons like?" I ask.

"As I said, they are a great deal larger. And they also breathe lightning."

"Whoa." My face slackens with amazement. Are you *kidding me?* Lightning-breathing dragons? *What?*

Then I remember: I saw them in my Earth-side visions. They were breathing lightning, but it wasn't like anything I'd seen before—it was less like lightning and more like a death-ray, ripping through sky and cloud with a terrible authority. As if it would be an insult to touch it and do anything less than cease to exist.

"Aye." He gives me a smile, amused at my unabashed geekery. "It's a different color than their outer scales."

"Cool." My eyes grow wide, but I'm not the least bit embarrassed. (Come on—if there's ever a time to let your nerd flag fly, this is it.) "Are there any dragons that breathe black lightning?"

"There are. Yellow, purple, red, green..." His amusement fades. "That was before the Tessellate failed. Its collapse wreaked havoc on the arcane tides. As dragons are sensitive to sorcerous upheaval, the majority became sick and exhausted. Lyderea killed hundreds in their weakened state."

"Did any of them survive?"

As we step on the road, Ren casts a quick enchantment, protecting us from the residual heat.

"Two that I know of." Gyrax raises his voice so he can be heard above the flames. "A blue and a green. They both reside in Aerie Denir, a city that juts from a sheer cliffside."

He's talking about the aerial metropolis I saw in my visions.

I open my mouth, about to elaborate, then I glance back at Lucky and Elier, trailing a few yards behind us. Who knows what they would do (or who they would speak to) for the right amount of money? They're really just mercenaries, when you get right down to it.

Gyrax's eyes don't leave mine. I get the sense that he knows what I'm thinking. My suspicions are confirmed when he says, "You're learning, Jon."

"Just leveled up." I throw a couple of punches at no one in particular. "Gimme a perk and some extra hit points."

My former dog rolls his eyes. "I never understood how a glowing screen could hold your interest."

"Show some respect," I chide. "Without video games, I wouldn't have a context for fantasy-world life—I'd cower and hide instead of trying to level up." I draw my dagger and slash the air, then make it disappear with a sleight-of-hand twist. "See? I'm probably like a fourth-level fighter/thief."

Gyrax laughs. "Who knew that *Diablo* and *Skyrim* could prepare you for Evermoor?"

"I know, right? *Elder Scrolls V* was a hint from the universe."

His expression turns thoughtful. "It very well could have been. Existence works in mysterious ways."

We continue down the road, watching the horizon give way to Naversé Township. Half the world—the prairie on our left—is still ablaze. Despite the inferno, I feel deeply at peace; it's all gonna burn, but something new will grow in its place.

Something good, hopefully.

Maybe even great.

12

Naversé is filled with cobbled roads, cozy houses, and shops that look like their names start with "Ye Olde." Under normal circumstances, I would find them charming.

Not today, though. The streets are empty, completely deserted. Every so often, I glimpse someone peeking through a shuttered window.

"Do you think it's a trap?" Elier scans the town.

"No," Ren says, "they're hiding."

I glance back at the smog-coated sky. If I saw wyverns going buck-nuts pyro, I'd probably be in hiding too.

"This is not to my liking," Lucky grumbles. "How can I earn when no one's about?"

Elier cups his mouth. *"We are naught but travelers!"*

No response.

"Enough of this," Ren mutters. "I need to find Terrelly."

As he starts forward, a portly man steps out from a door, hands raised. "Wind at your back and sun on your brow. My name is Biles Lom. I serve as unofficial mayor of Naversé Township."

I murmur, "Unofficial?"

Gyrax whispers, "In order to serve in an official capacity, you must be ordained as an Iaetrix Knight."

"Gotcha," I whisper back.

"Ren of the Barrens." Ren touches his forehead with his right index and middle finger, palm facing in, then moves his hand outward in a perfunctory greeting. "The wyverns have left, Kai Lom. Why is everyone still in hiding?"

"We didn't know if they were coming back." Biles gives us a wary look. "Still don't."

"Us? Knights?" Lucky spreads his arms in a *come-on-now* gesture. "We lack the armor and malice, Kai Lom."

"Did you run afoul of the local Justicers?" Gyrax asks.

"In a manner of speaking." Biles lowers his hands. "We always paid extra to their cursed tithe-men. This last cycle, however, we had nothing to spare. Our commerce has slowed—bandits and storms have taken their toll."

"But you paid what you owed?"

"Aye." An angry tic materializes high on his cheek. "And it wasn't enough. The Justicers threatened us—swore they'd return with a Darksickle sorcerer."

" 'Darksickle?' " I whisper to Gyrax.

"A mage who specializes in arcane torture," he whispers back. "They punish folk who don't meet quota."

Ah—he's talking about Pain Wizards. The half-men, half-smoke tormentors from my Earth-side visions.

"You are fortunate, Kai Lom," Ren says. "They burned the prairie and left you be. I'd count them as fools if they went any further—why saddle you with additional strife, when you reliably contribute more than you owe?"

Lom considers this, then grudgingly nods. "Your reasoning is sound, Ren of the Barrens. Forgive our caution—we are unaccustomed to Rainfire Knights."

"There is nothing to forgive," Ren replies. "You acted with prudence."

Lom turns and hollers, "It is safe to come out!"

People emerge from their shuttered homes. If they weren't so scared, I would find them amusing—like cartoon creatures taking teeny tiny steps out from their makeshift hidey-holes. But it's all too clear this isn't a cartoon; their faces are raw with pain and fear.

Ren clears his throat. "Master Lom, I am seeking a man named Terrelly Jindow. The last I had heard, he was residing within the Soothing Hand."

"I know of no such man. But you are free to look and see for yourself."

"My thanks, Kai Lom. May light find you in dark places."

"Aye, wanderer. May it ease your eyes and guide your feet."

A few blocks later we arrive at a red-brick house, about as big as a large McMansion. Unlike the townhomes lining the street, the Soothing Hand stands by itself, bordered by a yard and a neat garden. I recognize some of the plants—sage, lilac, ivy—but most are native to the world of Evermoor. A few give off feathery light. Others emit a whimsical hum.

(Cool. Never thought a flower could carry a tune.)

The door is marked by a hand-carved sign, decorated with an engraving of a hand above a tree. Ren lifts the clapper and knocks twice.

"Your name!" a woman calls.

"Ren of the Barrens."

"Your business!"

"I have come to see a friend: Terrelly Jindow."

A head-level slit slides to the left, revealing a pair of bright green pupils. They scan Ren, then give the rest of us a thorough once-over.

"A moment."

The eye-slit closes. We hear the owner of the voice walking away.

"Quite hospitable for a place of hospice," Lucky quips.

"Curb your judgment," Ren snaps. "Naversé is known for its flavored smoke, not a heavy Justicer presence."

"A charred prairie and some flying lizards?" Elier scoffs. "Soft warning, compared to what you would receive in Tellric or Jyde."

The latch unclicks, revealing a tall, pretty lady. "Wind at your back and sun on your brow. I am Perisa, assistant safewoman of the Soothing Hand. While you are here, I ask that you soften your voice and speak with repose."

We acknowledge her request with a scatter of "ayes," then follow her through a series of hallways. After a couple of turns, we arrive at a nondescript door.

"Once you are finished, exit the same way you came." Perisa gives us the touching-your-forehead greeting, then turns and leaves.

Ren glares at Lucky. "See yourself out."

"His Sourness has spoken." Lucky glances at Elier and jerks his chin toward the entrance. "Let us away before he throws a fit."

Ren stands where he is, making it a point to watch them depart, then reaches out and turns the knob.

The room is spare but comfy; furnished with two sets of drawers, a trio of lamps, and a plain wooden desk. The far-left corner is home to a bed, inhabited by a powerfully built, older Hispanic man. He's fast asleep beneath a quilt.

"Terrelly?" Ren steps toward the bed.

The man cracks a filmy eye. Confusion plays across his face, then slowly gives way to recognition.

"Rennarean Arteris," he whispers.

"Aye." Ren kneels and takes his hand. "I still draw breath, thanks to you."

Terrelly explodes with violent coughs. Ren twitches in, ready to catch him, but Terrelly mutters, "Cry off, cry off," and brushes him away. After taking a moment to regain his composure, he scans our party with a rheumy gaze.

"A Wolven," he whispers. "Your color and ridge...you are Fenric royalty."

"Gyrax Aclasian." Gyrax lowers to a knee and bows his head. "At your service, Kai Jindow."

Terrelly laughs—a hoarse, scraping bark. "Stand tall, Wolven. There is no need for bows and titles. Not in my presence."

Gyrax rises. "I disagree. To this day, my folk tell tale of Terrelly Jindow, Explorer Captain of the Wayfarer Advance. Before the Fracture, you thwarted myriad villains." He starts ticking points off on his fingers. "The Red Count of Scythe, the Lich King of Kade, the Elsars of Wreak...if not for you and your wanderer army, our world would have drowned in sorrow and woe."

"And what became of those storied wanderers?" Terrelly's voice is bitter and jaded. "The last two Wayfarers stand before you."

"You are not alone, Kai Jindow. I have been training my Wolven to—"

Terrelly interrupts with a dismissive wave. "Lyderea has crushed countless rebellions."

"Hope lives on," Gyrax insists. "Fair Folk are leaving their enchanted hides. Wildlyre are forging bonds and pacts. Even some Duelists have taken up arms."

Terrelly shakes his head. "After sixty years of pain and strife, I have come to understand a bitter truth: people will gather to grumble and squawk, but nothing will inspire them to actual change. I was at Sidehelm, Wolven, when the kings of Erendor turned their backs. After all their talk of honor and duty, they struck a pact with Arganti Knifelock."

"The world can change, Terrelly." Ren searches his face. "You taught me to say that before I slept. Have you forgotten the times we shared together?"

"I wish I had, Rennarean, for what I taught you to say was a thoughtless lie."

Gyrax clasps my shoulder. "All is not lost. Not according to the Vagabond King."

Terrelly scoffs. "Alijyar fled when we needed him most. His interest in our cause was a passing fancy."

"Before you stands the Prophesied Traveler."

Terrelly stiffens in surprise. "Aye?" He looks me up and down, then scoffs again. "You expect me to rally behind this boy?"

"Jon was born on another world."

Doubt flickers through his eyes. "So say you?"

"So says Alijyar."

I clear my throat. "Um...pleased to meet you, sir. Kai, I mean."

He pins me down with a pain-riven gaze. "I have met heroes aplenty, and most of them fell to a headman's axe. The ones who lived grew weary and slack—they lost their souls to smoke and drink."

"I'm no hero," I protest. "I'm just a man. Like you, like Ren, like..." I glance at Gyrax and mentally kick myself. "Like...yeah."

"Just a man, eh? Lyderea sacrificed her humanity to gain her power. If you wish to defeat her, you may very well have to do the same. Who's to say you won't become her? Or Shaddock forbid, something even worse?"

I fumble for an answer. Eventually I say, "Well...I've always got my dog. He's a positive thinker—gotta count for something." A nervous chuckle escapes from my mouth.

Total silence. (Great—I'm the Evermoor version of Michael Scott.)

Terrelly sits up in small, halting lurches. "The Avalon Clapfire. You still have it, aye?"

Ren nods. "You told me to guard it with my life. You never said why."

"According to Alijyar, the Prophesied Traveler will bond with Ailura. I wish to see if Jon can awaken her."

"I sincerely doubt it, but very well." Ren un-rigs a triangular pouch from his lower back. "Here."

"What uh…what is it?" I take it with both hands. (Whoof—heavy.)

"Open it," Terrelly instructs.

I unfasten the cover, then reach inside and curl my fingers around a hunk of wood. I pull it out and find myself staring at the bottom half of a giant revolver.

The chamber and barrel are both missing, but the grip, hammer, and trigger are all still there. It's way bigger than a regular pistol—the cowboy equivalent of a claymore sword. Beautiful scrollwork adorns the wood, aglow with a light that leaks through my fingers. The sorcerous radiance feels warm and even, a rhythmic pulse that steadies my hand.

Terrelly sighs in disappointment. "He isn't the Traveler. If he was, the arcane surge would be undeniable."

"Reserve your judgment," Gyrax cautions. "This is only half a weapon."

"His senses aren't quickened." Ren plucks the revolver from my grasp. "Perhaps that is a factor."

"What?" Terrelly's expression twists in dismay. "How could you possibly navigate life?" He shakes his head, baffled. "Unquickened senses…that cements my belief you are not the Traveler." He looks Gyrax in the eye. "And a boy who hails from another world, though curious and rare, does not justify the fire of war."

" 'Tis not a fire, Explorer. It is a building flood, ready to sweep through Evermoor and cleanse it of hate."

Terrelly glares at him. "My body is shattered, Wolven. My mind as well—it runs and slides like a broken yolk, thanks to Lyderea's Darksickle wretches. If you would avoid a similar fate, then cry off this senseless madness. There is no hope against the White Veiled Queen."

Gyrax's demeanor turns icy and harsh. "If you truly believe that, there is only one Wayfarer within this room. And it is not you, Kai Jindow."

Anger blazes in Terrelly's gaze. "Take your leave, you low-shadow harrier! I would cross into the Clear with a measure of peace!"

"You'll find none in here," Gyrax says coldly. He pivots on his heel and strides out the door.

Ren's mouth opens and closes. He's at a loss for words, completely dumbstruck.

Terrelly regards him with blatant disgust. "Lyderea has won, boy, plain and simple. Eke out a life while you still can. And for Shaddock's sake, don't have children—they do not deserve this blighted world!"

"Terrelly, I—"

"Go!" he snarls. *"I have nothing to say to you!"*

Ren walks out with a wooden expression. I follow behind and close the door. Before it shuts, I catch a parting glimpse of Terrelly Jindow. His head is bowed and his lip is quivering—both cheeks are wet with tears.

Based on what he said, I can't say I wouldn't feel the same.

13

Ren collects himself in typical Ren fashion: by staring furiously at nothing.

After nearly a minute of Silent Rage, I ask, "What's the Wayfarer Advance?"

"A body of folk who ranged long and far," Gyrax answers. "Known for their magic and swordplay, but even more for their bravery and wit."

"Like Jedi Knights."

Gyrax nods. "But less uptight. Their original goal was to uncover wisdom and spread it throughout Evermoor. That changed during the Crimson Wars, when they fought against the Queen as saboteur-scouts."

"And it changed again at the battle of Sidehelm?"

Another nod. "They were all but eliminated."

"What happened? Terrelly mentioned it, but..."

"The Unity marshalled at Sidehelm Pass, where they planned to—"

"The Unity?"

Gyrax sighs. "The Juric Unity: a widespread alliance that opposed the Queen. After long months of barter and treaty, the Kings of Erendor aligned with the Unity. Their armies comprised three-quarters of the attacking force."

"But they didn't follow through—they turned traitor instead."

"Aye. In their eyes, a Unity victory would come at a cost: the need to work with countless factions. Rather than bow to consensus and compromise, the kings secretly sided with Lyderea's generals."

"Wow. So they pretended to join the Unity...then fought them at Sidehelm?"

Gyrax shakes his head. "They didn't fight at all. Given the signal to charge, they sat back and watched. Afterwards, in a twist of irony, Lyderea betrayed the betrayers—she laid a curse upon the kings, sealing their souls into Sidehelm Fortress. To this day, they drift through the castle as restless haunts, known to all as the Watchers of Erendor."

"The Pass can twist a person's mind," Ren mutters. "And Terrelly crossed it many a-time. I wonder if that's what broke his faith. He never fought the Watchers, but..."

"It is certainly possible." Gyrax begins walking down the hall. "But I believe it was a matter of accumulated strife. Terrelly's hardships gathered and peaked, until he could no longer bear their grievous weight. Sidehelm was simply the final straw."

"He can still find his way," Ren says firmly. "I won't give up until he does."

Gyrax smiles. "And that is why you are a true Wayfarer. The last for now, but time may prove otherwise."

"How did you know?" I ask. "When you first met Ren, you nearly said it out loud."

"I saw a Talic decagram within his aura. It is known among his kind as the Lydiliant Glimmer, and it can only be given by a Wayfaring Master."

Ren cocks his head, curious. "The Glimmer is a bit of an exotic obscurity, even within the olden Advance. How did you recognize it?"

"My clan once cared for an injured Wayfarer: a man named Qynarius Burl. While he recovered, he taught us much of your culture and history."

"Burl gave me the Glimmer on my second birthday. He was one of many who fell at Sidehelm." Ren stares at nothing in particular, the weight of the world in his beaten-down gaze. "If Terrelly crosses into the Clear, I alone shall carry the mantle."

"Have faith," Gyax says. "Your mentor was once a formidable warrior. A spark lives on within his heart."

"I wish I could fan it back to life," Ren says morosely. "But seeing him now, I can't help but wonder if..."

"Leave it, Ren. Things will turn out for the best."

"I hope you are right."

They lapse into silence, which prompts me to ask, "What's the deal with the magic revolver?"

"Her name is Ailura Qartesi." Gyrax says. "She is a legendary weapon, capable of vanquishing high-demon energies."

High-demon energies. Wow.

He nods at Ren. "Give her to Jon."

Ren's face twists in protest. "I was told to protect her by—"

"—a man who is lost to despair and sorrow. Search your truest self, Ren: Jon and Ailura are bound by fate."

Ren closes his eyes and becomes absolutely still. After a long moment, he takes a breath and opens his eyes. "I...perhaps you are right. I've never had much Primal awareness, but I think I feel...some kind of *tug,* if I had to describe it. At the same time, I swore an oath..." He draws the revolver and examines it uncertainly.

"An oath to the light that wove us into being? Or to stiff-necked dogma and useless ritual?"

Ren studies the half-gun for nearly a minute, then sighs in resignation. "Here." He tucks the revolver into its pouch, unrigs it from his waist, and hands it over. "You'll need a belt to hold it." Out comes a belt from the depths of his carry.

"Uh...thanks." I don the belt, threading it through the loops of the gun-pouch.

Ren shrugs. "At this point, I'm willing to try anything."

Gyrax claps his shoulder. "Internal surrender: the first step toward grace and power."

Ren shrugs again. "If you say so."

I finish securing the pouch to my waist, concealing a rush of nerdish excitement.

Jon Dough: fantasy-world gunslinger.

Bad. *Ass.*

————

As we exit the hospice, Elier and Lucky—both leaning against the wall—straighten up and uncross their arms.

"My business is done." Ren looks at Gyrax. "Yours?"

"I am content. Let us head for Elerica."

"The Witchcraft City?" Elier asks. "Why?"

"To quicken Jon's sight."

"A hedge witch could do that. Why go to such—"

"He is a special case. It must be done by a high-level sorcerer."

"Why does he have unquickened sight?" Lucky presses. "I have yet to meet a human or creature that hasn't been quickened shortly after birth."

"An arcane injury," Gyrax explains, saving me the trouble of having to lie. "He was attacked by a Demakor."

Elier look stricken. "My condolences. I didn't know."

"No worries," I blurt. "I never really—"

Gyrax holds up a hand, cutting me off. "We head for Elerica. Unless anyone objects." He sweeps the party with his gaze.

The others exchange a noncommittal glance, then assent with a scatter of murmurs and nods.

"Good," Gyrax affirms. "Elerica it is."

————

Our path is dappled with spears of sunlight, filtered through a screen of rustling canopy. Every so often, a soothing breeze grazes my skin, caressing my face with a pleasant chill. The faint chirp of birds carries and echoes, adding an idyllic touch to our sylvan journey.

Nine days in, we hear commotion up ahead. It sounds like a quarrel—multiple guys arguing with a woman.

"I would rather not meddle in others' affairs," Ren grumbles. "Meddling and murder go hand in hand."

"A dispute is simply a hidden opportunity," Lucky replies.

"I agree with Lucky." Elier grins. "I welcome the meddling, along with the murder."

The woman's voice gets louder and angrier, then abruptly culminates in a ferocious shout.

Gyrax breaks into a four-legged gallop. The rest of us follow but he's way too fast; he slips out of sight in less than a second.

After a breakneck sprint, we stop at the edge of a forest glade, watching a green-clad lady swing her sword and cut the ties on her attacker's trousers. She kicks his butt and he stumbles away, holding the lip of his drooping pants. A dozen yards ahead, I glimpse four more men fleeing down the trail.

She turns around and my mouth drops open.

Standing before me is the most beautiful girl I've ever seen.

————

"If you're going to rob me, make it quick." She affects a yawn, letting her rapier droop by her side. Its single-gem guard is super elegant—silver-gold twists that form a shield around her hand.

Ren steps forward. "Erany?"

"Who are you? How do you know me?" She looks him up and down with doubt and suspicion.

She resembles a younger Taylor Swift, before Kanye and Jake and the sexual harassment. (Have I mentioned that I have a giant crush on Taylor Swift? Well now you know.) But even though she looks strikingly similar, she's not a twin. Her ears are pointy, for one, and she's dressed like Link from *Legend of Zelda*—green tunic, brown belt, brown leggings, but no cap.

"We fought through an ambush at Tyr Alídeen." Ren pulls his hood back. "Terrelly Jindow came to our rescue."

Her eyes widen. "Rennarean?" (Obviously, they share some history. Not gonna lie—I'm straight-up jealous.) "I came to see Terrelly. Is he—"

"Low in spirit, low in body," Ren says.

"I owe him my life. I must see him."

He shakes his head. "Nothing good will come of your visit."

Her lips tighten. "You have no say in what I do."

Ren scoffs. "You're as pigheaded as ever. I tell you, Erany, there is little use in—"

She points her sword at his throat. "Fetter your tongue, before I bloody your—"

"—trying to rouse a broken man!" He throws his hands up and groans in frustration. "Why won't you ever *listen* to—"

"—sour, low-shadowed *face.*" (Lucky's smiling with unabashed glee; he's found a fellow Ren-hater and he is *loving* it). Erany's voice rises to a shout. *"I have bled and suffered as much as you, but I have yet to give in to anger and bitterness! Now still your tongue and loose your blade!"*

"Fine!" Ren draws his sword with a furious swipe. "Just because you're a Fair Folk princess doesn't mean I'll bow and scrape!"

Her eyes flash with shock and hate. "I have never," her tone lowers into a dangerous growl, *"ever* asked any soul to bow before me. You have crossed the line, Rennarean, and I for one am cursedly glad that I get to put you in your—"

Gyrax steps between them, arms out. "Lower your weapons. Ren spoke out of turn, but that is no reason to—"

"Out of the way, Wolven." She levels her blade at him. "Or your head will roll across this trail."

Gyrax dips into a formal bow: right arm across his waist, left arm curled around his back. "Princess Eralindíany Ailahdi, of the Deláni Fair Folk. I am Gyrax Aclasian, Warrior Rex to the Wolven clans. Up until now, I have only seen you in my Ambassador's royal holographica. It is truly a pleasure to meet you in the flesh."

"Warrior Rex to the—" She lowers her sword. "You speak for the Wolven?"

"Only when they cannot speak for themselves. I am more of an advocate than a true politician."

She regards Elier and Lucky with a dubious eye. "You share travels with a Duelist and pickpocket."

"Thief!" Lucky protests.

She responds with a flap of the hand—*whatever*—and jerks her chin at me. "Your name. Speak it."

"Um...er..." I stutter for a moment, trying to think of something smooth and confident.

Gyrax, thankfully, comes to my aid. "His name is Jon. He was raised in seclusion during the Wars."

She examines me skeptically. "You seem unformidable, to say the least. Can you fight or cast?"

I almost tell her I'm good with a dagger, but I'm afraid I'll come off like a cocky douche-bro. "Um...I...I..."

"What's wrong?" she demands. "Are you listening to me?"

"I...I..." I gulp without intending to. "I—yes. I'm listening."

"What are *those?*" She studies my shoes. "And for that matter, what are you *wearing?*" (Dammit—I had to meet the crush of my life on a day where I'm wearing my weird-ass Earth clothes! Stupid, stupid, *stupid!*)

"Oh, um...they're called sneakers. These are jeans." I gesture at my legs, then at my chest. "This is a t-shirt." I can't remember when I felt this self-conscious.

She shakes her head in disgust and bafflement. "I advise you to find some boots and a jerkin. You look ridiculous."

"Sorry." Before my brain can filter my mouth, I blurt, "I can change now if—"

Erany pats the air, as if to say, *Calm down, creeper.* "I would rather not see what dangles and hangs."

My cheeks go from slightly flushed to flaming red. "No! That's not what I mea—"

"We are headed for Elerica," Gyrax says. "Would you care to share travels?"

"The Witchcraft City..." Erany slides her rapier into its sheath. "I wasn't planning on it, but you say that Terrelly needs healing?"

"At every level. His physical ailment is fairly severe, but it is nothing compared to his auric malady."

She curls a lock of hair behind her ear, causing my heart to beat a little faster. "Can he still be saved?"

"That remains to be seen."

Erany stares at the ground. Chirping birds fill the silence.

Finally, she says, "The City is filled with skilled physickers. Perhaps they can offer a magical remedy. Did anyone take his auric prints? If you are to commission a potion or salve..."

"Aye, it is a specialty I learned as a young pup. He dimmed his aura to conceal his pain, but I was able to descry it and capture his prints," Gyrax says. "It is why I speak with such surety—he might last a few more years, but it will not be pleasant. His mantic loci are completely ruptured."

Ren looks aghast. "Why didn't you say anything? We've been on the road for over a week!"

"I wanted to wait until you were calmer."

Ren clenches his jaw. "You have no right to—"

"Keep your hate at a low simmer? On the contrary, I believe it sensible and prudent. If you continue on in such a state, your perception will become completely undone."

Ren's hood slips forward, deepening the shadow around his eyes. "You are not my teacher, Wolven. Nor my keeper."

"You growl and snap like a rabid mutt." Gyrax's voice turns hard and stern. "The Reft has long since come and gone, but you act as if it rages through you."

"You...*you*..." Ren's lips bare into a snarl.

Erany chimes in. "He's right, Ren. You quest for peace yet deny it for yourself, much like Terrelly in his later years."

"Untrue, for I still stand for life and light. Terrelly—"

"Once said the same," she counters. "Change is coming whether you like it or not. Refuse to ride its fated waves, and you will drown beneath its merciless currents."

Ren looks down, no longer a livid teenager, but a humble young man. "You speak true, Princess. I plead thy grace in all matters, past and present."

"No need, Ren. I plead yours."

"All is forgiven." He meets her eyes. "Share travels with us. Your blade and mind would be most welcome."

"Since you asked so nicely, I bow to your wish." Erany throws him a smile, then echoes a saying I've heard before:

"Our crossing seems fated."

With the addition of Erany, we become a party of six.

14

It isn't easy traveling with a gorgeous, intelligent, warrior-princess. Especially since she loves teasing me about my willingness to strip. Whenever she does it, I flush bright red (which only makes her tease me harder), but after a couple of days, I start developing a thicker skin—my heart stops kicking into level twenty overdrive.

Lucky and Elier take her presence in stride. On Evermoor, it isn't uncommon for adventurous souls to travel together. Makes sense—why rot at home, when you can hit the road and seek riches and glory?

Predictably, Lucky tries sleazing into her royal graces, but every time he compliments her on (fill in the blank), she shuts him down with a dismissive scoff. She's not being catty; she sees through his crap and doesn't have a problem with letting him know it.

As the miles (or faires, I should say) roll by, the conversation turns to her childhood. Erany was born to a Fair Folk queen (Fair Folk means Elf, which is a legitimate term in Evermoor parlance, but more of an informal label bordering on slang) and a human bard, shortly before the Crimson Wars. After the fighting kicked off, Lyderea and her Knights invaded her home (Delán) and burned it to the ground. Erany escaped with the aid of her nanny, but her parents fell to Iaetrix Knights. Now she wants to even the score.

"I seek the Rosecraft Blade." She draws her rapier and carves a fanciful pattern into the air.

"You speak of a weapon?" Elier asks.

"Aye. A sentient sword. Born from a dewdrop and forged by lightning."

The Duelist gives her a skeptical look. "Lyderea covets relics of power. How do you know she hasn't already—"

Erany brandishes her left wrist, displaying a gold-weave bracelet with a red-lit gem mounted in its center. "This jeweled brace is Ryke'tari-forged—its clairvoyant locus is tied to the weapon. If she touched the Blade with her low-shadow hands, I would be the first to know."

"I see. Who gave you the bracelet?"

"A sage named Yondi. I did him a favor, which is another story for another day." She swings her sword in a slash-slash-thrust. "I suspect Lyderea doesn't know of the Blade. Or perhaps it is simply too much trouble, as it rests on the peak of Yom Dagur. Atop the summit is an enchanted circle, guarded by a golem and a dryad coterie."

"Seems risky," Lucky comments. "Easier rewards lie within reach."

"The eye of a thief is often blind, when it comes to what is truly valuable."

Lucky responds with an easy grin. "In that regard my vision is pure. I am dead-set on riches and wealth—a freedom agreed on by all with a brain."

"Not freedom," Gyrax interjects. "Bondage. The shackles may gleam and draw your gaze, but they trammel the heart all the same."

"I have no heart." Lucky shrugs. "I left it behind in my family's manor."

"I lack your conviction," Gyrax says.

"To each their own." Another shrug.

"Eventually, you will see that one affects all."

The thief laughs. "Well until that day, I choose to wallow in my greed and avarice."

A sorrow-tinged smile comes and goes, but that's the extent of Gyrax's reply.

"How much longer until we reach Elerica?" I ask.

"Another week," Ren says, "provided we don't run into any—"

A faint jangle reaches our ears: the jostle of armor, saddles, and sheaths. I glance over my shoulder and spot a quartet of Knights riding toward us.

"Easy," Gyrax cautions. "Let them pass."

The others assent, but Ren draws a dagger and reverses his grip. "They bow to Lyderea. We should—"

"Under their armor, they are simply men and nothing more. Now sheathe your weapon and let them pass."

Ren looks torn. Then he slides his dagger into its sheath. "Fine," he mutters.

"Was that so hard?" Lucky teases.

The Knights ride up and halt before us. "Wind at your back and sun on your brow," their leader declares.

"The same to you, Kai Justicer." Gyrax dips his chin, touching his forehead with his index and middle finger before bringing his hand out. (It's the same salute I've seen before—the Evermoor equivalent of a casual wave.) "How fare you and your dutiful colleagues?"

The Knight shifts atop his saddle. "We fare well, Master Wolven. But even so, I look forward to dusk, when I can doff my armor and slake my thirst. Where are you headed?"

"The Witchcraft City."

"For trade or pleasure?"

"A bit of both, perhaps, but definitely trade. Restoration as well, if we happen upon a reputable healer."

"Ah." The Knight nods. "Say no more. My body creaks from age and scars—each morning is a test of my will."

"I share your sorrow, Kai Justicer. It has been a day and an age since I have drawn the eye of a comely maiden. And judging by your weathered visage, I'd wager you know exactly what I speak of."

The Knight roars with laughter. "All too well, Master Wolven, all too well." The rest of the Knights grin and chuckle. "May light find you in dark places."

"And may it ease your eyes and guide your feet."

The Knights touch their foreheads and bring their hands out, just like Gyrax did a moment prior. We stand and watch as they disappear around a bend.

"That wasn't so bad, was it?" Gyrax favors us all with a brief glance. "At the end of the day, they want to shed their armor and enjoy a drink. Similar to what anyone wants, I imagine." His gaze settles on Ren, who maintains his silence.

Eventually, the wanderer mutters, "Maybe."

————

When we left Naversé, the forest around us was open and spacious. Now it feels downright oppressive, like thousands of eyes are secretly studying us. As we trek further into the darkening woods, the environment starts turning marshy and humid.

You'd think with bugs, lizards, and assorted creepy-crawlies, we'd have to wear netting or sleep in hammocks. But thanks to Ren that isn't the case; he blesses our party with arcane repellent. (He'd make a fortune back on Earth—how dope would it be to explore a jungle and not have to worry about bites or stings?)

Over the next few days, I see gaggles of lizards (Gyrax says they're called peryx) about two feet long, with super-stretchy necks that snap forward and snatch up prey. Lucky says they taste good with red-rub, but I have zero interest in testing his claim.

Other animals include dog-sized beetles—their thoraxes curve into a distinct bell-shape—who trundle slowly along, swiveling their antlered heads from side to side. Elier says they're called hapers (pronounced like "vapor.") If they feel threatened, they'll scream and run, and sometimes release a foul-smelling mist that'll make you stink for at least a month. Lucky tells me they taste disgusting, no matter how long you cook them or what you season them with. Once again, I have no desire to see if he's right.

There's other stuff as well. Shimmery dots with hazy faces (naya), vines that mutter, grumble, and cough (pengrips), and snakelike rodents with dozens of feet (burbies). All of them, Gyrax assures me, are fairly harmless. Apparently, there are bigger predators lurking in the bush (syoptrix cats) but by and large, they keep to themselves.

Erany chimes in, informing us she befriended a pack of syoptrix last year (because she had to hide in the woods after mouthing off to a Justicer). According to her, the cats have a rigid hierarchy; they're super respectful and etiquette oriented.

I cut her off with, "But will they eat me, is the question."

"Yes," Erany says, "but not out of spite. Syoptrix avoid you, so long as you're quiet and maintain your calm."

Lucky says, "I do not doubt the truth of your words, but I much prefer the civilized world. The wilds are like one big desert—nothing to steal, nothing to drink."

Suddenly, a woman demands: *"Who are you and what do you want?"* The voice comes from all around us, bouncing through the woods in a low-toned echo.

We instinctively form a six-person ring, snapping our weapons up into guard.

"Who goes there?" Ren shouts. "Show yourself!"

Dark blue mist swirls and churns, enclosing us all in its vaporous eye. When I stare at its surface, it bubbles and roils with hypnotic flow, skewing my perception of direction and depth.

"Who are you and what do you want?" This time, a female face bulges from the fog, appearing and vanishing in split-second flickers. *"Answer quickly, lest I strip the flesh from your cursed bones!"*

The rasp of metal echoes all around us—as if a million warriors just drew steel.

Gyrax slings his axe and raises his hands. "We are travelers and traders on our way to Elerica. Barter and rest are all we desire."

"Aye," Lucky adds nervously. "Travelers and traders, milady, travelers and traders. And just so you know, I like my flesh right where it is—I will consider it a favor if you leave it be."

The mist condenses into a violet-black whorl. A moment later, definition and color flood its center. Arms, legs, face...I find myself staring at a striking woman with a light-purple tinge to her enchanted skin. Her filmy black clothing shifts and shimmers, draping her body in smoke and fabric. If she weren't so scary, I'd find her attractive.

"Death and ruin lie ahead." She surveys our party with a black-rimmed gaze.

"Your name?" Ren asks.

"Nyanti Eldara, third Wise Woman of the Nightclaw Coven. Yours?"

"Ren of the Barrens. Naught but a wanderer."

She gives him a skeptical look but doesn't press him on it. "Elerica is lost. An army of Iguar drove us out."

Elier cocks his head, puzzled. "Iguar? If I am not mistaken, they are a flightless version of Khyranic Goblins. Even in the light of a Demon Blood Moon, they wouldn't last long against the Witchcraft City."

"These were led by Sytíshí Whisper Folk. Three of them."

The others exchange an uneasy glance.

I raise a hand, fingers curled. "Um, what's a Sicari Whisper Folk?"

Nyanti regards me with overt suspicion. "Elven shadow mages. And you are?"

"The Prophesied Traveler," Lucky says.

The rest of us gape at him.

Eventually, Ren finds his tongue. "No one told you. How did you—"

Lucky shrugs. "I am not without brains, Ren. Or should I say Rennarean Arteris, last of the Wayfarers."

Ren's mouth opens and closes. "I...I..." Calculation flits through his eyes—he's trying to decide if he should defend the lie or admit the truth. After a moment, the truth wins out.

"You have me at crossdraw," Ren says stiffly. "I plead your grace, Kai Lucknar."

"Oh cry off, Ren," Lucky says exasperatedly. "I deceive for a living. When someone tries it on me, it's plainer than day on the Sunswept Flats."

"The Prophesied Traveler?" Nyanti regards me again, only with twice the suspicion. "Impossible. You are merely a child with an odd sense of fashion."

"My sentiments exactly." Erany grins. (Why is it that I'm always wearing Earth clothes when I meet a hot chick from Evermoor? This is the second time now.)

Nyanti's gaze flicks across us. "A trio of royals, a Wayfarer, a Duelist, and a moonstruck boy who thinks he's a hero." She shakes her head in resignation. "Whatever you seek, I hope you find it. May light find you in dark places."

As she turns to leave, Gyrax stops her with, "Wait."

She halts in place, but doesn't turn around. "Speak, Wolven. Time runs thin."

"Perhaps we can help you reclaim the City."

Ren and Erany voice their agreement. Elier tilts his head, mildly interested, while Lucky shrugs and mutters, "As long as I'm paid."

Nyanti lets out a bitter laugh. "Against three Sytíshí? You have a high opinion of yourself."

"We are not amateurs, Sha Eldara. Should we catch them unawares, our advantage will be enough to lay them low."

"If you wish to commit suicide, it is no concern of mine."

"Then before we do, I would ask you a favor."

"Speak it." She cants her head, catching Gyrax in the periphery of her vision.

"Quicken Jon's sight." He give me a nod.

Nyanti is silent for a long moment.

Then: "Easy enough. Come with me."

15

"We fled to an outpost called Grifter's Ridge," Nyanti explains as she leads us deeper into the woods. "The magic is weak and faint compared to the City's." She mutters, "By flower and fae, grant us a way," then slowly exhales a weave of runes. They twine and curl before fading into a drift of blue-purple sparks.

Thanks to her spell, the shrubbery in front of us shrinks and parts, revealing a wide dirt road overshadowed by trees. As we forge ahead, the vegetation closes in a dozen yards behind us, hiding any trace of our physical presence.

"Impressive," Lucky remarks. "You are no hedge witch, that much is certain."

Nyanti hisses, as if to say *Child, please.* "I have completed every trial in *Elsinore's Fables.*"

"I take it that's good?" I whisper to Gyrax.

He answers with a nod. "If a hedge witch is equal to a small-town wrestler, Nyanti is as skilled as a UFC newcomer. Nothing name brand, but nothing to laugh at."

"And the Whisper Folk?"

"A couple notches higher. Fight-game veterans who know the ropes."

"So why are we endangering ourselves by helping her out?" I ask. "If these Whisper guys are that deadly, shouldn't we—"

"Jon." He stops and lays a hand on my shoulder. As the others march on, the bubble of parted vegetation elongates and stretches, keeping me and Gyrax within its curvature. "It isn't 'why are we helping her?' It's 'why *shouldn't* we help?' The first is unnatural, the second isn't."

"I'm sorry," I stammer. "I didn't mean to—"

"Yes, you did." His eyes are merciless and kind at the same time. "That's the first lesson. 'Ware the second."

My brow crinkles in puzzlement. "What do you mean? I don't follo—"

"Learn from your error, but do not condemn yourself. Or if you do, make it short. You will stunt your evolution if you insist on perceiving yourself as unworthy and low."

I try and reply, but nothing comes to mind. He beat me to the draw; I was already denouncing myself as a selfish piece of crap.

When I first got here, things seemed simpler. But the joke's on me—I'm just as confused as when I lived in San Francisco.

That's life, I guess. Irony abounds.

————

Grifter's Ridge feels uncomfortably familiar—like the scene in a drama where the hero is confronted with poverty and lack. Creatures and humans regard me with despair, anger, or blank acceptance.

Between greetings and check-ins, Nyanti informs us the Whisper Folk attacked five weeks prior. They surprised and overwhelmed the Arcane Defense Corps (a volunteer force of Elerican Wizards), which opened the way for their army of Iguar. Between her rundown and Gyrax's explanations, I start to get a sense of the bigger picture.

The Sytíshí (or Whisper Folk) are a group of Fair Folk exiles. After ignoring bans against certain enchantments, their respective tribes cast them out. Eventually, they banded together and continued their studies in the darker arcane. It makes sense they'd want to conquer Elerica, since the city is built around a powerful source of magic known as the hexflow spring.

As far as the reason behind the Iguar attack, it's anyone's guess. It could just be their warlike society (their minds are particularly vulnerable to the Crimson Reft—a residual variant of it resides in their auras). Or maybe they struck a deal with the Sytíshí. Or maybe they're under some sort of spell.

Like I said: anyone's guess.

Nyanti finishes bringing us up to speed as she guides us into an out-of-the-way tent. We take a seat on a circle of stumps, rough with cracks and splintery wood.

"Apologies." She fits a leaf-rolled cigarette to her inky-black lips. "We once sat on vine-woven thrones. These weathered stumps are a poor substitute."

"We are grateful, milady," Gyrax assures. " 'Tis a meager soul who cannot appreciate the simpler pleasures."

Nyanti chuckles. "A pretty sentiment. Would you care for a loken?" She reaches in her robe and produces a cigarette. "Any of you?" Her gaze swings around to everyone present.

The others accept with a scatter of "ayes," but I wave her off. Weed has left me with mixed impressions—I think I'll pass on the magical super-joint.

Gyrax nudges me. "Try it. It's good for your aura."

I laugh nervously and swallow my reservations. "Why not? All the cool kids are doing it." I give Nyanti an *I'll-take-one* gesture. She leans over and hands me a smoke.

The others snap their fingers under their cigs, sparking hot blue fire from their enchanted hands. Pretty soon, the tent is filled with a peaceful odor—the welcome ambience of homecooked food, paired with the chill energy of a Zen rock garden.

"Uh..." I look around, unsure of how to ask for a lighter.

"Jon." Gyrax beckons with a curl of his paw. I angle toward him, smoke in my mouth, and he lights the end with a fire-spark snap.

My first drag is deep and full; it floods my lungs with feathery warmth. Pleasant buzzing spills through my body, relaxing my muscles but leaving my clarity completely intact. It's like that pivotal moment when you let go of depression by complete accident—when your unconscious tension drops away, and you can finally breathe easy and light.

"I've never had better." Lucky studies his loken with mild wonder. "The arcane designs are nothing short of stunning." Erany and Ren voice their agreement.

Designs? Huh?

"Why can't I see anything?" I whisper to Gyrax. "I mean it feels good, but..."

"Your unquickened sight." He signals Nyanti with a lift of his hand. "Can you open Jon's aura?"

"Of course." By her matter-of-fact tone, I get the impression that opening someone's aura is hella easy. "Hold still." Glowing runes appear by her temples. "What is..." Her brow wrinkles. "This is incredible."

Cool. Maybe I'm the Evermoor version of Luke Skywa—

"Your auric energy is completely obstructed."

My Jedi fantasies screech to a halt. "What?"

"Could you at least try?" Gyrax asks.

The others look interested, but mostly puzzled. I stifle the urge to snap, *Thanks guys. Apparently, the only one who cares about me is my former dog.*

"I suppose I could, but..." Her eyes tinge with doubt and skepticism. "His meridians and loci are nearly petrified."

"Your sister Witches?" Gyrax prods. "Could they aid you in—"

She shakes her head. "Most are injured. And those who are hale are nursing the weak. But even so, even if they were flush with power and strength, it wouldn't matter—he is too far gone."

"If he were to bathe in the hexflow spring, then—"

Her eyes widen in shock and outrage. "How could you even— you would risk his unravelment! His mind is untrained!"

"But his spirit is sure. And strong."

"He could *die!*" she snaps. "The hexflow spring is no ordinary magic!"

"Jon is not an ordinary boy."

"So you say. Yet his only feature of any distinction is that his senses are clogged beyond repair. How do you even function?" She gives me a look full of pity and disgust.

I respond with a shrug. "I'm a hopeless derp. Woe is me."

She doesn't know what *derp* means, but she gets the sarcasm. "I didn't mean to judge. It is just that..." She trails off, struggling to find words.

"I know." I sigh. "I imagine it's like being deaf or blind."

"Worse!" she blurts. "I couldn't accept living like..." She takes a calming breath. "If your aura remains closed, your existence will become gray and mechanical. I would rather die than live with such tedium."

I grin sheepishly. "Makes sense. On my world, a lot of folks are chained to a de—ah, I mean, they sit in one spot for most of the day. Some get to work outside, but they're either underpaid or extremely lucky."

Elier taps ash from the end of his smoke. "What about sword-play?"

"A couple people do it as a hobby, but..."

"Are the inhabitants of your world as obstructed as you?" Erany asks incredulously.

I try and think of something witty (she still flusters me), but nothing comes to mind. "I mean...there's a few individuals with special powers, but they're usually seen as crazy or demonic."

"His orphic rigidity matches up with his claims," Nyanti states. "Lock someone's aura in monotone stasis, and their stagnation will attract a matching circumstance. It may not happen all at once—it would take place over the course of decades—but it would eventually become a physical reality. Is my assumption correct?"

I answer with a nod, a little chagrined, a little irritated. Her ruthless analysis feels a little on the nose. "Pretty much, yeah."

Everyone stares at me. If this were a laugh-track sitcom, you would hear chirping crickets.

After a hanging moment, I exclaim, "Come on, guys—it's not *that* bad!"

"It sounds terrible," Lucky says grimly, "on every level." His ebullient cheer has up and vanished.

"Your poor loci..." Erany murmurs. "I'm sorry, Jon. I didn't know."

"I'm not *dead!*" I protest. "You guys are acting like—"

"Hush. I doubt I can help you, but let me make certain." Nyanti takes a drag off her loken, then leans in and blows smoke in my face. I close my eyes, expecting it to sting or itch, but it's actually pleasant—a refreshing tingle that caresses my skin.

I open my eyes, watching as she waves the loken in deliberate arcs, etching silvery spirals into the air. Instead of dispersing, they hang and pulse with muted light, forming luminous curves and fantastic twists. Tiny runes appear in the smoke, tinted in shades of blue-green-indigo. A moment later, they contract into curls and wrap around me.

Whoa. *Awesome.*

As the runes begin to glint and brighten, I feel something twitching inside my brain—like a just-forgotten name, nagging insistently at the edges of my mind. Something's gonna happen, but I'm not sure what. Whatever it is, it's going to be—

Nyanti doubles over, gasping and panting. Gyrax rushes to her side but she extends an arm, keeping him back. The others rise from their seats, in varying degrees of shock and surprise.

"I can't...I can't..." She brushes hair away from her forehead. "There is no way to open his loci. Not without the hexflow."

The change in the Witch is jaw-drop stunning. Her cheeks are wrinkled and saggy, her eyes tired and rheumy. She just aged several decades in less than a second.

Then, much to my amazement, she starts to grow younger. Black creeps back into her withered hair, life crawls back into her desiccated skin.

"I injected magic into his aura, but it wasn't easy, as you may have deduced from my countenance and bearing." She straightens up and draws a breath. "It won't last long. This is only a temporary fix."

"Can you Shift your perception?" Ren asks. "Mentally, it feels like relaxing your gaze. Focus on me, but not in any specific sense— let thought arise without judgment or scrutiny."

I do as he says. Huh...his body is surrounded by hints of color.

"I see...*something...*" I squint harder, trying to will it into sharper resolution. Almost immediately, a mild headache forms on the right side of my brain. At the same time, the squiggles and orbs grow increasingly faint. I think I pushed too hard and closed off my senses.

"It's gone."

"His aura," Nyanti croaks.

Erany's lips part in amazement. "Deliac's Gleam...it's—"

"All right, all right," I grouse. "You've all seen my disgusting aura. Now will someone tell me why it's so damn interesting?"

Nyanti keeps staring. "It's just that... auras are indicative of causal structure."

"Pretend I have no idea what you're talking about. Because I don't." (Yeah I'm grumpy, but wouldn't you be too, if everyone was gaping at you like a sideshow freak?)

Gyrax elaborates. "Auras are loaded with runic information—the inhabitants of Evermoor use artistic writing as a means of communication. Yours, however..."

"It's almost..." Ren falls silent.

Lucky says, "It appears mechanical, but not without life. It is like..." He shakes his head. "There are no words."

Gyrax elaborates. "Yours is filled with stylized data. Like the alien scrawl of a science fiction civilization."

"Whoa..." I look down and try to Shift my sight again. Bladed outlines appear around my limbs and torso. "What the...man, this is *cool.*"

Suddenly, I feel a warm throb against my lower back.

I reach behind me and draw Ailura. The incomplete revolver is glowing and pulsing, spilling different shades of light across my hand.

Nyanti's face goes slack with astonishment. "Is that—"

"The Avalon Clapfire," Ren whispers. "And it seems to recognize him."

"Maybe it's true. Maybe he is the Traveler," Erany murmurs.

Nyanti regards me with doubt and unease. "Magic is fickle. Give it time before you jump to conclusions."

"Well? What next?" I look expectantly at the others.

Gyrax turn to Nyanti. "Will you accompany us? Without a guide, we would be deaf and blind in Elerica City." She opens her mouth, but he cuts her off with, "Consider the alternative: if you choose to stay, you limit the good you can do for your people. But if you travel with us..."

Her expression twists with conflicting emotions. "I suppose...I suppose you're right. A slow death versus...yes, I will guide your efforts." She sweeps our party with her black-rimmed eyes.

"We strike out tomorrow."

I can't help but grin—a high-level mage just joined our party. Bad. *Ass.*

16

Before Nyanti leaves our tent, she throws me a pair of grime-streaked boots. When I try them on, they shrink comfortably around my feet. (Man, magic makes everything so much better.)

The next morning, I'm woken by sunlight limning the door-flap.

"Hurry." Ren is already up and dressed. "Time runs thin."

Lucky sits up in bed, grumbling, " 'Time runs thin.' 'Time runs thin.' For the love of Ganshy, grace my ears with fairer words."

Ren adjusts the daggers strapped to his chest. "While we tarry, the Sytíshí tighten their grip on the hexflow. Not a concern for one such as you, seeing as you snatch the food from paupers' mouths, but—"

"Yes, Ren—I run around in the dead of night, denying babes their milk and bread." Lucky rolls his eyes in exasperation. "Cry off, will you?"

Nyanti pokes her head in through the flap. "If we step off now, we shall arrive in three days' time, roughly around noon. The higher the sun, the safer we are from Sytíshí magics."

"Do they build their spells off fear or terror?" Gyrax asks.

"Close but not quite. Their conceptual expression is better matched to a lack of sight—an inability to perceive the long-term good." Nyanti tilts her head, appraising Gyrax with newfound respect. "You seem knowledgeable in arcane philosophy."

Gyrax chuckles. " 'Tis a passing interest, nothing more."

"I know little of the arcane and less of philosophy, but I am ready to leave at your say. Taking advantage of your enemy's weakness—that is something I understand and appreciate." Elier shoulders his carry and slips outside.

"Gods, I'm tired." Erany rubs her eyes with curled fingers. "I would give a kingdom and a half for a cup of kepi. Some eggs and mutton as well."

"Typical," Ren scoffs. "Our lodging is a little too crude for her majesty's tastes."

Erany's face twists with anger. *"Watch your—"*

"Enough." Nyanti's voice is brisk and stern. "We need to leave. *Now.*"

Erany directs a Look of Fury at Wretched Ren, but he acts as if he doesn't see it. Part of me is pleased. Initially, I wasn't sure if they used to date, but that doesn't appear to be the ca—

"Are you ready, Jon?" Gyrax is standing by the door-flap.

"Um, yeah." I fumble with my shirt. "Just a second, I'll be—"

"Hurry," Ren calls.

I grab my stuff and rush out the door.

———

As we make our way through Grifter's Ridge, I'm struck by Elerica's ethnic diversity. I was born and raised in San Francisco—a city that emphasizes social justice and racial inclusion—so I'm well aware that *Lord of the Rings, Game of Thrones,* and *Dungeons and Dragons* are by and large devoid of minorities. (Well, D&D has expansions like Al Qadim, Kara Tur, and Maztica, but they were solely for uber-nerds like yours truly). Typically, anything fantasy hails from Western Europe, so it feels weird (in a good way) to see Evermoor breaking from traditional mores.

This bears investigating.

"Gyrax, I've noticed the humans are..." I trail off, struggling to find the right terminology. "They're not that different from what I saw on Earth. Racially speaking, that is."

Gyrax glances at me, amused. "Not just humans. Elves come in a variety of colors, though all are slender and pleasing to the eye. Evermoor is different from television fantasy—is that what you mean?"

"Yeah. I never saw diversity in swords and sorcery, but it's a different story here on Evermoor."

"A good choice of words," he agrees. "Because you're right—the story is different altogether. I could weary your ears with stodgy parables, but I'll spare you the pain and give you the short answer: much of what you see is a collective hallucination."

An incredulous laugh bursts from my mouth. "Say *what?*"

"Your environment responds to your deepest desires. That's the fundamental principle behind magic and creation."

"So why aren't I rich?" I counter. "I used to play powerball once a week."

"If that is what you wanted in the depths of your soul, it would have happened long ago. But the fact that it hasn't...are you familiar with the phrase 'Be dust upon your breath?' "

"Yep. Ren said it to me right after we met."

"Explain it. In your own words, if you can."

I study the sunlit sky, filtered through a lattice of purple-green canopy. "It means that a greater part of me—the part that breathes —chose my circumstances. And a smaller part of me—the dust— chose to experience them. It basically implies I should abide in acceptance."

Gyrax nods. "Exactly. Life is an art: feeling out when it's appropriate to analyze and plan, and when to let things take their course. That can only be done through acceptance and openness."

"How does this relate to fantasy-world diversity?"

"Earth was created by the part that breathes. And it's the same with Evermoor—we are simply reflections of a greater decision."

"Okay." I nod slowly; I can feel the concepts cohering together. "So diversity isn't about history or tradition, it's a realization of our collective psyche. Or Evermoor's, in this case."

"Correct. Now listen close and listen well: Evermoor chose a specific circumstance, but that needn't be a snare or a prison—it can set the stage for future adventures."

"So our lives are fluid. We aren't trapped by past conditions."

"Exactly. We weren't designed to be clockwork machines; we are riders and surfers of a fast-moving river. The currents may guide and influence our path, but we can row and steer in any direction. And if we so choose, we can see it's an ocean and not a river. But at that point, words can't describe what I'm actually referring to. Even 'transcendence' is just an abstraction, merely touching on what it implies."

"I get what you're saying," I venture. "I mean...I *feel* like I do, if that makes any sense."

"Perfect sense," Gyrax affirms. "Conscious thought has its limits. You must merge it with feeling to grasp the True."

"The True, huh? Cool name."

"It shall suffice," Gyrax says. Then he mutters, "for now."

I chuckle softly. "We veered way off topic. Into like, Eastern mysticism and holographic game theory."

"Call it what you want, but when you reference the basis for reality and consciousness, it inevitably leads back to the True." Gyrax shrugs. "That's just how it is—everything springs from it."

"Interesting."

I take a minute to let that digest, then scan ahead to see how the others are doing. Ren is deep in Silent Avenger Mode, while Erany and Nyanti are discussing the best way to fight the Sytíshí. A couple yards back, Elier and Lucky are trudging along in amiable silence, then it's me and Gyrax bringing up the rear. (Not gonna lie—I wish I was further up the line so I could talk with Erany. She is *so* pretty.)

As the hours pass and the trail narrows, the vegetation becomes increasingly dense. Black-leaf trees loom uncomfortably close, reaching over and across with their vine-draped limbs. I can't help but worry—there's eyes peeking out from the shadowy expanse, ringing us in with cat-slit pupils.

"Um...guys?" I cast a nervous look to either side. "Doubt you've seen *Aliens,* but—"

"Be easy, Jon," Ren grumbles. "They're just like syoptrix. So long as we honor their space and rhythm, they'll leave us be."

" 'Honor their space and rhythm?' How do we do that, exactly?"

Erany grins over her shoulder at me. "By keeping your clothes on."

"Oh come *on!*" I throw my hands in the air. "It's not like I—"

"Every forest has its own etiquette," Gyrax interjects. "And if I remember correctly, Elerican Sylvae are not aggressive." He looks at Nyanti. "Is that still the case, or am I mistaken?"

"You speak true, Wolven, but keep in mind that Sytíshí magics can twist your perception. They are designed to—"

Before she can finish, the bushes to my left burst apart. I catch a terrifying glimpse of fangs and claws, then Gyrax intervenes and tackles the beast. They go sailing off into the woods, growling and snapping like rabid wolves.

I grip my dagger and follow behind, heart pounding in my adrenalized chest. A second later, we catch up to Gyrax. He's sitting on top of a giant cat, coated in vivid green whorls and velvet black skin.

Gyrax tightens his hold on its paws, grimacing with the effort of pinning it down. "By the gods..." he grunts. "So...*strong...*"

Up until now, I've never seen anything that can physically challenge him. It's downright terrifying—if he had been a split-second slower, the cat would have torn me limb from limb.

Nyanti passes her hand over its face. It abruptly goes limp.

Gyrax rolls off and lies on the ground, chest working in massive heaves. I kneel by his side, keeping the cat in my peripheral vision. "You okay?" I can't tell if he's hurt or spent—it was all so *fast*.

"Fine," Gyrax wheezes. "Just a little..." He stops talking and coughs violently. "Just a little winded..."

The others form a ring around our attacker, keeping their weapons in low-medium guard. It gets to its feet and hacks twice.

Then, much to my amazement, it starts to speak.

"Damn Sytíshí...caught my mind in a low-shadow curse." Its voice is a cross between a rumble and a purr.

Nyanti steps forward. "Greetings, Felinx. My name is Nyanti Eldara." "

"My thanks, Witch. Without your aid, I would still be in the throes of unchecked rage. I am Yire Anon, Hunter Prince of the Tyrax Pride."

(Whoa. A talking warrior cat. Could life get *any* cooler?)

Nyanti dips her head. She touches her brow with the first two fingers of her right hand and then moves it outward, palm facing in toward her face. " 'Tis an honor to meet you, Hunter Prince. We seek to defeat the Sytíshí Whisper Folk."

Yire shakes his colossal head. "Unless you are a member of Circle SyCajister, you are sorely outmatched."

"If they reconfigure the spring, they will lengthen their reach by a hundred faires. You and your pride—"

"We know what's at stake. And it's not worth the risk."

"The Sytíshí will find you, sooner or later."

"Perhaps. But it's better to live now and die later. If you have any sense in that fragile head of yours, you will take your leave of this cursed forest."

"We are duty-bound!" Ren exclaims angrily. "Not just to Elerica, but to Evermoor at large!"

"The world has changed, human. Your convictions are meaningless."

"Do you mean to say that—"

Erany shoots a warning glance at Ren. "Lyderea need not rule these lands. Peace and freedom are still within reach."

"You offer little, half-Elf, aside from grand words and empty speech. Have none of you heard of Sidehelm Pass?"

"We have all heard of it," Gyrax says, "but that is no excuse to forgo hope. If we regain Elerica—"

The Felinx shakes his head again. "When I speak of Sidehelm, I speak from personal experience. I was there, you see. I saw the armies of Erendor turn their backs."

Ren tries to retort, but Gyrax interrupts. "He's said his piece. And we've said ours." He touches his brow with his middle and forefinger, offering the same salute given by Nyanti. "May light find you in dark places."

Yire considers him for a long moment. Then he rumbles, "May it ease your eyes and guide your feet." And swishes away into the brush.

Damn. I was hoping we could add a super-strong cat to our D&D party, but I guess it wasn't meant to be.

"Useless." Ren makes a disgusted sound, halfway between a click and a hiss. "We need to keep moving. Time runs thin."

And with that we set off. It could simply be my imagination, but the woods seem darker the further in we go.

After a couple of hours, I come to a conclusion:

Nope—definitely not my imagination.

17

On our third day of travel, Nyanti guides our party onto the road. We could have used it from the start, but the Sytíshí have set up roving patrols—avoiding the road was a matter of prudence.

It's a short walk from there to a guard-wall. Due to the sun and the arcane tides, it's safer to do this during the day. Still, I can't help but feel (since we're sneaking in) we should be entering at night.

The thing is, if we wait until dark, the Iguar will draw strength from the Demon Blood Moon and transform into augmented versions of their diminutive selves. Before that happens, we're gonna ambush the Sytíshí, signal to Elerica that we've vanquished the mini-bosses (I figure nothing short of Lyderea qualifies as a final boss) and that we need some help. Because if (when) we beat the Whisper Folk, the city will erupt with angry Iguar.

If this were a video game, we'd be doing things backwards. Instead of mowing through goons and capping things off with a climactic fight, we're going to kill the Sytíshí and (hopefully) escape with our lives in the ensuing chaos.

Complicating matters is the fact that Elerican aid isn't a guarantee. Nyanti begged and pleaded, but her fellow Witches wouldn't commit. So it might end up being Jon and his Adventurers against an evil horde of face-eating monsters. Good thing I'm a *Star Wars* fanboy—according to Han, I should never calculate the odds, and I might be able to bluff my way out of an enemy fortress.

(I pray to God that life is like Star Wars.)

Gyrax swings from handhold to handhold, scuttling up the wall and into a watch tower. A second later, he throws a hefty rope down from the parapet. Erany grabs it, braces her feet, and starts ascending in a slow, steady walk. Lucky, Elier, and Ren follow behind. Nyanti doesn't bother; she levitates up and over in an easy float.

I'm last. And just to be clear, I have zero experience in medieval rope-climbing. (Way to go, SFSU—why didn't you put that in your stupid curriculum?) So I clutch the line with a newbie death-grip, pinching it between my thighs so I don't slide down.

Yeah—I'm a real champion. And by champion, I mean idiot.

Ren leans out from the edge of the tower. "What are you *doing?*" he hisses. "Hurry. *Up!*" He jerks his hand in an impatient wave.

I grit my teeth, biting back an angry retort. Unlike the others, I wasn't raised in a D&D version of Outward Bound. Ren knows this, but it doesn't stop him from being a dick. I vow to find out what the Evermoor version of a noogie or swirly is, then spring it on him when he least expects it.

This I swear upon my life.

Ren hooks my arm and hauls me in, shaking his head in abject disgust. "As slow as you climb, all of Evermoor will age and die before we find the Sytíshí."

What a dick. (I said it before, but it bears repeating.) Instead of punching him in his stupid face, I respond with a tight-lipped, "Yep. Good talk."

He de-anchors the rope, tosses it to Gyrax, then climbs down the inner-wall ladder. I follow in his wake, touching the ground as Gyrax coils up the line.

"This way." Nyanti starts walking. We form a column and follow her lead.

Elerica (a neat array of buildings, townhouses, and the occasional hut with a thatched roof) is hauntingly empty. The vibe is markedly different from Naversé Township—even though Naversé looked deserted, I could still sense people in their shuttered homes. This is more like utter desolation.

As we progress, the streets fill with knee-high fog. It starts off as an occasional wisp, but a couple blocks in, it thickens into dense, ropy banks. My mind hearkens back to *Empire Strikes Back,* when Han flew into an Exogorth and didn't realize it until it was almost too late.

This isn't just emptiness, it's *absence.* An ache so deep I want to give up and stop. The others feel it too—every so often, one of them shakes their head and mutters quietly.

Something's wrong. Something's *off.*

"Gyrax." I force myself to take a step. And another. And another.

"I know, Jon. I know." His face is tired and heavy. "Keep going," he murmurs. "We have to keep going..."

Alarm races through me. It would be out-and-out panic if I wasn't muddling through this...

This...

Nyanti halts and kneels on the ground. Ren and Erany plop on their butts. Gyrax collapses face-first, drool trickling from his parted lips. Elier and Lucky try to crawl, then slump weakly onto their bellies. I take a couple more steps, but I can't resist—I sag to my knees beside Nyanti.

Why even try, when everything ends in death and sadness? There's nowhere to go, nothing to hope for. Just a hollow scrabble for temporary pleasure, which is snatched away soon enough.

"Jon," Nyanti whispers under her breath. For a second, I'm not sure if she actually spoke—she said it that softly.

"Jon." Her eyes tick up a bit at a time, settling on the mountainous horizon.

"What?" I breathe. Deadened fatigue radiates through me.

"We...have to..." She suddenly stiffens and clutches her chest. "Jon." Her face tightens. "We have to...have to..."

"What?" I instinctively reach for anger or fear. Something to dispel this God-damned haze. There's nothing, though. I'm a hollowed-out shell.

"What do we do?"

What *can* we do?

Before she can answer, the fog around us swirls to life, forming into a trio of albino Elves. Their skin is shockingly pale, their faces thin and narrow. Their eyes are glowing with sickly red light, accenting the purple-black clothing that runs along their frames.

The middle one asks, "What have we here?" His voice is feather-soft, barely louder than a soft murmur.

"Whisper...Folk..." I can barely get it out—my mouth is filled with invisible cotton.

"Adventurers, I think," the one on the left says. "Kill them quickly, Sarisyrin." His face shifts, as if it's partly comprised of pale white smoke.

"Soft, Rekhavy—this is our only entertainment since we took the city. Let's take a moment to savor their dread."

"How shall we do it? Sarisyrin looks at the one on the right. "Khyrell?"

He gauges our party with an emotionless stare. "Unravel their minds in a necrotic fugue. They're halfway there—might as well finish it."

"Very well." Sarisyrin smiles. "Sorry you have to die, but..." A nonchalant shrug.

"Jon," Nyanti hisses. "You have to stop them."

"How?" I murmur.

"You have to...you have to..." She trails off as her pupils unfocus.

Buzzing whispers fill the air, eclipsing my thoughts with disintegrating sound. I can't make out what they're saying, but each syllable erodes my conviction. The light around us warps and twists, bending the sun into a greasy smear.

"That's it..." Sarisyrin urges. "Let's look inside that soft-boiled mind...Jon, is it?"

Christ—he's rooting through my *brain*. Rifling through my thoughts and desires, peeling them apart into half-formed urges.

"A plain name, and with good reason. You scratch out fiction day after day, hoping in vain you'll write a story worth reading. Save your effort—nothing inspiring comes from the uninspired."

He's right. I should have stayed in San Francisco, collecting meaningless paychecks for the rest of my meaningless life.

His hair flutters and twists, a bleach-white fan around his eyes. "This is mercy Jon, pure and simple. You were designed to live as a rat on a wheel, occasionally glimpsing a better existence—a better existence you could never attain. Don't resist. This is so much easier."

Rat on a wheel, that's all I am. That's all I ever was.

I sit back on the ground, cross my legs, and fold my hands in my lap. My head slumps down onto my chest.

As my eyes droop closed, I give in to the relief of unfeeling oblivion.

18

There once was a boy named Jon Dough. His name was funny (it was what you called an unidentified corpse) but no one thought so. After a while, he realized it was only *technically* funny—in reality, it was sad and ironic.

It might have been funny if his life was intriguing and full of adventure, but that wasn't the case. He was born and raised in San Francisco—supposedly exciting and cutting-edge—but the city failed to hold his interest. He couldn't understand why people lined up for overpriced food, or bounced from trend to vapid trend. Nevertheless, Jon was dutiful. He studied for tests, volunteered, and built up a portfolio of extracurriculars.

Midway through high school, great sickness swept the Earth, exposing cracks and weaknesses in The Hallowed System. Mobs of people bickered and fought, afraid they would die or lose their jobs.

Jon did his best to ignore the strife—he bubbled scantrons, wrote essays, and conferred with his counselors. Society, in turn, indoctrinated him with part-time jobs and unpaid internships. Oh, he was also lucky: his parents covered his college tuition. Once he graduated, he had no debt.

Finally—he'd arrived at the Ocean of Young Adulthood.

Occasionally, Jon would experience a bit of turbulence (disease in the family, minor car accidents), but by and large, he enjoyed fair weather and easy currents. He landed a steady job at a solid company, partied a little (not too much), dabbled in drugs, and denounced both activities as relics of his twenties. When he eventually docked in The Responsible Lands (his early thirties), he met a beautiful girl named Addison Stone.

They did everything expected of a vibrant young couple. After they'd checked off a number of dates (and posted the requisite amount of cheery Instagram stories), they went on vacation in Northern California. Halfway through a candle-lit dinner, Jon knelt and proposed to Addie. She covered her mouth and burst into tears.

Jon rose to his feet and (remembering his training from countless romcoms) drew Addie in with a heartfelt kiss. Everyone watching broke into applause. Some cheered and whooped loudly, because who doesn't love a Responsible Couple?

Addie's friends played their roles—they cooed at her ring and her beautiful dress. A few were annoyed by the inconvenience (understandable, as wedding expenses don't just impact the bride and the groom), but they dutifully fulfilled their obligations, as none of them wanted to be Irresponsible.

When the big day came, the wedding went off without a hitch. Rejoice! For a man and a woman have become *even more Responsible!*

Unfortunately, one of Jon's peers wasn't as lucky.

Aiden Pazitsky, Jon's high school classmate, graduated summa cum laude from an Ivy League college. Over the next few years, he built an impressive resumé and earned a respectable sum. Aiden was a shining example of a **Corporate Go-getter!**

Alas, trouble was brewing beneath the surface.

For nearly a decade, Aiden abused cocaine and adderall, addictions he'd garnered while studying for tests. Eventually, he was fired for being high on the job—shunned and exiled from the Responsible Lands. When he couldn't pay rent, he moved in with his parents and made intoxication into a full-time career. They tolerated his presence for two full years, gave him an ultimatum (he ignored it) and kicked him out.

Jon began to wonder...could what happened to Aiden happen to him? He came to the conclusion it most certainly could. To guard against this ignoble fate, he had to increase his Responsibilities.

So he and Addie decided to have children.

Over the next few years, Jon and Addie transitioned into parents. So-and-so's kid was acting up. Those stupid school administrators were doing things the hard way. Honey, where are we going—Disney Land or Six Flags? I'm not sure. We should do some digging and see what's cheaper. Maybe Disney Land, if we can find the right discount.

Jon chugged along, easing into the roles of Swell Husband, Terrific Dad, and All-Around Good Guy. Addie, meanwhile, became increasingly distant, spending more and more time with her housewife friends. She had built a life all her own—a life that was separate from Jon and the kids.

After the lights were out and Addie was sleeping, Jon would stay awake and stare at the ceiling. Something was wrong, but he couldn't say what.

There are other worlds than these.

Jon began drinking.

Addie grew worried, but he put her at ease by delving into cigars and steaks, making eloquent observations about the notes in his wine or the sear on his cut. This wasn't addiction—it was *culture*. Soon, he managed to convince her he was becoming a Lovable Old Man. Addie felt great relief, for Lovable Old Man is a respected position in the Responsible Lands.

Deep down, Jon knew he needed help, but the mask of Lovable Old Man allowed him to conceal that unsettled part of him, the part that rattled its gilded cage. That deep-down part was small and quiet, but it still had a voice.

There are other worlds than these.

The alcohol kept it locked away, guarded by the spell known as At Least. At Least I have a home. At Least I'm making money. At Least I'm not [fill in the blank]. If Jon ever caught himself yearning for more, At Least would emerge from the depths of his mind and firmly remind him he was fine and dandy. Sure he had issues, but At Least he wasn't like Aiden Pazitsky, a casualty of the monster known as the Bad Luck Bogeyman.

The Bad Luck Bogeyman was the scourge of stability, the Reaper of the Responsible.

Should the Bad Luck Bogeyman ever come a-knocking, you knelt and groveled and prayed for mercy. And if you somehow managed to escape his wrath, you told your story to your Responsible Friends, who would nod somberly and call you brave. But if the Bogeyman was feeling just the least bit sour, he would tear through your life like a barbed-wire whirlwind, devouring jobs, relationships, and 401ks. Sometimes, it didn't matter who you knew or how much you worked, you were destined to experience ruin and tragedy. That's why you sacrificed your precious dreams—they were soul-forged tributes that kept the Bogeyman at bay, that kept him from demanding health or wealth or social standing.

Responsible Folk could choose their religion, do yoga or meditation or even smoke weed, but they were united in their worship of the Bad Luck Bogeyman.

Thus far, Jon had avoided the Bogeyman's shadow. That changed on a cold winter's night, when Addie was in the shower and he was lying in bed. Her phone lit up with a strange message—**"I can't WAIT to see you!!!"**—from an unlisted number.

Jon stared at the screen, wondering who couldn't wait to see his happily married wife.

Also: he was about to leave for a two-week business trip.

He waited for Addie to dry off and change, then asked about the text. Addie tearfully explained she was having an affair. After they ran through the script (yelling and screaming, threats and curses) they decided to give marriage another try.

Next came counseling and heart-to-heart talks, where they remembered why they had fallen in love. For the following year, they wallowed in the memory of their youth and lust, resurrecting the thrill of their whirlwind romance. But as the days became weeks and the weeks became months, it became glaringly clear that it wasn't enough—a copy of a copy just isn't as sharp.

Jon resumed drinking. Addie got hooked on prescription medication. It all culminated in a giant shouting match; Addie marched into his room while he was nursing a hangover and let him have it with both barrels.

Jon was a drunk, dead in the water at a mediocre job. He had once been a star, destined to make partner or maybe vice president, but now he was just another burnt-out drone. Where was the old Jon, the passionate Jon?

He retorted in kind: Addie had *killed* that Jon when she decided to sleep with another man. Just who in the hell did she think she was?

Yeah, that was the problem, Addie spat. That's why he drank in the morning and again after work (wouldn't be surprised if he drank *at* work, come to think of it). He said he'd put the affair behind him, but now, after all this time and supposed resolution, he had the goddamn nerve to bring it up again. What next—did he want her to wear a scarlet A?

The divorce was horrific; lots of crying, lots of paperwork. Addie got custody of both children, Jon got a payout for the house's equity. Just when it seemed like it couldn't get worse, Jon was fired. He moved his stuff into a dilapidated studio, and cut himself off from family and friends.

One night, while staring up at the darkened ceiling, he was haunted by the ghost of his younger self—he remembered he had wanted to be an author. Why not give it an honest try, now that he was unemployed and had nothing to do?

He cleaned up his studio, bought a fancy new chair and a state-of-the-art laptop, then got to work mining podcasts and blogs for the latest and greatest advice on writing. One puff of weed, twenty minutes of exercise, five-star nootropics and high-fat brain food...

None of it took. Jon sat for hours at a time, staring blankly at an empty Word document.

He fell back into his old routine: drinking himself numb, sleeping through the day, and bingeing others' creations on his HD television. Family and friends knocked and called, but he responded to their pleas with curses and shouts.

They stopped knocking. They stopped calling.

He couldn't pay rent; his money was gone. He'd sacrificed it to liquor and junk food and Netflix and video games. In return, they had soothed and distracted him. He had fostered the hope they would one day save him—fill him with purpose and newfound zeal —but it never happened. (A deeper part of him wasn't surprised; he deserved to rot for his sloth and inequity.)

Two months later, the sheriff came by and told him to leave. The man was polite, but Jon could feel his pity and disgust: here was a guy who had once been Responsible, then allowed himself to lapse into chaos and apathy.

When Jon took to the streets, he felt strangely at home. Over the course of his life, he had felt increasingly out of place, squeezed into a world of commercial expectations. That was no longer the case. He knew this wasn't where he was supposed to be (or *wanted* to be, for that matter) but it was slightly better than where he'd been.

Drugs weren't a problem. He would occasionally dabble, but he was much more comfortable with legal substances. (Alcohol and tobacco, specifically.) He knew it was absurd, but he wanted to try and respect the law. Even now, he clung to the Sword of At Least. At Least he didn't use heroin, At Least he didn't smoke crack.

Only later, when he was dying from cancer, did he realize that At Least wasn't a sword—it was a goddamn prison.

Jon was shackled by a chain of At Leasts. He could have escaped early on, when they were small and weak and hadn't rusted together, but the hour was late in his tattered life—all he could do was ride it out.

Unfortunately, things were about to get a whole lot worse. As he sank further and further into a destitute hell, At Least began changing into one of the most dreaded phrases in the English language:

If Only.

If Only he'd started his own business. If Only he'd stuck with writing stories. If Only he hadn't married early. If Only they'd put off having kids—built up their finances and traveled the world.

If Only.

Jon wandered the city, chanting softly under his breath. Occasionally prayer, but mostly a chain of At Leasts and If Onlys. And so Jon settled into his station, taking his place among the Irresponsible fallen. A few succeeded as painters or comedians or writers or singers, but they could generally be dismissed as flukes and rarities. Responsible Folk loved the art that sprung from these mavericks, but Responsible Folk were also fickle—they lauded artists for their vision and novelty, but even more for their failure and ruin. Because by and large, Responsible Folk hewed to the Curse of Comparison: that age-old malady that shackles happiness to an illusory hierarchy. And within that hierarchy, there was no better target than an Irresponsible success.

Jon had once known that comparison was a game—a dualistic play that was meant to be fun and full of light. But as his life crawled toward its unenviable end, he couldn't remember this axiomatic truth. Existence was devoid of hope and potential; it was a downward spiral into bitter disappointment.

A decade later, disease began spreading throughout his body, forming into hard nodules that bulged from his skin. These unsightly tumors grew and festered, marring his once-handsome face with lesions and sores.

Jon couldn't care less. It was predictable, actually—the latest torture in his miserable journey.

He began his last day alive like any other: by waking in a heap of smelly trash. A part of him knew he was approaching the end, and wanted to give writing one last try.

During the morning rush, he walked into Starbucks and stole an unattended laptop. People yelled, Jon fled. He slipped around the corner and hid beneath garbage. Once he was safe, he crawled from the filth and opened the computer.

Microsoft Word...he couldn't see it anywhere on the—

Ah. There it was. He clicked the icon, opening a blank document.

For a long time, all he could do was sit and stare. In the void of this page was untouched promise—the potential for every story ever and never written. How could he have abandoned this for a cushy house and two point five kids? Those were offshoots—leaves and twigs from an inexhaustible tree. Instead of watering his True-deep roots, he had chosen to tend his outer trappings.

His fingers settled on the keys.

Then he was struck by a surge of fear. Why should anyone read what he wrote? What had he done to earn their attention? He wasn't special; just a wasted ghost who was no longer welcome. He should give up now—lay down and die on the street.

His hands curled into fists.

A moment later, certainty bloomed inside his gut. This was his chance to make a statement. It didn't matter if he was a homeless phantom—he was going to follow his goddamned heart.

There are other worlds than these.

As his hands uncurled, he felt something stir inside his soul, transmuting into shadows of half-formed thoughts. His feelings combined with churning cognition, mixing together into ideas and words.

And then he felt it—a sensitivity in his fingers that told him he was ready. He let them dance across the keys.

There once was a boy who liked to dream. Then he was told his dreams were wrong. He let fear and worry guide him along, but he only became sadder and sadder. After many years of hiding his sorrow, it all came out in a terrible flood. Life turned bad, but he was given a chance to make things right—to channel his dreams into a story.

This is what he wrote:

My
　　Dream
　　　Is
　　　To
　　　　　Be
　　Care
Free

19

Man, what happened? The last thing I remember is that freaky Whisper guy, muttering something-something-something about being a rat on a wheel. Think I fell asl—

"On your feet, Jon!" Gyrax hauls me up. *"You broke the enchantment and hurt the Sytíshí! We need to kill them before they escape!"*

A dozen yards away, Nyanti, Erany, and Ren are throwing blasts of light from their outstretched hands. The Whisper Folk are lined up across from them, responding in kind. I don't understand magical combat, but judging from the Sytíshís' pained expressions, I think they're getting their asses kicke—

"Jon!" Gyrax shakes me. *"Go help Elier!"* Then he sprints toward the arcane battle.

I swivel around, glimpsing an arrow as it flies from Lucky's bow. Elier's standing in the middle of the street, cavalry sabers out and cocked, staring down a horde of Iguar.

Frying pan, meet fire.

I sprint to his side, flipping my dagger into an icepick grip. *"I'm coming, guys! Don't worry, I'm—"*

"There!" Elier points his saber directly behind him. *"Hold there!"*

"What should I do? Is there anything I—"

"Here they come!" Lucky fires, shooting two arrows at the same time. A pair of Iguar collapse and crumple.

"Stay close, Jon!" Elier shouts. *"Stay close and watch your ba—"*

Nyanti interrupts with a high, haunting note. Blue streams of light arc in front of us, peaking brightly before they explode. The discharge forms into a magical barrier, punching hundreds of feet up and rushing out to either side. Its inside fills with undulant hues, painting the air with mother-of-pearl blaze.

One of the Whisper Folk shouts a phrase—it booms through my mind like Saruman's voice—and a searing white line runs up the barrier, splitting it in two while shrinking the left and right edges until they're confined to the street. Instead of a single wall, now it's a pair of them swinging inward, creating a gap for the goblins to enter.

Nyanti counters with a phrase of her own, freezing the walls at a diagonal slant. The gap is only four feet wide, enough to accommodate a couple of Iguar. Now, instead of a barricade, we're working with a channelized kill-zone. (Thank you, *Starcraft,* for giving me a primer on battlefield strategy).

Elier steps into the gap, spinning and twisting his cavalry sabers. *"Behind me, Jon! Kill the ones that slip my blades!"*

"Yep! Got it!" My focus is drawn to my adrenalized chest, where my heart is pounding like a runaway drum. Just gotta hope they don't—

One gets through.

My arm and hand react on their own—entangling, diverting, and stabbing before I consciously register I've actually done it. I finish my attack by shoving the Iguar; its throat leaks blood as it falls by the wayside.

"Good, Jon, good!" Lucky bullseyes a trio of goblins. *"Stay keen!"*

Under normal circumstances, I'd roll my eyes and respond with sarcasm. *Stay keen—you don't say?* But this is the polar opposite of a normal circumstance—I feel like puking and pooping and screaming in terror.

"Elier!" I yell. "If you want to switch out, I can—"

"Stay where you are!" Elier lunges into a sweeping slash, decapitating an Iguar at the base of its neck. Its head tumbles left, its body slumps right.

"They're climbing the walls!" Lucky screams.

Handfuls of goblins are scaling the townhomes, intent on bypassing the magical barrier. Thanks to the kill zone and Elier's swords, they haven't yet flanked us. But if they cross the roofs and drop to the street...

Elier kills two with a spinning swipe. A third Iguar ducks his saber, shoulder-rolling sideways with its sword and shield.

"Kill it, Jon—KILL IT!"

I kick it in the shield as hard as I can. It flies back into the barrier, causing colorful dazzle to erupt from the contact. Before the goblin can regain its bearings, I launch my shoulder into its chest. It hits the barrier again and crumples to the ground.

Elier shoots me a furious look. *"What are you—FINISH THEM, Jon!"* He hop-skips sideways, spearing the Iguar through its throat.

The reality of what I'm doing suddenly hits me. This isn't *Skyrim* or *Call of Duty,* this is *real life.* I just killed a living being and helped Elier kill one of its companions. Even though it was in self-defense, I—

"Get ready!" Lucky shifts his fire to the edges of the barrier, where Iguar are scrambling down the townhomes.

"Can't hold—" Elier spin-kicks an Iguar in its face, *"—much longer!"*

"I as well!" Lucky shouts. A flurry of arrows streak from his bow, killing the first six assaulters that drop to the cobbles.

Suddenly, Gyrax interrupts with some much-welcome news: *"We've got them on the run!"*

I glance over my shoulder. Two of the Sytíshí are speeding away, transforming into a slash of zigzag blurs. Every time they change direction, they briefly resolve into a solid shape. Nyanti and the others are dueling with the third (Revakhy, I think). His feet are spread and his forearms are crossed, forming an X in front of his face. The gesture seems connected to the violet-black forcefield flowing across him—whenever they hit it with one of their spells, his crossed arms shake and tremble.

Revakhy closes his eyes and waves his arms, gathering the forcefield into his palms. As it intensifies, Gyrax, Ren, and Erany shake the air with a chorus of chants, flinging fire, lightning, and patterned streams of roiling energy. Without the protection of his arcane forcefield, the blasts hit Revakhy full-on, brightening pieces of his body into multicolored embers. His sinew and muscle are clearly visible, his bottom jaw is stripped of skin.

"CAST HARDER!" Ren shouts. *"HE'S GOING TO—"*

Revakhy—half skeleton at this point—pitches forward and slings the concentrated forcefield. It gathers mass as it speeds toward us, lit by an umbra of amethyst blaze.

Gyrax howls, *"DOWN!"* and leaps forward, scissoring his legs as he hurls a spear made of blue-green shimmer. It strips away the last of Rekhavy's flesh and turns his bones into a billow of dust. At the same time, the Sytíshí magic lets off an ear-piercing whine—

EEEEEEEEEE

—and detonates in the middle of the ravaged street. A chunk of pavement hurtles toward me, eclipsing my vision before the world goes dark.

———

Someone's shaking me. Hard.

A moment later, I realize it's Gyrax. *"Jon! We need to run!"* Nyanti—unconscious or dead—is draped across his right shoulder.

Murrgh...head is still fuzzy. Did we just—

He shakes me again. *"Get UP, Jon!"*

Oh yeah—Iguar! Sytíshí! Magic duel!

"Yep, got it!" I shout at full volume. I can barely hear—everything sounds like I'm swimming underwater. I rise to my feet and stagger sideways, assaulted by waves of nauseating vertigo.

Oh man, my freaking *head...*

"GO!" Gyrax shoves me, pushing me forward. At the same time, he swings his axe from hip to shoulder, slicing an Iguar into bloody halves.

Further up the street, Lucky is hanging off Ren and Erany, clutching their shoulders as they help him limp across the cobbles. Mid-step, the half-Elf princess twists in place, chucking a crackling orb that sails past my face and blows apart a handful of Iguar.

I run up beside Erany. "Is there anything I can—"

"Take my place," Erany orders. She ducks out from Lucky's arm and guides me under the crook of his elbow.

"Easy—*easy!*" Lucky grimaces. "Would you two slow dow—*AH!*" He hop-skips twice, jerking his injured leg up to his waist.

"Can't," Ren says tightly. "Time runs thin. Jon, heed my count so we can walk together. *One* two, *one* two—"

Lucky twitches and limps in time with our gait, dragging his bad leg along as best he can. It's far from smooth, but at least the three of us are moving in unison. After a block and a half, Ren draws his sword and holds it out to the side.

"What are you *doing?*" Lucky spits.

"Draw steel, Jon. If one of those Iguar gets past our friends, we need to make sure it breathes its last."

"Seriously?" I throw him a panicked look. "Dude, I'm not a good fighter in the best of conditions—I doubt I can do it while I'm carrying Lucky."

"Draw, Jon. And say a prayer to the gods you hold dear."

Damn. Shit just got real.

I reach down and draw my dagger. Never thought I'd die from bloodthirsty goblins, but—

Ren swivels and decapitates an Iguar. I should be shocked by the sudden violence, but it surprisingly has the opposite effect; I feel aloof and disconnected.

"Keep going." Ren unhooks from Lucky's arm.

Lucky responds with a chain of expletives, condemning Ren as a low-shadow akersnatch and to give him a gods-cursed warning so he can stay off his gods-cursed leg.

As I adjust my footing to bear Lucky's weight, I look back at the others. Erany chucks two more explosives, causing dirt to rain down all around me. A bit of it slips between my lips, flooding my mouth with bitter earth.

Then a goblin hurls a twine-wrapped bundle. It flies into the window next to Gyrax, but he's too busy casting to pay any attention.

"Gyrax, watch ou—"

The building blows outward in a blast of rubble.

Gyrax and Nyanti soar through the air. They bang into a house on the other end of the street, then crumple into a pair of lifeless heaps. Lucky swears and curses, shouting something-something-something about his injured leg, but it barely registers. My best friend is unconscious or dead. I need to—

A second later, Gyrax pushes to his feet.

Thank. *God.*

He shakes his head, growling and muttering under his breath. Nyanti—ironically woken by the deafening explosion—leans heavy against the wall, shielding her face with a bent-armed hand. When she sees the Iguar flanking Elier, her eyes widen with shock and horror.

"Come hither!" she shouts. *"NOW!"*

Everyone stops fighting and sprints toward her.

The Witch stands tall, bending her fingers into impossible gestures that defy my understanding of human anatomy. Spotty green light trails her hands, forming into slashes that converge into an oval.

"Hurry!" Ren screams. *"Nyanti, you need to hur—"*

The oval detonates, flattening into a wave that cuts through the street. As the others disintegrate, I realize this is the end. Nyanti knew it and spared us some pain by killing us all. I can't decide if I'm grateful or—

My vision whites out, then the world goes dark.

20

Is this the Clear? High stone walls, bare wooden floor...

No. It's just an unfurnished room.

Elier and Lucky are sitting on their butts, looking dazedly from side to side. Ren is slumped against a wall, palming his head.

"Gods...hard to *think*..."

"Nyanti." Gyrax nods at the Witch, lying on the floor a few feet away. Her eyes are rolled back—the whites shine from her sockets in a sightless stare. "She teleported us into a safe location."

"You call this safe?" Ren straightens up. "The Sytíshí could be anywhere—the next room over, even!"

Erany crouches beside Nyanti. "She cast the spell in too much haste...lost control and absorbed the feedback."

Gyrax hunkers down next to her. "Her loci and meridians are out of alignment. We need to adjust them, or the pressure will kill her from the inside out."

"Like a blood clot," I venture, "in a vein or an artery."

"Exactly." Gyrax nods. "Only a lot more painful, especially to someone as sensitive as her."

"I have performed a few healings, but I am no expert." Erany turns to the others. "What about the rest of you?"

They shake their heads. *Nope.*

"Keep an eye out for danger," Gyrax tells them. "Erany. You, Jon, and I will aid Nyanti."

"Me?" I stammer. "I'm no healer!"

"You are much more than that." He gives me a knowing look.

An involuntary scoff bursts from my mouth. "What? Dude, I don't know what you're—"

"You broke the Sytíshís' Black Weave Trance. And in so doing, you wreaked havoc on their auras and spun us back into being. That's the only reason we're still alive."

"Because I…" Pieces of my dream come rushing back. "Because I plinked some words onto a stolen laptop?" My brow wrinkles in confusion.

"Don't be reductive." Gyrax waves his hands over Nyanti's face, causing the air above it to gleam and brighten. "That was Laiddinic power, honed from the stories you wrote as a boy. It was that skill—that ability to create and narrate—that saved our lives. Literally, in this instance."

Literally. "Nice entendre," I reply. "What do I do?"

"What *can* he do?" Erany's expression twists in puzzlement.

Gyrax beckons me over. "Hold out your hands. There are powerful loci inside your palms. I'm going to link them to Nyanti's aura."

"All right." I kneel beside him and hold out my hands. (Feels kinda hokey—like I'm a con-artist faith healer.)

He turns to Erany. "Ready?"

"Aye."

He turns back to me. "We're going to dive into her psyche. I'll do my best to untangle the damage, but there's a good chance you'll have to do most of it."

"Gyrax, I have zero experience with auras and mind-stuff. What if—"

"Do your best."

His palms glow red, flaring noisily with a loud *fshhh*. Erany's hands follow suit. After a couple seconds of tense silence, he draws her attention with a jerk of his chin.

"Open Jon's senses as much as you can."

"Act in haste, for it won't be easy. He's about as fluid as a dried twig." She closes her eyes and begins to chant.

An electric jolt shivers my spine. Suddenly, I'm able to see Nyanti's aura. Her glyphs and designs are snarled together—a magical version of a mangled body. I don't understand what any of it means, but it's all too clear that something is *wrong*.

[Easy, John.] Gyrax's mouth doesn't move; he's speaking into my friggin' *mind. [Stay calm and centered, or you risk life and sanity.]*

[Uh, how do I—] I'm about to ask how to engage in telepathy, then I realize I just did it. *[Right. Never mind.]*

Gyrax blazes with luminescence. *[Don't get lost. Keep a tight hold on your sense of self.]*

Doesn't sound hard. I'm pretty sure I know how to—

And then I'm sucked into a mental whirlwind, fighting to remember who I am.

21

Isn't fair going to set things right find the Rosecraft Blade—

[Get OFF ME!] Erany shoves me away.

I tumble into a blear of apathy, overcome by a wave of despair. Then a smile blooms and abruptly takes hold, vanquishing indifference with a sweep of contentment. Oh man, everything's going to be *just fine.* I was stressing out for no reason whatsoeve—

[Jon.] Gyrax clamps onto my psychic scruff.

My mind stop racing. *[Whoa.]* I perform the disembodied equivalent of pressing a hand to my heart. *[Where am I?]*

[Between solid focus and immateria.] Erany projects. *[How are you even—.]*

[Enough.] Gyrax snaps. *[There'll be time for that later.]*

[But are you sure he can—]

[You saw how much he hurt the Sytishi. Without him, we would all be lying dead in the street.]

She wants to know more, but she doesn't press further. Beneath her desire, I can sense deep-rooted hints of respect and wonderment.

I stretch out with my perception, the equivalent of looking around in this hella weird state. I occasionally glimpse a fleeting picture, but for the most part, all I get are vague impressions. As far as space and time, I have a definite sense of being *somewhere...*

I flex my will and reach for clarity.

An image appears in my mind's eye: we're clustered around Nyanti's body, hands splayed above her head and chest. The three of us are painted in psychedelic blaze, a photo negative brimming with chroma. My vision is bordered with colorless tines, drifting and floating in a tidal rhythm.

[Hurry. UP.] Erany emotes the impression of clenched teeth.

[Sorry.] The essence of *flustered dork boy* washes through me.

[Time runs thin.] Gyrax raises an eyebrow (or projects the feel of it, to be exact). *[Ready?]*

[Yeah.]

He aims our consciousness toward Nyanti. At first we're caught by a gentle pull, then we pick up speed and whirl into her psyche.

————

I'm deluged by a flush of random memories. Laughter, tears, adoration, resolve...my response is instinctive: I start weaving them into a linear narrative.

Nyanti was raised in a family of Witches. When she was an infant, her parents communed with her through Primal energies—a tug of emotions and subtle urges. Once she was able to speak and walk, her mother enrolled her in Shylan's School for the Magical Ar—

Gyrax's voice cracks through my brain. *[Enough. We aren't here to comb through her past.]*

[Uh, right. Sorry.]

[We must undo her points of twist—the blocks and kinks in her auric body.]

[How?]

[Unwind your perception and merge it with mine.]

[Um, okay. And how do I do that, exactly?]

*[Please—**hurry.**]* Erany adjusts and braces against us. The tension is palpable through our link.

[Don't overthink it.] Gyrax chides. *[Follow my lead through feeling and instinct.]*

He closes his eyes and becomes...*blurry* is the best I can describe it. He isn't concentrated in a single location; his presence is cloudlike.

[Okay, here goes.] I still my being. Almost immediately, *Happy Gilmore* rises to the fore—that scene where Kevin Nealon tells Adam Sandler to "be the ball." God, those '90s SNL movies were so damn *funny*.

Gyrax senses my wayward thoughts. *[Jon.]*

[Yep, yep—sorry.]

I try to relax but it doesn't work; I'm caught in a muddle of past reflection. Murderous Iguar, magic duels, Nyanti's injuries...I can't believe I'm in a parallel dimension where humanoid warriors fight with swords and spel—

[Jon.]

[Huh?]

[Don't force it—abide in it.]

Abide in it. Right. (Shouldn't be hard, I've seen the *Big Lebowski* a kajillion times over.) Instead of denying my fear and worry, I acknowledge their presence and let them be. I'm a *little* calmer, but I'm not really sure if...

Something shifts deep inside me—as if invisible weights dropped away from my head.

Gyrax gives an approving nod. *[Good. Direct your focus on to me.]*

We swirl together, like when you're playing sports and unconsciously bonding with the rest of your team. You know where they are without even looking.

[Now reach for Nyanti.]

Piece by piece, I build a Nyanti-like feel inside my awareness. Pretty soon, I can sense her presence: her dark beauty, her kind heart (I *knew* she was nice) and the general "Nyantiness" of it all.

[That's it.] Gyrax says. *[Now feel for the cracks along her aura.]*

I expand a little more...then reflexively contract. Jesus—if she were a trauma victim, her bones would be broken in a hundred different places.

[Easy, Jon. Stay—]

And then I hear her tortured scream: like talons scraping against a chalkboard.

[AAH!] I clap my ears, twisting violently from side to side. *[AAAAAAHH!!!]*

Gyrax is telling me to slow down and breathe, slow down and breathe, but he might as well be shouting in cracked-out gibberish. Because Nyanti's screams aren't just audible; I *become* her terror and utter helplessness, I *become* her frenzy and hysterical panic.

[Gyrax!] My breath hitches in my chest. *[I can't I can't I can't—]*

She screams again. This time, I join in.

[JON!] Gyrax wrenches my composure back into place. It's almost as disorienting as Nyanti's agony—everything settles with bewildering speed.

[Better?] He regards me warily.

[Yeah.] Man, that was *intense*.

[You must bear her pain. I wish there was some other way, but there isn't.]

[I...okay.] Deep, steadying breath. *[Let's do this.]*

We merge back together, sharing impressions and sentiment as we swirl and combine. Once we're synced, we reconnect with Nyanti.

The Witch crashes into us like a ton of bricks. For a split-second I try and fight her, then I laser in on staying calm.

Gyrax says, *[This won't be pleasant. Come closer.]*

Gyrax and I press together, linking idea and thought, intention and motive. As we blend and fuse, Nyanti's screams tear through our mind. Me/Gyrax relax a bit more, coiling into a ball of spring-loaded purpose.

[Good...focus...relax...good.]

Once we're aligned, we latch on to her dislocated psyche. Gyrax wordlessly communicates what he wants to do next, to which I respond with a disembodied nod. We grab everything we can and hold on tight.

[On the count of three.] Our focus becomes razor thin.

[One.] he/me says.

[Two.] me/he breathes.

[THREE!]

We swim through her breaks, snapping and cracking them back into place. Occasionally, we channel pure aggression into her traumas, forcing loci to line up with their parent meridians. We're making progress but it's not gonna hold—I can sense this is just a temporary fix.

Gyrax confirms this with, *[She's too disjointed; she's going to unwind. You need to rewrite her wounds.]*

*[Wait—**what???**]* Feverish terror rushes through me. *['Rewrite her wounds?' What does that even **mean?** Why didn't you tell me before—]*

[You would have overthought it! Jon, do it NOW! She's starting to loosen!] Sure enough, I can feel her slipping.

[Can't. Hold. Much...LONGER...] Erany grits her teeth.

I flood the Witch with my spastic awareness. As pain erupts throughout her loci, she meets my attention and issues a plea.

*[Jon. **Please.**]*

That does it—my mind steels. Nyanti's my friend. I can't let her die.

So I charge wholeheartedly into her damage, letting my desire and will flow over her torment. Narrative pours from the depths of my soul, filling Nyanti with belief and trust, with my absolute faith in her natural wellness.

And that's what I focus on: not her wounds, but her organic integrity. I envision her rifts as golden opportunities, as avenues to weave her back into strength. My apologue dances throughout her being, bringing her slowly but steadily into alignment.

[Jon.] She stares at me, astonished. *[How are you—]*

[Shh.] Sweat drips off the point of my chin. *[Not finished.]* I continue envisioning her as she deserves to be—singing, dancing, laughing, playing.

A minute later, I relax my grip. I think I'm done.

Gyrax sighs in relief. *[Get back to your body.]*

[Thank Ishay.] Erany breathes.

————

I open my eyes and gasp in shock. I'm completely soaked—drenched in a sheen of sour perspiration. A bit of it plips onto Nyanti's face.

She wrinkles her eyes and raises a hand. "Jon. You're sweating on me."

"Oh!" I scuttle to my feet and laugh nervously. "Sorry. Didn't know I was—"

She sits up and groans. "Be easy. If not for you, I would still be lost in a maze of agony."

"Right. Of course." I awkwardly snort-laugh and immediately hate myself for it. "No worries—all in a day's work."

She gives me a tired smile. "When I first heard about the Prophesied Traveler, you are not what I imagined."

Erany rubs an eye with the heel of her palm. "Do you truly believe that Jon is the one?"

Gyrax dusts himself off. "Now more than ever. That was Laiddinic power, as the day is bright and the night is long." He looks around, puzzled. "Where are the others?"

Ren and Elier are nowhere to be seen. Lucky's fast asleep; half-lying, half-sitting against the wall.

"Lucky!" Gyrax reaches over and taps his cheek.

"Uh?" His eyes flutter open.

"The others. Where are they?"

Lucky shakes his head, groggy. "Hunting down the remaining Sytíshí…" A pained moan escapes his lips. "My cursed *leg*…"

Nyanti kneels beside Lucky. "Here." She extends a glowing hand, almost touching him, then moves it down the length of his thigh. "That should help."

He grunts in acknowledgment. "Thank you. It feels better already."

"A partial healing, but it'll do for now." She reverses course, moving her hand toward his hip.

"What? No!" Lucky glares at her. "Finish the job!"

"I need to conserve my arcane energy. We are trapped in a castle with two Sytíshí, not to mention—"

"I am *wounded!*" Lucky snarls. "And I am not being paid to be a soldier or savior! My agreement was to travel with the Wolven and watch his back, not stand toe-to-toe against a pair of gods-cursed Whisper Fo—"

"—the horde of Iguar crawling through the city," she continues calmly. "If I heal your leg, I'll shrink our chances at gaining the hexflow. We should all hold counsel before I commit to such magic."

"This is absurd," Lucky hisses.

"You'll get what you're owed." Gyrax cracks his neck. "I'm going to look for Ren and Elier."

"Me too," I say automatically.

"No." He unslings his ax. "The Sytíshí are not to be trifled with."

"I just saved your life! *Everyone's* life! If not for me, then—"

"This is different," Erany cautions. "We are in pursuit of desperate monsters. Like cornered animals, but far more deadly."

"I—"

Suddenly, the door bangs open. Elier and Ren come staggering in, leaning heavily against each other. Ren lowers Elier onto the floor, then collapses beside him. Erany and Gyrax run into the hall, but Ren calls them back.

"We chased them into the lower catacombs," Ren wheezes. "Collapsed the walls with a majeric wave."

"We have to finish them," Nyanti insists. "It will be much worse if we let them go."

"Agreed." Gyrax nods. "Nyanti. You, me and Erany will search the building and—"

"What about me?" Ren asks heatedly. "I am no stranger to arcane combat!"

Gyrax shakes his head. "Guard our injured. Elier and Lucky can't fight off an Iguar, much less a pair of Sytíshí Whisper Folk."

"I can still kill Iguar," Elier mutters.

"My point is—"

Before he can finish, the room floods with violet-black mist.

22

The others are shouting, but I can't make head or tails of what they're saying—I'm deep in the grip of mind-rending pain. And from what I can hear, so are they.

"You killed our *brother!*" Khyrell shrieks. He clenches his fist, causing my muscles to snarl into knots.

"AAAAHHH!!! STOP!" I scream without meaning to. I just want to *get away.*

"Not until I've peeled you apart." He bares his teeth in a sick grimace.

My tendons and ligaments jerk and twitch, threatening to tear off fascia and cartilage. I flop on my belly and try to crawl, but my fingers skew in different directions, popping and cracking like miniature fireworks. As much as that hurts, it doesn't compare to what happens next—my head starts twisting from side to side, triggering excruciating pangs as it pushes my range of motion to its absolute limit.

I'm about to break my own neck.

Then, through a film of tear-blurred vision, Blindfold Guy (the ninja-mage from my Earth-side visions) appears in a flash of green lines. He doesn't resolve into flesh and blood; he remains transparent like a *Star Wars* hologram.

"Knifelock!" Khyrell tightens his grip, stealing my breath with a surge of agony. "We were just about to—"

Knifelock's hand flashes to his waist, drawing a dagger with stage-magic speed. Khryell manages a panicked *"NO—"* before the back-curving blade punches several holes in his upper chest.

The pain in my body immediately ceases. *"HUUUHHH—"* I push to all fours and vomit forcefully.

Sarisyrin flings an upturned hand in Knifelock's direction, releasing a bolt of crackling yellow. Knifelock swats it away with casual indifference.

The Sytíshí opens his mouth to speak, but Knifelock grabs his throat and lifts him up off the deck. A second later, his vertebrae begin to break—*CR-CR-CRACK*. His eyes roll back, his tongue lolls out.

Elier and Erany stagger to their feet, bringing their weapons into sloppy guard. Knifelock gives them a disinterested glance, then blinks out of existence.

For a long moment, no one moves.

"What...what just happened?" I stare at the others.

"Arganti Knifelock," Ren rasps. "We're lucky..." He coughs up a glob of bloody phlegm. "We're lucky he didn't kill us."

"Not worth his time." Erany sags to the floor.

Gyrax's eyes flick back and forth. He's working the angles, trying to make sense of what he just saw. Finally, he says, "Aye. We were lucky."

"What now?" Lucky asks.

Nyanti peers through a third-story window. "The Iguar are going door to door."

Ren walks in a short circle, pausing briefly at each window so he can see for himself. "They're canvassing the city from the outside in. The center is quiet, but it won't be long before that changes." He squints into the distance. "They've buttressed the walls with inward-facing zigzag earthworks."

I raise a half-bent arm. "What does that mea—"

"They want to keep us from escaping. Gods, they're *everywhere*..." His lips and fingers move in a quick, silent rhythm. "Tens...maybe hundreds of thousands. Terrelly trained me in tally and score, but this is well beyond my scouting abilities. There are far too many to gauge an estimate."

Elier asks, "Options?"

"Create a diversion, flee in the chaos," Gyrax offers. "But that will be risky, seeing as you and Lucky are both injured."

Wait—Elier's injured? Then I notice his blood-soaked pants. Something mangled his left leg.

The Duelist meets my gaze and grins wryly. "Khyrell's handiwork. I took him by surprise and tried to fillet his spine. He returned the favor by savaging my flesh."

Erany jerks her chin, catching Nyanti's attention. "Have you signaled your sisters?"

"I have, but they haven't responded."

"Then it's settled," Ren says. "If we link our auras and weave a spell, our combined energies could—"

"We have an alternative," Nyanti interjects.

Six pairs of eyes settle on the Witch.

"In the past, I have held palaver with a powerful spirit: a Nelithy Elemental named Arinia D'sae. In the span of a minute, she can inflict as much damage as a kingbreaker siege engine. If we're lucky, she might convince her husband—Aiethic Tyanmore—to help us as well."

"What are you waiting for?" Lucky snaps. "Summon her!" He flaps a hand in disgust. "If we had avoided Elerica, we wouldn't be stuck in this low-shadow mess."

"If we had avoided Elerica, it would have remained in Sytíshí hands," Ren counters.

"*Who CARES?*" Lucky shouts. "I can tolerate this idiot thinking Jon is the Traveler—" he flings an arm at Gyrax, "—but when the rest of you actually start to believe him..." He hisses through his teeth in frustration and anger. "Listen close and listen well: none of you are heroes, saviors, or martyrs! *Get that through your Nok-damned skulls!*"

Ren grabs the thief and slams him up against the wall. "From the very beginning, you have cheerfully excused your greed and avarice, claiming that faith and fortune would see us through. Why not grin like you always have, and tell us that all will be fine and fair?"

Lucky's face twists into a sneer. "Listen to you. If you could only hear how *stupid* you sound, you wou—"

"Enough." Erany pushes them apart. "The odds are against us as it is. If we bicker and gripe, we might as well surrender to the Iguar outside."

"What about Knifelock?" I ask. "He helped us once. Could he do it again?"

Uneasy glances all around.

Ren breaks the silence with, "He's a Nightkeeper, Jon. And not just any Nightkeeper—Lyderea Fairdyle's right-hand captain."

Gyrax clears his throat. "Ren is right. There might be more to what we saw, but now is not the time to explore it."

"All righty then." I turn to Nyanti. "Let's get to summoning that Nelithy Elemental."

"It's not that easy," Nyanti cautions. "If she agrees to help, she will demand a tribute."

"Joy," Lucky grumbles. "This keeps getting better and better."

"What kind of tribute?" Gyrax asks.

"A substantive investment of arcane energy. And the only way I can offer it is—"

"—if we are able to access the hexflow spring," Erany finishes.

Nyanti nods. "If I call her without it, she will devour us all. Nevertheless, Arinia may be our safest bet. The Iguar are canvassing from the outside in. And Elerica is built around the spring, which also happens to be the center of the city. That means—"

Ren concludes. "It's our best chance at avoiding Iguar."

"Correct. If we head for a wall or one of the gates, we are certain to encounter a massive horde. Maybe not if we head for the spring."

Worry tinges Lucky's voice. "Elier and I are both injured. Are you going to leave us behind in this low-shadow castle?"

Nyanti looks him in the eye. "That would be prudent. If I refrained from healing you, I would be able to cast stronger battle-magic. That would serve us well on our way to the hexflow."

"How is that a concern when I'm sitting in this room like a bloody piece of huntbait?"

"Our only other option is to take you with us. But in order to do so, I would have to perform an intensive curative, and that would more than halve my ener—"

"Then it's settled," Lucky says brusquely. "Heal us. Do it quickly."

Ren steps forward, palms out. "Lucky, think: with stronger magic, we could move faster and reduce our peril. Healing your leg might seem tempting, but if we circle back for you after we summon Arinia, we could establish a safer route of—"

"You would leave me to die while you run for that hexflow?"

"No, that's not what I—"

"Enough. Heal me, Witch." He looks pointedly at Nyanti.

Ren tries again. "Lucky, just—"

Erany cuts him off with, "He is requesting aid, Ren. That is it and that is all."

"But—"

"Elementals are spirits, not machines," Gyrax states. "Arinia might not accept our tribute."

"We are close to walking the razor's edge," Ren argues. "We must be ready to make sacrifices. And if that means we leave Lucky and Elier—"

Gyrax steps closer, casting his shadow across Ren's face. "Remember your lineage, Wayfarer."

Ren's face twists in frustration. "I..." Then he hangs his head. "Very well."

"Heal me first," Lucky orders. "Since I was the first one injured."

I glance at Elier, expecting him to be irritated by Lucky's behavior, but the Duelist shrugs with typical stoicism. "Either way is fine by me. If I am to die by an Iguar's sword, then so be it."

Lucky scoffs, as if to say *what an idiot*. It's to be expected, but I'm surprised into anger nonetheless. Evidently, Ren feels the same: he tightens his jaw and clenches his fists.

Nyanti kneels by the thief, stilling her hands above his leg. She closes her eyes and begins to chant. At first it's a murmur, but then it picks up—a slip-slide of vowels and sibilant consonants.

"Gods," Lucky hisses. "It *hurts*. Is it supposed to hurt? Nyanti?"

She doesn't answer. She just keeps on chanting.

Lucky dips his chin and squinches his eyes. A second later he blurts, "What are you *doing*? Why does it—*aah!*" He thrashes and flails, but Gyrax and Erany pin him down. *"Let go of me!"* he demands. *"Let go, you gods-cursed—"*

Nyanti's chant grows in volume, expanding into a double-toned elegy that echoes through the room. Blue-green light spills off her fingers, wrapping his leg in throbbing luminescence.

"Get off get off—AAAAHH!!!"

As soon as she finishes, Lucky scrabbles to his feet and grips the hilt of his cutlass. After a hanging second, he lets go of his weapon.

"Thank you," he says stiffly. "I feel much better."

Nyanti ignores him and kneels beside Elier.

"Make it quick." He closes his eyes and swallows hard.

"I'll try."

The light purls off her fingers and fills his wounds. His expression tightens...then his eyes crack open in wary surprise.

"What..." He looks down at his leg, then at Nyanti. The Witch doesn't move—a bead of sweat trickles down her cheek, lining her face with a crescent of moisture.

"That should do it." She rises to her feet.

Elier stares at her, dumbfounded. "It...it almost felt *good.*"

"You and Lucky are worlds apart," Nyanti explains. "His psyche is rife with deep-seated scars, whereas yours appears to be relatively clean."

Lucky mutters, "Or it could just be your lack of skill. I know mud-town hedge witches that are better at physicking."

"Predictable," Nyanti sneers. "I wouldn't expect you to lay claim to your weakness, even if doing so would make you stronger."

Ren draws his sword and heads for the door. "I'll take lead. I have ranged through peril many a-time—my experience and instincts will keep us safe"

Nyanti cocks her head, puzzled. "Have you been here before?"

"No."

"Then how will you know where to guide us?"

"I memorized the layout when I looked out the windows. The hexflow temple was easy to spot—it's built on a circular street ringed with statues."

"Very well, Wayfarer. I trust your training."

As Gyrax passes by Nyanti, he says, "Thank you."

"This isn't over, Wolven. Save your thanks until it is."

"Learn to celebrate the smaller victories. Sometimes, they're all that stand between you and the Clear."

Nyanti half scoffs, half laughs. "Come." She jerks her head at me. "Let's get this over with."

I fall in behind Gyrax, unsure of how to feel. In the span of a day, I lived a nightmare version of my Earthling future, killed a handful of murderous goblins, and healed an Elerican Witch with Laiddinic powers.

Atriya's contract flashes through my mind:

SOMETHING DIFFERENT.

Truer words were never written.

23

As we make our way through a grid of corridors, I realize that everything around us is made of wood. The walls and floor are mostly petrified—meaning they're technically stone—but it all looks alive. *Feels* alive would be a better way to put it.

"Are we...are we in a tree?" I whisper the question, but it still sounds loud in the pin-drop silence.

Ren shushes me with a finger against his lips. Gyrax, however, doesn't seem to mind. "We are," he says at normal volume. "An old-world glamourwood. Judging by its size and its breadth, I'd say it has lived for at least ten millennia, maybe twenty."

"Glamourwood, huh? Didn't see it back in the city."

"They fade and dim when the sun is high, then brighten and liven as dusk approaches. That is why it escaped your notice."

"Whoa. Very cool." I'm also glad he didn't shush me. Thanks to Gyrax's canine senses, he would be the first one to detect a threat, so it's safe to say we're in the clear.

Ren, irked by our lack of doom-and-gloom silence, shakes his head in mild disgust.

Whatever, bro.

The Witchery isn't all up in my face yelling SUNDAY-SUNDAY-SUNDAY, but as we advance through the glamourwood, it becomes increasingly noticeable. I spot several labs filled with occult-y altars, grimoire-laden shelves, and jars of ingredients that look gross, exotic, or both.

Eventually, the corridor feeds into a serpentine labyrinth, full of twists and turns and winding forks. I'm glad I'm in the rear—I would be hopelessly lost if they asked me to navigate.

After a couple more minutes of Witch-castle spelunking, I whisper to Gyrax, "How do you know we're going the right way? I know Ren memorized the outside layout, but—"

"There are auric diagrams inscribed in the air. He's following the ones marked 'exit.' "

Auric diagrams—of course. If this were a party, I'd be the loser hanging out in the corner, nursing a half-empty cup and bobbing along to the music.

The labyrinth opens into a foyer. There's benches and chairs scattered throughout, but they're not independent of the castle itself; they're grown from the walls and the symbol-lined floor. The main entrance—a double-gated door adorned with richly colored vines—is the focus of architecture.

Ren squares up with us. "Once we're outside, we need to be quiet." He dips his head, mulling something over, then looks me in the eye. "There is no denying it Jon—you have shown your worth. I want you to know that before we venture into further peril."

I'm shocked into silence. Typically, Ren communicates with resentful glares and sullen grunts. His compliment catches me completely off guard—so much so that a lump of emotion begins growing in my throat.

Before I can reply, Ren says, "Remember: it will be over soon." He unlatches the door and leans into its edge. The hinges groan as it yawns open.

I think he's trying to comfort us. Didn't work, but I'll keep it to myself.

————

The fog is still here, but it's only an inch or two high. Unlike before, I can now see the ground, which I consider a huge plus—when it was deeper and thicker, I kept thinking about Luke and his buddies in the Death Star trash compactor. I am so not a fan of stalk-eyed tentacle-monsters.

(Tentacles. Blech.)

It isn't long before we hear some Iguar heading toward us. Ren darts into an alley and motions for us to follow. A second later we're lined up behind him, pressed tightly against the alleyway wall. I hear the jangle of armor and an angry epithet—"Yah GEBBIN tebbit!"—as they continue on past.

Ren pokes his head out, studies the street, then beckons with a hand. *Come on. The coast is clear.*

Everything's magnified. Every breath and footstep—even the rustle of clothing against skin—is utterly deafening. I can't get a comfortable grip on my dagger; my fingers continually adjust, trying to find the right amount of tension.

We're being quiet, but the Iguar aren't. The air is filled with growls and snaps, accompanied by the clatter of weapons and gear. I wish I knew what the hell they were saying. I'd really like to know if it was casual conversation, or something along the lines of *the humans are around the corner. Pretend to keep going so we can circle behind them.*

Ren holds up a fist. We freeze in place.

A squat-bodied goblin rounds the bend, wielding a serrated sword and a disc-shaped shield. It seems annoyed and preoccupied, like it's been ordered to carry out an irritating task.

Ren lunges forward and cuts off its head.

More goblins pour toward us. My companions rush them, stabbing and decapitating with vicious speed. Before I know it, twelve Iguar are lying dead in the street.

It happened so fast...I didn't have a chance to throw a strike.

Ren wipes his sword on a prone body. He locks eyes with us, places a finger against his lips—*shhhh*—then straightens up and continues walking. The others clean their blades and fall in line.

Then something yells, *"YAAWK!"* flooding my brain with instant terror.

No time to think—I dive sideways as Iguar burst from the house to my right. I finish my roll in a semi-crouch, ready to fight, when I see a doubled-edged long-knife whipping toward me.

This it. I'm going to di—

An arrow hits the knife in its double-tined guard, striking a spark off the gritty black metal. Both missiles fly diagonally past me.

Lucky and his short bow just saved my life.

I push off the ground and charge my attackers. My blade slips in and out as I rotate and strike, rotate and strike. Keep the pressure on so I can force a gap, thrust my dagger into unarmored flesh, because that's the easiest way to do the most damage—

And then it's over. The last Iguar falls backward, a runny red wound in place of its eye. My foot twitches up and kicks it away, just like I was taught: after a critical hit, gain some distance, because you never know how long it will take them to die.

Suddenly, my mind downshifts. I stop thinking about parries and counters and loading my weight for follow-on moves. I bring my hands to my chest and stare at the bright red grime coating my fingers. I know it was us or them, but—

Elier says, "Well done." The others murmur their assent.

Lucky looks at my face, then at my hands, then at my face again. "Welcome to Evermoor." He claps my shoulder and walks away.

Gyrax's eyes are sad and knowing. He opens his mouth like he's about to speak, then shakes his head and takes his place in the column. I wish he'd spoken, but I get why he didn't.

There aren't any words. This has to be felt.

24

We make it two more blocks before we're spotted again. As we crash into their rounded shields, my mind loops into a desperate frenzy. It's all a blur of metal, blood, and snarls until—

"Hhh!"

A back-angled sword grazes my arm. Without thinking, I flip my knife into an icepick grip and punch it through a shoulder, clavicle, and neck.

Up ahead, a mob of Iguar round the corner. This time, they're accompanied by a pair of ember-eyed dogs. Their skin is made from char and ash. Curls of fire wisp from their nostrils.

Nyanti shouts, *"Diabolin Hounds! Use aqueous magic to counter their heat!"*

Lucky yells, *"Don't know any! What do the rest of us—"*

"THEN STAY OUT OF MY WAY!"

One of the hounds charges Gyrax. He slaps his left wrist with his right hand, causing a rippling blue gauntlet to envelop his arm. His attacker clamps down on his spell-armored wrist, jerking violently from side to side. Gyrax staggers, nearly pulled off-balance, then accelerates into a spin and throws the dog like a discus.

Ren and Lucky whirl and slice, covering each other in a brutal duet. Elier and Erany are doing the same, only with a lot more elegance. I'm just trying to stay alive—flailing and thrashing without any semblance of aim or accuracy.

I stab an Iguar, kick another, then a third one smashes my chest with its shield, sending me tumbling across the ground. I skid to a stop, rise to a knee...

And lock eyes with a demon hound.

Uh-oh.

It lopes toward me, burning ash-ringed footprints into the cobbles. Just before it hits its stride, Nyanti slams into its ribs. As they barrel-roll away, thick vapor pours off their bodies. The muggy haze makes everything bleary, but I can still make her out as she knees it twice, then cracks its jaw with a power-charged hand.

Gyrax hauls me up by my collar. *"This way!"*

I stumble through the turmoil, swiping and stabbing random attackers. Gotta keep running, gotta keep fighting, just focus on the nex—

Suddenly, the wind picks up and disperses the fog. Nyanti doesn't miss a beat; she sprints a dozen yards ahead, leaps high in the air, then turns around and lands in a single-kneed crouch, punching the street with her blazing fist. Jigsaw cracks erupt from her strike, whipping back toward the Iguar in undulant waves.

I hope that's enough. It was impressive as hell, but I'm not sure if it did any dama—

The buildings give way on either side, filling the air with snapping beams and tearing walls. Mortar and shingle crash down on the Iguar.

Okay—*that* was enough.

Or maybe not. The surviving goblins—the ones a bit further back—are still in pursuit. I can barely make out their armored silhouettes, scrabbling across the dusty wreckage.

"Hurry!" Nyanti calls.

As we resume our flight, Iguar horns blare and carry. I'm being hunted and my body knows it—all I want to do is to run run *RUN.*

Goblins emerge from townhomes and huts, flooding the street with bodies and weapons. Erany slashes the air with her non-sword hand, projecting a plume of billowing flame. It burns a couple, but most just screech and shuffle back. We take advantage of the disruption by smashing their line, killing a handful, then trampling the rest. Without slowing down, Gyrax picks a javelin out of his shoulder and chucks it back at its thrower. It hits the Iguar with tremendous force—its feet fly up in a wide V.

Nyanti shouts, *"Ren, make sure we're going the right—"*

"This way!" He takes a hard left onto a building-lined avenue. Iguar pop out from the corners and doorways.

Exhaustion unfurls throughout my limbs, draining my strength and eating my speed. We're holding our own, but the instant we let up—

A pair of hounds pounce at Gyrax. He crosses his arms in a brawny X, forcing them to bite his wrists instead of his neck. Fire takes root across his arms, set ablaze by their hellfire fangs.

He growl-shouts a curse in gutter-speak Wolven, then bangs their skulls like a pair of pots. Each blow is sickeningly loud; they bark, squeal, and let him go. He follows up by stomping the first one's spine—I hear the gunshot *CRACK* of snapping vertebrae—then skip-steps forward and kicks its partner in the ribs. It voices an ear-splitting yelp as it soars away.

"Gyrax! Are you—" I slip a chop and grab the back of my attacker's head. My blade slides home but I barely notice.

He stares at his palms and utters a chain of whispers. Bright green lines surround his hands, forming symbols and runes an inch above his skin.

"GYRAX!" I thrust-kick an Iguar, then punch my knife through its gullet.

A few more steps and I halt before Gyrax. Man, his arms look *bad*...they're burnt and cracked, leaking blood and fluid.

The runes combine into glimmering circles, then tighten down onto his wounds. He flexes his right hand, grunts in satisfaction, then tries his left. Judging by his expression, it hurts like hell.

I ask, "No good?"

He shakes his head. "No. But if we catch a reprieve from these Nok-damned goblins, I'll be able to—"

Erany sidekicks an Iguar into three of its peers. "Gyrax! If we combine our auras and cast a crux-melded spell—"

"Can't!" he shouts. "My arms!"

She backhands an Iguar, sending it spinning to the ground. "Nyanti! We need to break their tempo! We can't keep—"

"Say no more!"

Nyanti extends her arms, clutching the air with quivering fingers. Glowing orbs fill the street—swelling, crackling, and exploding like bombs. The runes surrounding them unspool in a twitch, swamping the block with arcane writing

Dozens of Iguar are caught in the blasts, quickly reduced to smoking husks. As an added bonus, clusters of orbs go off in the townhomes, breaking them apart into blocks and beams. The goblins beneath are pelted and pummeled, then pancaked flat by falling walls.

Nyanti reels and falters, her balance stolen by the quaking earth. Ren swoops in and hooks her arm, helping the Witch keep her footing. She clasps his hand in both of hers, then gives him a look that says it all: *I'd thank you if I could, but I'm too damn tired.*

I know exactly how she feels.

Out of nowhere, a moment of quiet descends upon us. It's not quite silence—I can still hear those damned horns—but it's close enough. Without speaking, we shuffle inward and form a circle. Unspoken understanding flows between us: we're lucky to be alive, even luckier to be whole and intact.

"Good." Ren takes a steadying breath, looking at each of us in turn and nodding approvingly. "It is far from over, but we have given fair account of ourselves. Take heart and hold faith, for those low-shadow Iguar know it well."

"Aye." Elier smiles. "I'm glad I came along. Much better than sitting in a tree."

"Tell that to my hands," Gyrax says wryly. "Didn't want to use this just yet, but…" He reaches in his carry and produces a glass jar filled with floating sparkles. He pops the top with a flick of his thumb, then turns it upside down onto his injuries. The burns lighten and disappear, leaving bald patches of healthy skin.

"You could have healed me with that!" Lucky exclaims. "Why didn't you—"

"Wolven only, thief. It would have stripped the muscle from your bones."

"Should have used ale. Ale heals all, regardless of designate." Elier quips.

Everyone chuckles or flashes a grin. It isn't that funny, but we've all been operating at the edge of our capacity. Lucky is the only one who isn't amused; he lets us know it with a Grinch-like scowl.

"This is no time for cheer."

Ren bursts into hearty guffaws. I'm not sure if it's genuine mirth or he's simply trying to piss off Lucky, but one thing's for sure—it's infectious as hell. The rest of us laugh while Lucky glowers.

"Are you done?" he snaps. "We have better things to do than lounge about and jest."

Everyone stares at him…then we all give into another fit. Not just hearty, but downright raucous this time.

"Be grateful, Lucknar," Gyrax admonishes. "We are stealing merriment from dire circumstances—the most daring theft a man can commit. You would do well to rejoice, for you stand at the height of your larcenous craft."

Lucky opens his mouth to retort, but Ren interrupts with, "Enough. We need to keep going."

"For once I agree." Lucky nocks an arrow onto his bow. "We have an hour of daylight, maybe less." He looks at Nyanti. "How long until we reach the spring? Can we make it before dusk?"

"Typically, it would take half an hour. But we must try and be stealthy, which will slow our progress by a considerable degree."

Lucky groans in frustration. "Can I please just get a yes or n—"

She holds up a finger, cutting him off. "I believe we can make it, but more importantly, we *must*. Come nightfall, the Iguar will assume their Dark Moon aspect."

I rub the back of my neck. "I know that's bad, but on a scale of one to ten, how bad are we talking?"

"Their size and strength will roughly double. In some cases, their durability will increase by a factor of ten."

"Got it." I raise my hands in mock-surrender. "Sunlight good. Moonlight, not so much."

"Essentially."

"Nothing changes." Gyrax hefts his axe. "Tread light and talk soft. Eliminate threats as fast as you can."

"Aye," Nyanti agrees. "I can break another rush, maybe two, but the rise of the moon will dim our chances."

"Time runs thin, now more than ever," Ren says. "Eyes open, weapons close."

He takes his place at the front of our line, scanning empty buildings and shadowed doorways. As I follow behind, inevitability washes over me. Weirdly enough, I find it comforting—we've placed our bets and rolled the dice.

All we can do is see this through.

25

Six blocks in, a stream of oncoming Iguar forces us to duck inside a building. Every time we try and leave, more Iguar come bustling along, dashing our hopes and straining our nerves. After our fifth try, the sun dips below the skyline, painting its edge with a red-orange glow.

My teeth start grinding; it takes a conscious effort to make them stop. "Ren, if we don't leave soon…"

"Thank you," he hisses, "for stating the obvious. Yes, I'm well aware—if we don't leave soon, they will grow twice as large and tear us apart."

My cheeks flush red. "I wasn't trying to—"

"Easy, Jon." Gyrax lays a hand on my shoulder. "We must choose the right moment, or it will all be for naught."

"I know, I know." I shake my head, frustrated. "It's just that—"

"Relax. Enjoy this." His lips widen into a grin.

"What?" I can't believe he's *smiling*.

"Savor your hardships lest you dwell in regret, wishing you had seen them for what they truly are."

"And what are they?"

"Opportunities." His eyes flick up as Ren signals with a bent-armed wave. "Come. Let us see what fate has in store."

————

We move with quiet urgency, striking a balance between stealth and speed. Strangely enough, I feel incredibly lonely. Despite being surrounded by my adventurer friends, the world is reduced to the swish of cloaks, the tread of boots, and the insistent thump of my adrenalized heart. I'll take it, though, if it means—

An Iguar bugle sounds from behind us.

"Run!" Ren pounds forward, cloak flaring as he picks up speed. The rest of us follow, chased by horns and the rattle of armor.

A second later, the streets explode with hundreds of goblins. Their presence causes a palpable disturbance—I can actually *feel* them closing in.

"Start casting!" Gyrax bellows.

Lucky throws a chain of glowing red ovals. Some earn a yelp, but most blow apart and do little to no damage. Elier's more versed in combat magic; he carves rune-laden flourishes into the air, projecting black-purple waves from his cavalry sabers. The spells are meant for personal defense—each one vanishes after ten or twenty yards—but whenever they hit, bones snap and skin unravels. At the front of our line, Ren twists his fingers in hypnotic circles, projecting several jags of searing blue lightning. The energy jumps from Iguar to Iguar, revealing their bones in an x-ray flash. Directly behind him, Gyrax throws spear after spear of blinding white light; each one pierces half a dozen Iguar before they disappear. Lines of goblins scream and fall, punctured by his invasive projectiles. Last but not least, Nyanti and Erany project laser-like beams from their rune-circled hands. Whenever they hit, they trigger massive detonations, launching bodies and dirt into the sky.

The air sizzles, the ground quakes. The entire world is breaking apart, exploding at the seams and tearing at the edges. I wish I could help, but all I have is a single knife. Maybe I could throw it, but—

"Keep running!" Nyanti screams. *"We're almost there!"*

Then, in a deceptively gentle shift of light, the sun disappears below the horizon.

Gyrax shouts, *"The sun is out, the sun is out! 'Ware your flanks!"*

I spot a sudden gap in our seven-person column. Someone stopped casting but I can't tell who. I think it's Lucky, but—

"Help!"

Definitely Lucky.

A strong breeze clears the air, revealing the reason behind his plea: one of the Iguar threw a bola—a rope with weights on either end—wrapping his feet in a tight-bound coil. Now he's sitting on his butt, sawing at the line with a double-edged dagger. To make matters worse, five Iguar are running straight at him.

Gyrax crashes into them as I catch up to Lucky. I saw frantically away at the Iguar bola, putting my bodyweight into my knife. The line holds for a gut-wrenching second...then snaps apart with an angry twang.

"Come on!" I lurch forward, holding the thief by the crook of his arm.

As smoke billows and chaos reigns, my dread blooms into full-on panic. How close are we? Because if we don't reach shelter in the next few seconds...

[Jon.]

What the hell?

[Draw me.]

I gasp, "Who are you?" then suck in a lungful and manage, *"What* are you?"

[Ailura Qartesi, the Avalon Clapfire. Draw me—we're running out of time.]

The moon pokes out from behind a tower, spilling pale light across the street. When it touches the Iguar, they grow a couple feet taller, filling out their armor with a wet, ripping groan. Their eyes change too—from wide yellow circles into nasty red glints.

They're no longer goblins. Now they're orcs.

Elier continues cutting them down, but our moon-powered foes are noticeably fiercer; they're deadlocking his swords with alarming frequency. Lucky, meanwhile, has gone full-on caveman—he's sitting on an Iguar, stabbing it manically with his bloody cutlass. Another Iguar tries to attack him, but Gyrax snaps its neck with a ferocious backhand, hitting it so damn hard that its head spins around.

[Jon. Draw me.]

Elier curses as a serrated dagger slices his thigh. Gyrax leaps forward with his arm cocked back, torquing his legs as he grabs the back of an orc's head and drives its face into the ground.

[DRAW ME!]

I flick the button on the revolver's pouch cover, then dig inside and clutch the grip. As I level the half-gun, a ball of emerald light appears in place of its cylinder, washing the streets in swamp-green radiance.

I pull the trigger.

The ball of light catapults outward, expanding into a wave of aquamarine blaze. Handfuls of Iguar are caught in the blast, thrown backward with jet-engine force. A bunch of us—me included—are knocked off our feet and onto our butts.

Eerie calm takes hold in my brain. Man, it'd be nice to just lay here and—

"RUN!" Nyanti screams.

I stumble to my feet and rejoin the column. Maybe if I ask for another assist...

[Ailura?]

Nothing.

"Keep going!" Nyanti shouts. *"It's just around the corner!"*

The street opens into a spacious square, home to an imposing, cathedral-esque building. Just like the castle, it's formed from the trunk of a building-sized tree, interspersed with stone and stained-glass murals.

"There it is!" Ren cries. *"Jon, shoot them again!"*

I turn around and raise the half-gun, but its unchambered top stays cold and dark.

"Can't!" I scream. *"She's not responding!"*

Ren curses in a foreign language, then spits out a booming sound that sounds like an axe chopping a cord of firewood. He levitates a foot off the ground, then hurtles like a missile toward the cathedral. Mid-flight, the air in front of him catches fire, forming a brilliant shield around his face and chest. He tucks inward, aiming his shoulder at the double-door entrance, and—

WHUNG!

—rebounds off it.

He gets to a knee, smacking the cobbles in sheer frustration. *"Gods! They're warded!"*

"All together!" Gyrax yells. *"Link auras!"*

Nyanti and Erany throw a couple more spells, then face the doors and begin chanting in tandem. Glowing runes circle their hands, ringing their features in purple-green shine. Gyrax and Ren blast a few more Iguar, then join in the chant.

Galvanic energy builds and intensifies—the atmospheric charge of a late-summer storm, only a thousand times stronger. After a hanging moment of whipcrack tension, the combined spell releases with a roar, taking form as a giant ray.

The doors slam open with a gunshot bang. I scrabble inside as fast as I can.

"CLOSE THE DOORS!" Gyrax shouts. *"KEEP THEM OUT-SIDE!"*

He takes the right, we take the left. For a nerve-racking instant, both doors refuse to move...then grudgingly relent with a deep-rooted groan.

Gyrax orders, "Ren! Nyanti! Lay them low if they try to push through!"

Ren and Nyanti fill the gap, casting a barrage of hasty magic. A moment later, the hideously slow doors (or so they seem to my panic-flooded brain) slam shut with a decisive BOOM.

Gyrax spins his axe, whirling sideways toward the knotted tie-down holding up a twenty-foot deadbolt. He slices through the rope—

"*rrrRR**RAH!***"

—causing the stone bolt to drop into a brace, barring the door shut with deafening finality. Howls and wails erupt from outside.

"How long will it hold?" I ask nervously.

Nyanti points at the deadbolt, now glowing feather white. "As stout an enchantment as any I've seen. Unless they're friends with a SyCajister mage, we're safe in here for at least a month."

Lucky blurts, "A *month?* I can't stay in this low-shadow temple for—"

"Watch your tongue," Nyanti warns. "This is the heart of Elerica. Show some respect."

Lucky waves dismissively. *Bah.*

Gyrax appraises the marble-coated chamber. "Where is the spring?"

Nyanti sits on an iron bench, formed from twists of gem-laden metal. "Down the hall. Inner sanctum." She tilts back and closes her eyes. "We'll get to it later. Right now, I need to rest."

Ren gestures angrily at the entrance. "We're just going to wait? They're right outside!"

"Cry off, Ren." Gyrax slings his axe. "She needs to recover."

"But—"

"If she tries to summon with errant focus, she could easily conjure an army of fellspawn."

Lucky mutters, "For once, I agree with Ren." But that's the extent of his protest.

We all take a seat on one of the benches. Gyrax crosses his arms, letting his head droop to his chest. Erany curls on her side and starts to snore. Ren and Lucky lean forward, elbows on their thighs, and stare furiously at the ground.

I close my eyes and try to snooze, but it's not gonna happen. I just escaped an army of monsters, several of which I killed in hand-to-hand combat. Oh, and let's not forget: I vaporized a bunch with a magic revolver.

My mind circles back to recent events: the Sytíshí attack, healing Nyanti, our fight with the Iguar...I can't stop thinking about how—

And then I'm asleep.

————

I rub my eyes, clearing them of gunk. Holy crap...feels like I was hit by a runaway train...

"Jon?" Gyrax walks over. "Are you well?"

"Yeah, I think so." I meet his eyes with a bleary gaze. "Haven't been this sore in...well, *ever*, really."

"You expended a great deal of energy."

"You don't say." I rotate my arms in small circles, wincing reflexively. Each one feels fifty pounds heavier. "Man, I am *tired*...not sleepy, just totally beat down..."

"Walk slowly—that should help."

"Okay." My gait is stiff and bow-legged. "Ugh...how do you get used to this?"

"If your perception is flexible, it can expand to accommodate nearly any circumstance. Your body and aura will naturally follow."

"I see."

My muscles creak and pull, drawing a groan from my chapped lips. After a few laps around the foyer, my legs start to loosen. Awesome. For a minute there, I was afraid I was going to end up like Abe

Simpson, complete with a limp and quavery voice. I'm still sore, but not the kind of sore where you think twice about moving.

"Nice." I reach up and crack my neck. "I can run and fight at least."

"Good." Gyrax glances at Nyanti and Erany, who are chatting quietly in the corner of the chamber. "There's a good chance you will have to do both."

"But not if Nyanti summons the Elemental, right?"

"I'm not sure if it will come to our aid. And even if it does, there might be too many Iguar for it to—"

"Gotta have faith, right?" I shrug cavalierly, tapping my inner eighties action hero. "Things will work out."

Gyrax grins. " 'Be dust upon your breath.' "

"Yessir," I assert. "And if you can't breathe, then sack up and give it a try, because you might just hit it out of the park."

"Good man." He claps my shoulder and gives it a squeeze. "Nyanti will do the brunt of the work. Erany, Ren and I will provide assistance. Everyone else will stand guard."

"I thought we were safe in here."

"Summoning an Elemental is not without risk. The arcane flux could shut down the wards, in which case—"

"We go right back to fighting face-eating monsters. Gotcha."

Lucky pipes up: "Oy! When are you going to summon Arinia?"

Nyanti regards him with blatant disgust. "Let us once more into the fray...so you can grace us all with your complaints and cowardice."

"I've been accused of worse throughout the years." Lucky palms his back and arches his spine, eliciting a bony crack from his lower vertebrae. "*Ah.*" He twists his neck from side to side. "Much better."

Nice to see he's doing well. I suspect it's because he's a fair-weather optimist, but I'll take fair-weather optimism over dickhead cynicism.

Nyanti beckons, and we fall in behind her. She leads us through an ornate door, then into the mouth of an echoey corridor.

Enchanted stained-glass lines the walls, lit by a soft, arcane glow. The beginning of the hall depicts farmers and settlers. The middle shows them fighting off beasts. Toward the end, the images portray a growing city: gradual construction of buildings, streets, and fixtures.

The hall concludes with a wrought iron door, interspersed with pieces of colorful glass. I have no idea how it opens—it doesn't have a knob or any sort of handle.

Nyanti, thankfully, has it covered. She kisses her index and middle fingers, causing a rotating sparkle to shine from their tips. When she touches the door's oval centerpiece—a magenta inlay with a twist of blue strands—the shine from her fingers flows into the glass, imbuing its patterns with sinuous luster.

The latch clicks back. The door creaks inward.

Arinia D'Sae, here we come.

26

The hexflow feeds into an oval pool, around twenty yards across at its widest point. The water is ringed by eight striking rocks, all mounted on six-foot poles. Each rock is as big as a strongman's stone, rough and craggy with unpolished color. Their cradles, however, are smooth twists of gold and silver, mingled with streaks of ocean-blue metal.

"Whoa," I whisper. "What are those?"

"Orphic polestars," Gyrax says. "Cut from anexium and infused with fae-shine. They serve as amplifiers for those who know how to tap their potential."

"And for those who don't?"

"If they're lucky, nothing happens. If not..." He trails off and shrugs.

"Gotcha." I nod. "Fall down go boom."

"If by "fall down go boom" you mean 'flay your soul until it's a mere shadow of its former self,' then yes."

"Could've just stuck with 'fall down go boom.' "

"Lend me an ear," Nyanti calls.

We bring it in.

"Typically, summoning an Elemental involves a seasoned coterie of Elerican mages. But we are short on time and long on peril, so we'll need to make do with what we have. In this case, that would be me, Erany, Gyrax, and Ren." She looks at Elier and Lucky. "Unless you wish to partake in an interplanar summons. Are either of you familiar with Kaenodian augury?"

They both shake their heads.

"As I thought. During the summons, we will be physically vulnerable. I doubt the Iguar will breach these walls, but it is best to be prepared."

Elier dips into a sweeping bow. "I shall ensure your safety, milady."

Nyanti cracks a smile. "My thanks, Duelist." The Witch clears her throat. "Jon, be ready to help. You and your..." She struggles to find the words, *"abilities* might come in handy."

"Yep." I give her a double thumbs-up. "No problem." (Little confused as to what my abilities are, exactly. They seem to be along the lines of magical storytelling)

"Good. Mages, draw in close. Our mental design will be an Aglecktian dial..."

The casters huddle together, leaving me, Elier, and Lucky standing off to the side. After a couple minutes of uncomfortable silence, I decide to strike up a conversation. Unfortunately, my idiot brain defaults to a time-tested icebreaker:

"So...how 'bout them Knicks?"

Lucky and Elier give me a mystified look, then shake their heads in mild bafflement. *Just Jon being Jon. What a derp.*

Jerks.

Thankfully, the others are ready—they surround the water in an equidistant circle.

"As we discussed." Nyanti closes her eyes.

For a long moment, nothing happens. Then I hear a low-voiced hum. At first I'm not sure if it's my imagination, but my doubt falls away as Nyanti raises the pitch. A second later, the others join in.

One by one, the polestars erupt with colored flames. Nyanti, eyes still closed, drops her voice a couple of octaves. The polestars respond by dimming and fading, leaving a pulsing glow in their craggy centers.

Right on cue, the pool starts to roil and bubble. Steam rises off its surface, then coalesces into a woman's face. Distinctly Black, with an attractive haughtiness in the cast of her eye.

"Nyanti Eldara. It has been a day and an age since last we spoke." Her voice is otherworldly, filled with resonant tones and multilayered echoes.

Nyanti bows. "Arinia D'Sae. I am honored by your presence."

"As you should be." Arinia's lips curve into a smile. It quickly fades, giving way to mild puzzlement. "What is happening outside the temple? It sounds dreadful…" Understanding blooms in her transparent gaze. "Iguar. Hordes of them."

"Aye, milady. It is why we summoned you. And perhaps your husband, if he is willing to help."

"Alas, my heartmate is busy. As much as he would enjoy demolishing goblins, it cannot be. What do you offer?"

"I have been granted agency of Elerica City. Accordingly, you may have your fill of these enchanted waters."

Arinia radiates doubt and skepticism. "That won't buy much. Five minutes of battle-focused magic, no more."

"I accept." Nyanti traces a circle with her index and middle fingers, marking the air with an orange corona. The magical halo sizzles and hisses, leaking ember-bright sparks into the pool.

Then—slowly, deliberately—she inscribes a light-woven rune in the center of the circle: a blood-red letter steeped in velvet black flames.

"As High Coven Witch, I scriven this warrant to seal our bargain."

Arinia flares blinding white. "Your warrant is just. I pledge aid and combat in return for your tribute."

"So it is. So shall it be," Nyanti intones. The circle and rune break apart, leaving a scatter of glittering flickers.

Arinia grows a torso and limbs, morphing into a glossy humanoid. She doesn't have clothes, but the R-rated bits are nowhere to be seen—she's like a life-size Barbie doll, only her body is made of mother-of-pearl shine.

"For the next five minutes, I am yours to command." The iridescent figure strides out of the spring.

"Very well," Nyanti says. "Clear us a path."

———

Arinia dissolves into flowing mercury, streaming out from the chamber in a quicksilver coil. It's hypnotic to watch: twisting curves of airborne shine, twirling and winding toward the—

"Jon!" Ren is already running for the entrance. "Come on!"

I catch up a moment later, right before Arinia smashes through the doors. As she reassumes form, she's immediately swarmed by ravenous Iguar.

Their mistake.

The Elemental's strikes are relaxed and indifferent—lazy backhands, sometimes even just a flick of her fingers. Whenever she hits, a gunpowder clap erupts from her touch, lighting the air with a violent flash.

As casual as she is, the resultant damage is anything but. Iguar fly through windows and walls, portions of their body burnt to ash. Occasionally, she'll grab one by the throat and lift it up off its feet. The prolonged contact triggers a series of angry detonations, causing their heads to pop off and roll across the ground.

Gyrax says tightly, "Get ready to run." Then he cups his mouth and yells, *"Arinia! We need a path, dammit!"*

She continues wading through legions of orcs, blasting them apart with firecracker slaps. **"Their numbers are vast—I do not think I can kill them all. I can slay them faster if I amplify my presence, but it will halve my time as a physical being. Your choice, mortals."**

Gyrax looks at Nyanti, who responds with a noncommittal shrug. *What do we have to lose?*

"Do it!" Gyrax shouts.

"Very well."

An orange flux jets from Arinia, enveloping the Iguar and burning them down into fine particulate. Some shriek a warning and break for the townhomes, but for the vast majority, it's way too late. Before they can run, deadly magic sweeps their ranks.

"There!" Gyrax points at a gap in their decimated lines. *"That's our opening!"*

We pour outside in a feverish sprint. As soon as we clear the temple steps, an onslaught of Iguar emerge from the buildings. Thankfully, Arinia has another trick up her extradimensional sleeve: in the span of a second, she grows a hundred feet tall, dwarfing the city with her luminous form.

"TAKE SHELTER!" Arinia booms. *"THIS WILL BE NOTHING SHORT OF CATASTROPHIC!"*

"Inside!" Ren points at the nearest townhome. *"GO!"*

Gyrax drops to all fours and gallops ahead of us, smashing the door with his tucked shoulder. As it flies off its hinges he flows into a roll, coming up on a knee and twirling his great axe.

Four Iguar are waiting inside. He parries their swords and spins in place, killing them all with a brutal flourish. We pile in behind him as their bodies hit the floor.

"MORTALS!" Arinia bellows. *"GET READY!"*

She rears back and inhales mightily, backlit by the glare of the cloudless moon. I can hear—and *feel*—the air being drawn into her lungs. Invasive cold shivers my skin, tickling the deep-down space between my ears.

Then she cranes forward like a Tyrannosaurus Rex, expelling a flood of lethal sound. Pressurized death whooshes outward, detonating Iguar by the handful. The ones closest to Arinia are reduced to slime, while everyone beyond that vomits and spasms.

This is incredible. I never thought I'd ever see anything like—

Oh shit—the wave.

It's headed *right for us.*

I shout a warning, but it's lost in a muddle of blurry haze. My ears, nose and throat instantly swell, engulfing me in a feeling of unbearable fullness. God, it feels like my organs are going to *rupture...*

Luckily, the sensation begins fading almost immediately. The lump in my throat dwindles and shrinks, the swelling goes down in my nodes and sinuses. I'm not alone; everyone else is in varying degrees of sickness and recovery.

"THIS NEXT SPELL WILL BE MY LAST! IF YOU WOULD KEEP YOUR GUTS INSIDE YOUR BODIES, I SUGGEST YOU CAST A CIRCLE OF PROTECTION!"

"Come on," Gyrax manages. His eyes are leaking yellow-green gunk, the fur on his cheeks is matted with tears. "Erany and Ren—build the circle's leftmost half. Nyanti, you and I will take the right."

The others agree with a scatter of "ayes," and spread out accordingly. Erany and Ren take west and south, while Nyanti and Gyrax take east and north. As they carve sizzling grooves into the floor, chains of runes form over their knuckles.

"TEN SECONDS, MORTALS!"

Four separate curves shine from the deck—they're about halfway done.

"FIVE. FOUR."

I grind my teeth as the curves inch toward each other. Each second seems like an eternity.

"THREE. TWO."

The lines meet, completing the circle. At the four points where the lines have joined, a quartet of characters—a little like Mandarin and a lot like Gothic—materialize above the floor, spinning twice before they brighten and vanish.

I tense up, waiting for Arinia to call *ONE,* but it doesn't come. Instead, she straightens and draws a giant breath, kindling sear-bright shine within her core. At the same time, a high-pitched keen builds around us, squeezing my ears and the backs of my eyes. Whatever she's planning, it's gonna be pretty damn epi—

And then she howls into the full-moon sky, burning with terrible, unfiltered light. Ephemeral energy lashes off her, slashing the Iguar with murderous brilliance. Mobs of orcs split and erupt, filling gutters with bones and sludge.

"That's *right!*" Lucky bares his teeth. "Rip the skin from their cursed *bones!* Ha! This almost makes my injury worth it!"

I'm trying to figure out if I should be elated or disgusted, when one of the tendril begins drifting toward us. *"Oh shit!"* I dive to the floor and curl into a ball.

As the appendage sweeps our protective shield, it becomes momentarily visible—we're not just sheltered in a two-dimensional circle, we're standing in a half-dome made of staticky red lightning. Once the tendril clears its edge, it goes back to being invisible.

"Very courageous," Erany remarks dryly. "You may be the Traveler, but you may also need a change of pants."

"Easy, Jon." Gyrax lends me a hand. "We need not fear Arinia's magic."

"Oh yeah, for sure," I reply bluffly, trying to hide the tremor in my voice. "I knew that. I was just testing my uh...you know—it was just a test. Yeah."

Erany laughs, then echoes what I said in a deep, oafish tone: "It was just a test. Yeah."

I grin and blush, but still—I'm gonna count this as a win. I'm alive and whole, and I got some good-natured teasing out of a beautiful Princess. (Maybe she's flirting? Fingers crossed. Jesus, Jon, this is life and death—stop thinking about your half-Elf crush!)

Outside, Arinia's tendrils whip into a storm, a vortex made of light and wind. Due to the chaos, I can barely see the remaining Iguar. They're dim little shadows, exploding and bursting in rapid fire time.

A moment later, the carnage stops. An imprint of Arinia remains in the air, frozen in place against the moon-lit sky. As she turns transparent, the stars shine through her chimeric outline...

And then she's gone.

<h1 style="text-align:center">27</h1>

Nyanti trots briskly along, leading us through the spell-ravaged streets. I try (but fail) to ignore the snap of bones when someone steps on a charred skeleton, or the wet *sploosh* of liquefied Iguar.

On our way to the hexflow, I felt oddly lonely, despite being surrounded by my badass friends. I was drawn into my own little world, enveloped in an isolated quiet that defined my existence. Now, however, it's the exact opposite: I feel deeply connected to everyone else. We shouldn't be alive, but we beat the odds and here we ar—

A scatter of bugles sounds from behind us.

Jesus Christ, how are any of them still alive? Arinia D'Sae was our ace in the hole. If they bog us down, we're up shit creek without a padd—

A pack of Iguar dash out in front. Nyanti breaks right, but a dozen more Iguar cut us off. (And let me just say, they are *way* more terrifying in their Dark Moon aspect. When they were four feet tall, the danger came from their strength in numbers. Now they're like roided-out hillbillies with an extra helping of Ugly McNasties.)

I glance from side to side, stepping back toward the others. Slowly but surely, our column shrinks, until we're clustered together facing outward.

Elier sighs. "I suppose this is it. Pity."

"See what comes of your bleeding hearts!" Lucky rages. "If we hadn't stopped in this low-shadow city, we'd be safe and sound in—"

He continues ranting, but I'm not listening. This definitely sucks, but if I had to choose between our current predicament and forty-plus years in a neon-lit office, then—

"Jon." Erany cants her head, catching me in her peripheral vision.

"Huh?" I turn slightly toward her.

"I'm glad I met you. Passing into the Clear doesn't seem so bad—not with you standing by my side."

Whoa—what?

What?

"Um...yeah. Same," I manage.

Wow. I mean *wow.* Yes, I realize I'm about to be beaten and eaten, but I haven't stopped crushing on Eralindíany.

"Uh, Erany?" Butterflies ripple through my stomach.

"Yes?"

"If we survive...I mean, after we make it out of here, do you...uh..."

Come on, Jon—*DO IT.*

A bead of sweat trickles down my temple. Forget the Iguar—Erany *scares* me. Not just because she's super pretty, but also because she's a *warrior princess.* I bet she could break my legs and neuter me senseless. (Probably in a single move, no less.) I bet she could—

"Jon?"

Get it together—breathe, Jon, *breathe.*

I take a breath that becomes a gulp. "After we make it out of here, do you...do you want to go out for coffee or something? Like, just the two of us? On a...a date?"

Without meaning to, I squinch my eyes shut. I force them open as she says, "Jon, look at me."

I do as she says. God, she is *beautiful.* Taylor Swift without any of the hairless cat vibes she sometimes gives off in bad photos. Golden blond hair, light purple eyes, soft mouth and delicate jaw...

"I am unfamiliar with the word *coffee,* but I would love to drink kepi with you, if you'd have me. And yes—just the two of us."

Yes—ohmygod *YES!*

The fatigue in my body disappears, vanquished by a surge of horndog energy. At the same time, my heart kicks into Super Saiyan overdrive.

Erany's lips twitch with amusement. By the look of it, she knows exactly what kind of effect she's having on me (on my raging hormones, to be precise). "But let's tend to the Iguar, aye? We've sent a great many into the Clear. The ones before us deserve the same."

"Yep. Right." I throw her an overzealous nod. "Let's. *Do this.*" I'm going out with Erany, come hell or high water. And these dickfaced uggos will *not* screw that up.

The uggos in question halt ten feet away, regarding our party with glinting red eyes. Lucky's been cursing and swearing during my exchange with Erany, but I didn't hear a word he said—I was totally focused on asking her out.

Some of the Iguar taunt us with smirks. I couldn't care less.

Bring it on, turdholes.

Suddenly, Lucky yells, "Brace yourself, there are more—"

Commotion breaks out among the orcs. At first, I think Lucky's right—something else has joined their ranks—but then a flash of doubt crosses my mind. It sounds more like—

Gyrax shouts, "Take heart, friends! The Felinx have come! The Felinx have come to fight by our side!"

Felinx? My mind goes blank, then I remember the giant cat we met in the woods. It was strong enough to wrestle with Gyrax. If *those* things are here, we might just have a fighting chance.

"MAKE WAY, LITTLE ORCS! MAKE WAY FOR YIRE ANON!" The air erupts with terrifying growls. "TURN TAIL AND RUN, LEST YOU WISH TO DIE BY CLAW AND FANG!"

A handful of cats flicker into view, mowing down Iguar with frightening speed. Something about them (how can something *that* big move *that* fast?) is arrestingly primal; I have to stifle the urge to freeze in place.

"We'll meet them in the middle!" Elier shouts. "Ren, Erany, Lucky—watch our backs! Gyrax, Nyanti, Jon—we'll form a wedge and charge north! Ready? One, two, th—"

"Hold!" Nyanti shouts. "Look to the south!"

I swing around, watching a blitz of magic bloom and explode. In between a chain of indigo flares, I spot a flutter of hooded cloaks.

"Elerican Witches!" she cries. "Elerican Witches have come to our aid!"

Nearby Iguar shuffle toward us, taking half-hearted swings with their clubs and swords. The Felinx and Witches clearly have them rattled. Me, on the other hand, I'm on top of the goddamn world— ready to kick some ass and earn some alone-time with Erany.

"On three!" Elier yells, cutting and stabbing with newfound enthusiasm. "One! Two!"

We all roar, *"THREE!"* and arrow into the Iguar horde, smashing them apart like a well-aimed bowling ball. I find myself smiling as I parry and slash, kick and sweep. Inappropriate? Maybe. But keep in mind that a few minutes prior, I was ninety-nine point nine percent convinced that a black-steel blade was gonna chop me in half.

And also: my date with Erany.

So yeah, sorry not sorry—I don't really care if I'm being "inappropriate." To be perfectly honest, I don't really care about anything right now, including this mob of big-ass Iguar. Bring it on Knights and Whisper Folk, Wyverns and Nightkeepers. I could go toe to toe with Lyderea herself.

Because I asked Erany out, and she *just said yes.*

———

I almost feel sorry for our orcish opponents. No one wants to die from a super-strong claw or a twentieth-level fireball. But a deeper part of me—the part that breathes—knows that I don't have to worry. The scales are balanced in the Eventide Clear.

After we mop up the stragglers, Gyrax slings his axe and heads for our Felinx savior. "Yire Anon! Come hither, you scraggly-haired nip-snorter!"

Yire rears back, batting him with powerful swipes that would kill or cripple a full-grown man. Gyrax guards his face like a seasoned boxer, then clinches Yire and hugs him fiercely.

"Damn Felinx!" Gyrax laughs. "I should have known you would come!"

"Release me!" Yire flails, trying his best to squirm away. "You smell *TERRIBLE!*"

Gyrax laughs harder, squeezes tighter, then lets him go. They give each other parting swats (once again, hard enough to take a grown man's head off) and take a step back, half-laughing, half-growling.

"Couldn't let you have all the fun." Yire's tail swishes back and forth.

"I'm glad you didn't." Gyrax brushes dirt off his jerkin. "I had just made my peace with Fenrus and Bau when you and your pride came to our rescue."

"Speak not of debt." Yire waves dismissively. "If it wasn't for you and your friend Nyanti, I would still be deep in a Sytíshí curse. I did a poor job expressing it when last we met, but you inspired me, Gyrax. Enough to enlist the aid of my kin." Yire clears his throat and drops his gaze. "After you freed my mind, I...I did not respond in a noble manner. I plead your grace, Kai Aclasian."

"Aye," Gyrax says gravely, "It would have been a dire twist if the Sytíshí retained control of the Witchcraft City. Yet the sight before me is far more troubling."

Yire turns his head, averting his gaze. "Have at me, Wolven. I deserve nothing more than—"

"That a haughty Felinx would admit to wrongdoing...it makes my stomach turn in disgust." Gyrax crosses his massive arms.

Yire looks up, eyes wide with uncertainty, then lets loose with a harsh, barking laugh. Gyrax tries to keep cool, but his lips widen into an unrepentant grin.

"Ha! You nasty unwashed dog-man! You...you..." the cat shakes his head and chuckles throatily.

"Be at ease, Yire. We all slip and occasionally stumble."

Yire arches up, grasping Gyrax's paw with both of his. "You set an august example, Wolven, and not a moment too soon—I believe our world is on the cusp of change. We should both see that it changes for the better."

"I am heartened, Yire, for I share your view. Your involvement in the Unity is of immense value, as my warriors are young and know little of the Wars. If they could hear from someone who was actually there, I think they would—"

Yire and Gyrax stroll out of earshot. Lucky and Ren are nowhere to be seen, while Nyanti and Elier are openly flirting, standing next to a battered house. The Duelist is leaning against a doorframe, gracing the Witch with a rakish smile. She's half-sitting on a broken wall—closer than necessary for casual conversation—curling a lock of hair behind her ear.

Those two? I chuckle softly under my breath. Never would have thought.

I ease onto a chunk of shattered stone, reveling in a wash of bone-deep contentment. I just finished my first side quest, and all my friends are alive and well. Lyderea is still out there, but—

"May I sit?"

Oh my god—Erany.

Anxiety twists my tongue into a knot. "Y'g'head whurvery-ouwan'…"

She cocks her head, puzzled. "Beg pardon?"

I clear my throat and mentally kick myself. "Yes." I force myself to enunciate clearly. "Yep. Mm-hm. Take a seat." (God, I am *so STUPID.*)

"Thank you." She sits beside me, resting her elbows atop her thighs. "According to Nyanti, the rest of the Iguar are fleeing the city. Without the Whisper Folk, they had no answer for Elerican magic."

"That's awesome," I offer. "Glad to hear it."

For a long moment, we're both silent.

"Sun's up," she comments. "A welcome sight."

"*So* pretty," I blurt. (Jesus, Jon—calm the hell down!)

"I thought I was going to breathe my last. I was sure of it." She searches the sky with her lavender gaze. "Right before the Felinx and Witches, I had an epiphany: I never considered what I wanted for myself. Revenge and duty have governed my path."

Her thoughtful tone soothes my apprehension. "Yeah…yeah, I think I can relate. I mean, evil tyrants didn't kill my parents, but up until recently, my entire future seemed mapped in stone." (Typically, I would never have the balls to compare my life to half-Elf princess-hood, but gimme a break—we just survived the mother of all battles.)

"That's exactly how I felt." She lets out a sigh. "As a tot, I was harried and badgered by royals and tutors. They were always emphasizing my highborn station—how my actions would determine the fate of the many."

I find myself nodding as her words strike a chord—expectations can be as constricting as a vise. "On my world, they put you in school for twenty or so years, getting you ready to enter the workforce. If you stray from that path, people condemn you as irresponsible."

"What if you stray and find success?"

"They call you lucky: a genius or a fluke. People sing your praises or turn jealous and spiteful. In either case, they make you an outsider and push you away. Maybe not intentionally, but..." I conclude with a shrug. "That's just how it is."

"Hmm." She's silent for a bit. Then: "I was always an outsider—the Fair Folk children teased me mercilessly."

"Why?"

"My rounded ears and faded eyes. The adults never said anything, but I could tell that deep down, they felt the same way as—"

"I'm sorry, what?" I'm surprised into laughter. "They teased you because of your ears and your eyes?"

"Deláni possess rich violet eyes. Mine hold color, but nothing close to a true-blooded Elf."

"That...is a *ridiculous* thing to hold against you."

"You're the first to say so. It does me glad to hear it from your lips."

"I'm also a minority, but I was raised in an area where they didn't judge me for it."

She scuffs the dirt with the toe of her boot. "I wish my world was more like yours. In that respect, at least."

"Don't get me wrong—there's plenty of places where my appearance wouldn't fly, but where I grew up, it wasn't an issue. Funny." I shake my head and chuckle softly.

"What?" She turns toward me.

"It's just..."

I return her gaze with a level stare. This is the first time I've been able to appreciate her beauty without getting nervous. It feels more than nice—it feels *right.*

"Just what?" she prods.

"I prefer life on Evermoor. There's downsides for sure, but...I like it here. I like who I am. I like what it makes me."

Erany responds with a radiant smile. And wonder upon wonders, it isn't sarcastic or teasing. "Jon, I—"

"Look at you two lovebirds!" Lucky appears out of nowhere, causing me to topple back onto my hands.

"What do you want?" Erany glowers at him.

"I swear to God, Lucky—" I rise to my feet, ready to punch him for screwing up my Intimate Moment. "If you came over here just to—"

"Nyanti wants to see you. Both of you."

We exchange a glance. *Us? Why?*

"Hurry," Lucky says impatiently. "Time runs thin."

"All right, all right," I grumble.

He leads us down the street and around a corner. Nyanti is conversing with a six-foot lady dressed in the same fashion as her: long flowing robes, only gray instead of black. Unlike Nyanti, she doesn't have sleeves. (Could be a power move—even from a distance, I can see she's in shape.)

"Here they are." Lucky gestures at us and walks away. (Probably so he can steal someone's carry. I hope they catch him—I hope they punt him in his kleptomaniacal nuts.)

"Wind at your back and sun on your brow." The lady gives me a once-over. She's tall, beautiful, and...holy *CRAP* is she strong! Like Crossfit strong—her arms are cabled with sinuous muscle.

"I am Lyné Anir, High Sygress of Elerica City."

Erany dips into a sweeping curtsy. "It is an honor to meet you, Sygress Ani—"

Lyné grabs her scruff and pulls her straight. "Do not bow, half-Elf. Your sniveling flattery turns my stomach."

Erany's face twists with anger, but it's quickly replaced by grudging admiration. "As you wish." Erany gives her a dangerous smirk. "But remove your hand, Sygress, or I'll take your fingers and most of your palm."

Lyné smiles and lets her go. "You and I will get along fine."

"I believe so as well." The Princess cracks her neck.

Lyné falls quiet and examines me carefully. Whoa—her pupils are blue-green-indigo, mixed with night-black swoops. Seeing them up close I feel kinda spacey...

"This is the Traveler?"

"Aye, Sygress." Erany's expression is a blend of affection and amusement. "I wager his presence falls short of your forecast, but—"

"No, I believe it." Lyné's pupils gyre clockwise, then reverse direction. "Those who dismiss him would do well to remember that greatness springs from humble beginnings. I did not begin life as an Elerican Sygress—I grew into the position a day at a time."

Erany opens her mouth, then quickly shuts it. A slight flush reddens her cheeks, causing me to feel a petty flash of pleasure. Ha! That's what you get for doubting your boy Jon! (But please God please—don't change her mind about going on a date with me.)

"I shall quicken your senses," Lyné states. "It would be prudent to do so before you depart for your home."

"Right," I nod thoughtfully. "Yeah, we should definitely do the sense-quickening thing before—say *what?*"

"You are going back to Earth." Lyné's gaze settles on Erany.

"And you will accompany him."

28

I gape at Lyné for nearly a minute. Eventually I manage, "What do you mean, we're going back to Earth?"

"Come." Lyné starts walking.

"Don't worry Jon." Erany matches my steps. "We can go on our...what did you call it?"

"Our date."

"Right. We can do it later."

"Oh man." Not just a date, but a date on *Earth!* Homefield advantage, baby! "We could go to Fisherman's Wharf, Sutro's Cliffs, or the Nineteenth Hole down in Hollister. Dunno if you have redwoods here, but—"

"Jon." She pecks my cheek. "Later."

I freeze in place like a jacklit deer.

She kissed me.

She *kissed* me.

Do I kiss her back? Wait, no—say something smooth. She hasn't been exposed to Earth-style flirting, so I could probably get away with a cheeseball line. Come on, Jon, seize the day! Be the change you want to see! Live, laugh, lo—no, that's Karens, you idiot!

Just *say something!*

"I like your sword!" I blurt. "So *cool!*"

"My sword?" Her grin falters.

"Um...I mean...ah..."

Much to my relief (and chagrin), Lyné interrupts with, "If you two are finished..."

We walked several blocks but I barely noticed; I was laser focused on trying to impress Erany.

"Be easy, Jon." She squeezes my arm. "We can talk about my sword when we go on our date."

I resist the urge to facepalm. "Right," I mutter. "Uh...yeah. Let's do this, brosef."

She gives me a skeptical, WTF look (probably wondering what "brosef" means), but before she can speak, I hurry into the temple.

God, Jon.

You are *such* a moron.

———

For the past few days, I could happily ignore my supposed destiny, thanks to a barrage of life-or-death problems. But now things are different; I don't have to worry about anything aside from my own quickening, which will aid me in my quest to defeat Lyderea.

Which will determine the fate of *an entire world.*

So yeah—no pressure.

As we file into the hexflow chamber, Lyné spits a sibilant phrase, causing the darkened polestars to flare and blaze. Different colors reflect off the pool, painting the walls in a lattice of shadows.

Suddenly, beams of energy project from the spheres. They collide and combine above the water, merging into a pulsing ball of light. Kind of like the ending of *The Fifth Element,* only a hell of a lot cooler and way more intimidating.

Lyné steps in. "Take my hand."

Erany, sensing my hesitancy, gives my arm another squeeze. "Take heart, Jon." (Man, I should fake being hesitant on a regular basis— getting squeezed by Erany is better than a cold mountain dew on a hot summer night).

I clasp Lyné's hand and walk forward. At first it feels like regular water, then buzzy tingles run up my legs. They're pleasant and soothing, but they fail to calm my frazzled nerves. It's not every day that you wade into magic with an Elerican Sygress.

"Stay with me, Jon. Abide in serenity."

"Be dust upon your breath, right?"

She responds with a smile. "Yes. Exactly."

I put one foot in front of the other, focusing on the lap of water and the rhythm of my steps. Every so often, Lyné gives an approving nod, as if to say, *you can do this.* Not gonna lie, I'm grateful for the support. With the exception of Gyrax, everyone has treated me like a bumbling idiot at one point or another.

Before I know it, I'm standing in front of the magical nexus, watching threads of neon snake off its surface. Lyné steps back into the locus, closing her eyes as her skin makes contact. I flinch without meaning to (an irrational part of me expects her to explode or combust) but the Sygress remains whole and unharmed, silhouetted by a gush of blinding energies.

"A moment, Jon. I must harmonize these dynae."

"Take your time." I force a casual nod. "Been reppin' dynae harmonics since back in the day."

Her face is backlit, but I can still make out the cast of her features. There's a bit of amusement and a whole lot of *Please stop talking. Your adorkable babble hurts my will to live.*

She draws a measured breath. Color flows from the nexus into her mouth, lighting her torso with vibrant coils. The radiance unfurls throughout her body, revealing the shadows of organs and bones.

I got nothing. I mean...wow. Wow, wow, *wow.*

Her eyes glow increasingly brighter, to the point where they eclipse the glaring nexus. Then she speaks in a double-toned voice:

"Jon." Her blanked-out gaze locks onto mine. **"Take my hand."**

When our fingers touch, the nexus peaks in a supernova flash.

————

At first, all I can sense is peace and stillness. Then I'm plunged into a psychic maelstrom.

[Hey, I'm not okay here!] My thoughts brim with fear and alarm. *[We need to stop—like RIGHT NOW!]*

Immediate strain erupts between us; she's using her will to keep me in place. Before I can descend into outright hysteria, she radiates a blast of serenity and calm, lowering my panic by a couple of notches. The fear is still there, but it's not overwhelming.

Almost immediately, it starts to build again. Unease turns to dread, dread turns to distress, distress turns to—

[Enough.] the Sygress hisses. ***[ENOUGH!]***

Lyné's presence weaves through mine, a magical version of cold water invading your nose and causing everything connected to it—ears, throat, jaw—to go batshit haywire. She's prying me open, stretching me out with pure aggression. I think I'm going crazy. I think I'm going to die. I think I'm going to flat-out unrave—

And then it stops.

I stumble back, letting go of her hand. "Whoop! Oh *shi—*"

And plunge bodily into the knee-high pool. Much to my surprise, it feels warm and welcoming. For some weird reason, it only felt cold when I was standing up.

Wow...the water...it's *glowing.* Filled with fractals and tight-wound symbols, almost as if it's one big spell...

Erany grabs my collar and hauls me up.

"HuuUUUUHH!" Oxygen hits, transforming into a fizzy head rush. "Whoa." I clutch my chest and almost fall, but Erany hooks my elbow and keeps me steady.

I glance back and forth between her and Lyné. They're both surrounded in archaic script, moving and shifting in time with their breaths.

"Jon? Are you well?" Erany peers at me.

"I...yeah." A self-conscious laugh. "It's just that I can see your auras now and it's..."

"It won't last." Lyné twists the air with her hand, causing the polestars to blanch and darken. The nexus fades in time with the stones, leaving a buzzy outline hanging in the air.

"Wait, what?" Sure enough, the arcane designs are growing fainter by the second. I palm my head with both hands, giving into anger and frustration. *"Why?"*

"Don't worry—I am sure it is temporary." Erany turns to Lyné, eyebrows raised. "It *is* temporary, is it not?"

"You ask a simple question for a complex answer. Your quickened senses will come and go. It is part of your—"

"Why?" I demand.

Lyné holds up a finger and gives me a stern look. A very 'Sygress-like' look. "Let me finish. Jon, you are not the Traveler."

"What are you—"

"But you could be, if that is what you want." Her gaze bores into mine. "The decision is yours: claim your potential, or let it fade into whimsy and dream. Your aura reflects that. Its openness mirrors your state of being—how fully you have chosen to embrace your mission. But until you abide in perfect acceptance, your senses will vacillate between mundane and fantastic. Don't take it as a threat, because it isn't—it is freedom incarnate, for you can choose to stop at any moment."

That *does* sound appealing. I've fought hordes of Iguar and escaped from a Sytíshí mind-prison. Now they're asking me to save their world, which, when you think about it, is absolutely, unequivocally batshit cra—

I look at Erany and my doubts fall away.

"No way." I shake my head. "No *way*. I have a giant opportunity here. I'm not gonna let it slip through my fingers." Right on cue, my quickened sight revs up and sharpens.

Lyné's lips curve into a smile. "Just be sure that you know what you mean by the word 'opportunity.' Romance doesn't qualify."

"Could we get to the Earth stuff?" I'm a little peeved—Lyné's acting like I'm a tweenage schoolboy, gaw-gawing over an Instagram supermodel.

Lyné crosses her arms. "Be wary—Lyderea's agents are aware of your presence. I am not sure how, but—"

"Knifelock," Erany states. "We met his simulacra."

I raise my hand in half-hearted protest. "Yeah, but he didn't attack us, he—"

"Had his reasons," Erany says firmly. "He is a Nightkeeper Captain. He was *not* acting in our best interests."

"As I was saying," Lyné continues, "Lyderea's agents will follow in your wake."

"How do you know this?" Erany asks.

"Long hours spent by the scrying pool. They have built transmundane paths into the bleed. Every one of them leads to Earth."

"No worries." I throw her a cocky grin. "Pretty sure we'll be able to spot them. Sword-wielding monsters aren't that common in downtown San Francisco."

"Their appearance will shift," Lyné counters. "Lyderea will hide them in veil and shadow, which will translate into an Earthly disguise. They may appear strange, but not completely out of place."

"Great." My smile disappears. "So we'll be watching our backs the entire time."

"Yes."

My hopes of date-night fall away. Instead of dinner at House of Prime Rib, we'll have to settle for week-old sewer pizza. This is like discovering your highly anticipated getaway was just replaced by a marathon study session.

A marble of pure white light forms above Lyné's hand, flaring with enough intensity that I have to fight the urge to turn away. The marble sounds with a muted *pfff,* then burns through the air and traces a longish outline. It quickly fills in, detailing the upper part of my arcane revolver.

"Ailura Qartesi." Lyné says. "The other half resides on Earth."

"So when do we leave?" I prod. (Maybe date-night is still in the cards. Okay, so House of Prime Rib is a little much, but we could still do Super Duper Burger, or at least—)

"Soon. But gaining the Clapfire isn't the end. The Princess must find a weapon for herself."

Lyné gestures again. In place of the revolver, a slender sword begins to take shape. Its guard is formed from vine-like twists, while the blade is forged from rune-scriven metal. A soft-glowing ruby shines from the pommel—it isn't a jewel that belongs in a store, but a rough-hewn gem pulled straight from the earth.

"The Rosecraft Blade." Excitement is audible in Erany's voice.

"Aye." Lyné nods. "Once you complete Ailura Qartesi, Alijyar SyCajister will send you back. Upon your return, you must win the Blade from its dryad coterie. Their guardian, a stone golem, will not let it go without a fight."

"Come on." I throw her an easy smile. "You're talking to a Deláni Princess and the Prophesied Traveler. I doubt they'll give us that much trouble."

Erany and Lyné judge me with blank gazes. Gazes that say, *you are unspeakably, unconscionably stupid.*

"Right...uh, good talk." I clear my throat.

"Brace yourselves. Your departure beckons."

"When are we leaving?"

"Now."

"*Now?*" I pick my jaw up off the floor. "I mean, I know you said 'soon,' but...what about the others?"

"What Jon means to say," Erany puts a reassuring hand on my shoulder, "is that we must talk with our friends before we leave."

"Very well." Lyné gives a slight nod. "Go and palaver. I will be here waiting."

———

It doesn't take long to explain our task. By Earth standards, I sound insane, but hey, this is Evermoor—a world where blindfolded ninjas fight monstrous bugs.

Elier is the first to offer his forearm. I reach out and grasp it.

"Good luck on your journey. May your steps lighten, may your spirit brighten."

"Thanks." I rub the back of my neck, embarrassed. Evermoor lingo is so poetic compared to Earth-speak. "Um, good game. You know, with the Iguar and all."

Elier smiles and pats my arm. He knows I'm a doofus, but he's not gonna say it. True friendship, right there.

Lucky wishes me well, then it's Nyanti's turn. "Enjoy your sojourn." She looks at Erany and gives me a wink. "Both of you."

I'm about to bluster there's nothing between us, where did she get the impression that...and then I check myself. Yeah, I'm hot for a Fair Folk princess, and from all indications, she feels the same way about me. So why hide it?

"Oh you know I will." I return her wink. "Just like you and Elier."

She acknowledges my comment with a soft chuckle. As she turns away, Ren walks up and offers his hand. "May light find you in dark places."

I clasp his forearm. "And may it ease your eyes and guide your feet." (Bam—nailed it.) "What about Terrelly? Can you find a way to heal his—"

"I am a Wayfarer, am I not?" He tilts his head, amused. "Now that the Witches can access the hexflow, I am confident in their ability to brew a remedy. But it is not your concern, as you must complete your own quest. Come back safe, so you can harry me with more of your insipid questions."

"You're joking? *You?*" I recoil in astonishment. "Will wonders never cease."

"Remember, Jon: eyes open, weapon close." But he says it with a smile.

Ren turns to leave, then Gyrax envelops me in a furry hug. "Stay keen, Jon."

I squeeze him back. "You too buddy. I'll be fine, but thanks for the concern."

"Aye." He steps back and crosses his arms. "We'll all be fine." He glances slyly at Erany. "Do not come back until you two kiss."

"Dude!" I throw a mock-punch.

He dodges and laughs with mischievous glee. To my chagrin, Erany laughs right along with him.

" 'Ware his trickery!" Gyrax warns. "Avoid video games like they were the Reft—once he starts playing, it'll be a day and an age before he stops!"

"Oh come *on!*" I shake my head, exasperated, then prompt Erany with an inquisitive look. "Ready?"

"Yes." She threads her arm into my elbow, sending a tingle up the back of my spine. Her hand drops away as we enter the temple, but the memory of her touch remains on my skin, lighting my nerves with a sweet sense of yearning.

Lyné is standing right where we left her: in the middle of the pool, surrounded by weaves of slow-drift symbols. "You've said your farewells?"

"We have," I reply.

"Very well. Come hither." She holds out her hands. We take them in ours. "It will be quick."

My gut lurches. Every time I've been close to a "super-spell" (a mass-discharge of arcane energy, like when I healed Nyanti or Arinia went beast-mode), I've been taken for a mind-bending ride. I really, *really* hope this won't be as disorienting.

The bones in her hands glow white-cored blue, shining through her flesh and spilling through our fingers. With a conscious effort, I force my body to remain still. If I botch her magic, we might end up in a monster's digestive tract or smack in the middle of a dying star syst—

She darts forward, covering our eyes with her glowing palms. All I can see is sparkling radiance, leaking past my lids and flooding my sight.

A panicked burble flies from my lips. "Hey wait, could I get just a second to—"

Then I lose my balance and splash into the pool. Suddenly, I'm surrounded by darkness. I have a brief sense of being—

(elsewhere)

—before I'm ejected onto the grass. A quick look around and I realize...

Holy crap.

I'm back in Golden Gate Park.

29

This is where I met Alijyar SyCajister; the same pond I almost drowned in. I wonder if there's something to that, or—

"Jon?" Erany asks shakily. "What now?"

What now, what now…

Shit.

I left my car at Lafayette Park. They probably towed it, but what the hell—might as well go and double-check.

"Come on." I help her up, then take a moment to undo my cloak. Luckily, I crossed over wearing my Earth clothes (with the exception of my boots) so I won't raise eyebrows. Erany, on the other hand, is dressed like a fighter/mage half-Elf. Oh well, it can't be helped. For the time being, it's her only option.

"This will attract unwanted attention. Can you stick it in your carry?" I bundle my cloak and hold it out.

"Of course." She drops it in, then does the same with hers.

San Francisco is seven miles long by seven miles wide. Walking across it takes three or four hours, which is nothing on Evermoor. Despite that, my Earthling proclivities make themselves known—I feel like we should be taking an Uber or Lyft. Unfortunately, my phone disappeared when I crossed into Evermoor, so hailing a ride is out of the question.

As we make our way through Outer Richmond—a gridded neighborhood lined with two-story homes—Erany looks around in wide-eyed wonder. I'm afraid that someone will comment on her clothes or the sizable rapier hanging off her hip, but thankfully (and oddly), no one says anything. That changes at Van Ness Avenue, when a quartet of twenty-somethings—two boys and a couple of girls—point and laugh at her.

Uh-oh.

Her face darkens with whoop-ass rage. Before she can act on it, one of the guys yells, "Cool costume! Love the ears!"

Her anger vanishes, replaced by confusion. "Costume?"

I shrug, miffed. "Don't ask me. I'm not sure why they would—"

Wait a sec...I survey the stores, then mentally kick myself.

Halloween decorations.

I spent several months traipsing through Evermoor, but only a few weeks passed on Earth. In science fiction, they always talk about how time and space are a lot more fluid than we've been led to believe, but...

I cradle my head, fighting off vertigo.

"Jon?"

"It's okay." I give her a wan smile. "Just a little thrown. Up is down and black is white, you know?"

"Um..." Her brow furrows.

"It means a sudden change in what you think is familiar."

"Oh." She returns my smile. "That needn't be fell. Thus far, I am thoroughly enjoying the strangeness of your world."

"Really? I mean, yeah...I guess it's cool if you've never seen it." (Ooh, here's my chance.) "Hey, are you hungry? Wanna grab a bite?"

She curls a lock behind her ear. "Later, perhaps. Lyderea's agents might be watching."

"Right. Good point." (Jon, you are an *idiot.*) Also, I couldn't buy food even if I wanted to—I lost my wallet when I crossed into Evermoor. I hope it's still in my car (which I really, *really* hope is still at the park).

As we take a left onto Sacramento, I realize we went too far east. No big—it's only a couple more blocks to Lafayette. Shortly after we course correct, the park's green-coated slopes come into view.

"What the—" I stop dead in my tracks.

My car...it's right where I left it.

"Is something amiss?" Erany gives me a puzzled look.

"No. Yes. I mean, I'm not really sure..."

Irritation tinges her voice. "You're not making sense."

"Sorry, it's just that..." I gesture at my undisturbed Hyundai. "If you park your car past the designated cutoff, someone's gonna tow it. Look—it's written right there."

I point at a sign that says I better move my car in two hours—and make damn sure it's somewhere else on the 2nd and 4th Tuesday of every month so they can do a 10am street-cleaning—or I'll face the wrath of a dead-eyed meter maid.

Erany squints at the sign. "The sigils are blurry, but I think I can..." She squints harder. "Something about time limits?"

"Yep—time limits." Curiosity rises to the fore. "Wait, you can't read the letters?"

"I can, but..." She shakes her head. "They're written in Scopic, but for some reason, I can't bring them into focus. I suspect it's because I am foreign to your world. I am not an expert in interplanar travel, but..." She shakes her head again. "My presence has disrupted the arcane tides. Of that I am sure."

I angle closer and inspect the wipers. Holy...are you *serious?*

No ticket! I can't believe it!

A small part of me finds it funny. I've seen wyverns and wizards, Elves and goblins, yet my unticketed car is *freaking me out.* I'm pretty sure it's a Pavlovian response; if you live in the city for any length of time, you hear plenty of horror stories about tickets and towing. (I once got towed during my senior year and the penalties were equal to a month's worth of rent. When I went to the impound, a European couple was begging the clerk to waive their fee—if they ended up paying, they weren't going to be able to afford their hostel. The clerk, however, remained unfazed.)

The door clicks open. Huh—why isn't it locked?

I peek inside and spot the keys, dangling from the ignition where (I think?) I left them. Not only that, but my phone is still there, mounted to the dash. I don't understand...why didn't someone grab it for themsel—

And then I see it: a piece of newspaper by the gas pedal, covered in grime and ragged sharpie. I reach in and smooth it out.

THERE ARE OTHER WORLDS THAN THESE.

Alijyar SyCajister. Goddamn. I chuckle softly under my breath.

"Jon? Is everything fair?"

"Alijjyar—he took care of my car while I was gone."

She appraises the Hyundai. "Do I sit inside, or..."

"Yeah. Over here." I walk to her side and open the door. "Grab the handle and pull it back. And this is for when you wanna get out." I jiggle the interior lever.

"I see." She lowers into the car. "Thank you."

I hop in the driver seat when it suddenly hits me: my wallet. It's a long shot, but maybe...I reach over and pop the glovebox.

Insurance, registration, Jiffy Lube receipt...

There it is!

I stuff it in my pocket, grinning like an idiot. Not just my car, but my phone *and* my wallet! Thank you, Alijyar!

"Strap in." I click my seatbelt into its receiver. Erany watches and follows suit, albeit a lot slower and with more hesitation.

"All right, here we go."

The engine starts, cueing my musical playlist. Erany yelps, bracing against the dash with extended arms.

"Sorry. Should've warned you." As I turn down the volume on *I Think He Knows,* the display informs me it's October 30th, the day before Halloween.

"You very well should have." She gives me a smile, half playful, half relieved. "You owe me, Jon. Honor your debt lest I smack you ruddy."

"Promises, promises."

I put the car into drive, causing her to flinch once again. As I step on the gas, my mind flashes back to Lyné's warning: Lyderea's agents are somewhere out there. But my half-Elf crush is riding shotgun, Taylor Swift is playing on speaker, and what do you know—the sun's breaking through the afternoon clouds. I think a little cheer is entirely appropriate.

"Whence comes this song?" Erany asks. "Are there hidden minstrels inside your carriage? 'Car,' I mean?"

"Nope." I shake my head. "Cars are fitted with lightning-powered machines called 'electronics.' They're capable of performing multiple functions, one of which is playing music."

"Amazing." She stares out the window, transfixed by Japantown. "Are the buildings machines as well?"

"Not really." I sneak a glance at her. She's flattened her hands and nose against the glass. It's kind of adorable—very childlike. "But they're filled with electronics to the point where...yeah, I guess you could say they're partly machine."

"Deliac's Gleam," she whispers. "No horses, just cars."

"Oh we still ride horses," I say, "but they aren't that common. Unless you're rich or a mounted police officer, there's no real reason to keep one around. If we go to the Presidio, you might see some cops on horseback."

"Cops?" Her brow wrinkles in confusion.

"Sorry—I meant law enforcement. Roving peacekeepers."

Her gaze sharpens. "Like the Knights on Evermoor?"

"Not really." Then I catch myself. "I mean, some of them, yeah, but..." I chew my lip. "It's complicated. A couple years back, there was a lot of unrest directed at cops. They're not all bad, though. Some are, while some are decent and ignore the bad ones, which makes them bad in a sense, but..." I blow a frustrated sigh. "Like I said: it's complicated."

Erany falls silent. Then she says, "I think I understand. The Knights are taught to harass and extort, but I don't believe that all are malicious. Not at heart, anyway."

"Exactly. Some are caught in past momentum, trapped by the weight of their obligations."

"Perhaps." She looks sideways. "You haven't seen them at their worst. They razed Delán without mercy or quarter."

I reach out and grasp her knee. It's not calculated; I do it instinctively. "I'm sorry." And I leave it at that. I can't feel her pain, but I can at least acknowledge it.

"Thank you." She covers my hand and gives it a squeeze.

Butterfly tremors flood my stomach, transforming into a roil that fills my chest. Call it puppy love, call it what you want, but man, this is *intense.*

"Um, right." I retract my hand and clear my throat. It's the least sexy noise in all of existence—my voice cracks as I *a-a-HEM.*

She straightens in her seat, amused and bewildered. "What was *that?*"

"I..." My lips widen in a self-conscious grin. "I mean..."

A second later, we break into howls. As we both laugh with unabashed glee, a soul-deep part of me revels in the moment. The sky is aflare with pink-orange hues, the crush of my life is riding beside me, and Taylor Swift is singing like an angel.

There's nowhere else I'd rather be.

———

"This is where you live?"

"Yep." I flick a switch, clicking on the overhead lights.

"How curious." She stares at the recessed lighting. "You said they're machines? Not magic?"

"Correct."

"Aye," she mutters. "If they were magic, I'd be able to see their auric signature, but..."

"Oh!" I snap my fingers. "I wanted to ask: can you still cast spells? Or is that Evermoor only?"

She holds out her hand and stares at her palm. Her fingers tremble, then a coil of rune-bordered light swirls into being. "I can." She closes her fist, dousing the light. "But it takes more effort."

"Does that mean Lyderea's goons—"

"Are in the same predicament? Possibly. What about you? Are your powers—"

I click my tongue and hiss through my teeth. "Can we talk about it later? I'm still getting used to regular magic. This whole thing about bending reality..."

"Of course." She smiles warmly. "Take things moment by moment, step by step."

"Thanks." I return her smile, then sit on the couch and stare out the window. Aaah...forgot how nice it was to relax at home.

"Jon?"

"Hmm?"

"Do you have access to water? I would cleanse my skin of grime and muck."

"Yeah. Over here." We head to the bathroom, where I show her the ins and outs of using a shower.

"Thank you. I'll take it from here." She smiles mischievously. "Unless you care to join me."

My mouth goes dry. "What? No. Yes! I mean—"

"No? Yes? Which is it?" she teases.

"I...I meant to say—"

"Be easy. I was merely jesting." She puts her hands on her hips and studies the shower. "First I will bathe, then we shall determine what to do next. Perhaps we could buy some machine-city cuisine. We would have to eat it here, of course, to remain safe from Lyderea's folk."

"Right. Of course." I don't need a mirror to know that I'm blushing—my face feels like a red-hot coal.

"Jon," she says patiently.

"Yes?"

"*Out.*"

"Um, yeah—sorry!"

I trudge back to the couch and plunk down, thumping my fists against my forehead. Ugh, ugh, *ugh*. That was the polar opposite of smooth and sexy.

Ten minutes later (ten godawful minutes of the most intense self-loathing I've ever experienced) Erany comes walking out. Man, she looks *good*. Doesn't matter if she's fighting Iguar or just standing there, she's so damn *pre*—

"Why are you smiling?" She cocks her head, grinning faintly.

"Oh, uh—I didn't know I was. I was just thinking...never mind. Hey, maybe we should get you a new set of clothes. For the next two days, people will be celebrating Halloween, which means they won't think twice because they'll think you're in costume. But after that..."

"I suppose. Pity—I like my garments." She looks down and sighs. "But I see why your folk would perceive them as strange." She crooks an eyebrow. "The denizens of this world favor loud, dysfunctional garb. Should I be wearing similar attire?"

"Um...something similar, yes. But there's a wide range of choices —I'm sure we'll find you something appropriate." (Super tight yoga pants, hopefully). "Also, let's keep your sword in the trunk of my car."

She shakes her head in resignation. "As you wish. It boggles my mind that no one on Earth carries a sizable blade."

"Probably different in Texas or Florida." She gives me a puzzled look, but I follow up with a dismissive wave—*not worth explaining.* "We're not big on swords or daggers, but pretty much everyone carries one of these." I take out my phone and click the display. The background is a shot of Gribbles in his walking gear, smiling happily into the camera.

"The device from your car." She takes it in her hands and studies it carefully. "You called this a 'phone?' "

"Yep. It can play music, project your voice through other phones, and call for help if you're injured or threatened. It's also got games and access to the interne—uh...a communal source of information."

"Interesting..." Her brow furrows as she swipes and clicks. "And it's powered by lightning?"

"Yep."

"I see," she mutters. "It appears to be magical, yet it has no aura. Fascinating."

"I'm going to shower, then we'll get you some clothes. Here—" I run her through the basics of touchscreen tech. "That's pretty much it. Feel free to mess around."

She gives a distracted nod. As I walk to the bathroom I chuckle softly—she's hunched over my phone, googling at the screen like a little kid.

————

After I finish, I walk back out. She's still fiddling with my phone, only her expression is one of mild disgust.

"What's wrong?" I ask.

"Nothing. It's just..."

Uh-oh. Did she open a porn site? God *dammit,* Jon! What were you *thinki*—

"It's too *much.*"

"Too much?" Now I'm confused.

She holds out the phone. I pluck it from her hand and slip it in my pocket.

"The phone. Your world. It's all too *much*. I can barely read the characters, but they're crass and overwhelming nevertheless."

"Oh." I laugh in relief. (Thank *God* she didn't open an x-rated site.) "Yeah, I know what you mean. There's a growing consensus that people should limit their time on their phones. Otherwise, it starts to mess with your mind."

"I feel unbalanced," she mutters. "Using your device seems to have..." She stares at the wall. "It seems to have dulled my magical perception. Sharpness and clarity are in short supply."

I Shift my perception as far as I can, catching glimpses of the scrollwork in her aura. "Sorry, I'm not sure what you mean. My quickened sight is at quarter strength, maybe less."

She stands up and stretches. "I still need clothes. Do you have them here, or..."

"Nope. We'll get 'em at the mall." I suddenly remember she has no idea what that is. "Which is another word for...marketplace."

"Very well." She nods at the door.

"Lead the way."

30

As we stroll through the mall, Erany barrages me with rapid-fire questions, all a variation of, "what is *THAT*?" Typically, shopping would make me grumpy and tired; I never, *ever* thought it could actually be fun. (Well, credit's due where credit's due; playing chaperone to a gorgeous half-Elf is a great way to offset Earthling consumerism.)

After a bit of browsing, we start hunting for wardrobe. Her first pick—a bunch of military stuff from a tactical equipment store—is a hard no.

"Why not?" She glares balefully. "This garb is rife with pouches and pockets—plenty of room for tools and weapons."

"Nuh-uh." I pry the clothes away and start putting them back. "You won't blend in—you're not a prepper and you don't play airsoft. Look." I turn and wave, encompassing the oodles of college students, high-schoolers, and yuppiefied families. "Not a single person in defcon four."

"Defcon—"

"It means wartime footing."

She crosses her arms. "Perhaps they should be."

"No, they *shouldn't,*" I reply heatedly. "People should be free to live how they please, as long as they're not hurting anyone else."

Erany looks stricken. "I'm sorry, Jon. I plead your grace. It's just that..." She rubs her eye with the heel of her palm. "While other kingdoms fought and suffered, Delán sat and idled pretty. The White Veiled Queen saved us for last."

I cock my head, puzzled. "Last? Why?"

"To divide and conquer. She sent us a chain of honey-tongued emissars, each declaring she would leave us in peace. The Deláni Ancestri took her at her word." Her lilac eyes grow heavy and sad.

"Ancestri...those are your leaders, I'm guessing?"

She responds with a nod. "When we joined the Unity, it was too little, too late. If we had acted earlier, we could have sent Blade-shadows to Sidehelm Pass. They might have made up for Erendor's treachery..." She shrugs and sighs. "If, perhaps, and maybe. Who can say what truly would have happened?"

I step in and give her a hug. Normally, my heart would shoot into red-line overdrive, but come on—first and foremost, Erany's my *friend*. We've fought together, traveled together, we've...

We've...

This. Feels. *Amazing.*

I lean into her warmth, resisting the urge to sigh contentedly. We stay like that for what seems like an eternity, even though it's less than a minute.

"Jon."

"Hmm?" I almost shush her. I really wanna savor this.

"You're drooling on me."

I jerk back as she points at a damp spot on her shoulder. Right where I put my stupid, drooly lips.

"Oh!" I blurt. "Oh, crap! I'm sorry!"

She borrows a phrase from my Earthling vernacular: "It's okay." Then she grins faintly and shakes her head, as if to say, *I can't believe I find you attractive.* "Let's finish our barter, shall we?"

"Of course," I say hurriedly. "Gotta save Evermoor."

"That we do." She flashes me a smile.

My knees go weak, my head goes light. I clear my throat, trying to hide my fluster, but I'm pretty sure she sees right through it.

We get back to our task, picking out clothes that'll allow her to pass as an average nineteen-year-old. Not too emo, not too sexy, not too anything. She could blend in anywhere, which is exactly what I'm hoping for.

Halfway through, she tries to put some shirts in her carry, but I shoo her off. Call me old-fashioned, but lugging her stuff makes me feel like a real boyfriend.

As I walk beside her, holding two full bags of newly purchased clothes, I drink in every smile, every grin, every stare she directs at some new piece of Earthling strangeness. And with each flip of her gold-glimmer hair, each time she throws her head back and laughs, I fall a little deeper in—

"Out of the way! *MOVE!*"

We both swing around. Four guys are hustling toward us, brandishing kitted-out submachine guns. There's something weird about them; they're a little *too* commando, like movie-crafted versions of—

"Lyderea's thralls!" Erany hisses.

"What? How do you—"

"Come on!" She grabs my elbow and hauls me along.

Two shots ring through the air. Pandemonium erupts all throughout—screaming and shoving, frantic movement in every direction.

"How are they—"

"Less talking, more running!" Erany pulls on my sleeve, nearly yanking me off my feet.

I push off the floor to keep from falling (miraculously, all the clothes stay in the bags), then we squirt through the mall's four-door entrance, chased by a burst of staccato gunfire. Directly behind us, panes of glass crack and disintegrate.

"Get to the car!" I gasp.

"Where is it?" Erany swivels, frantically trying to spot my Hyundai. *"Where—"*

"I don't know!" I fumble for my keys and click the beeper, but the cars in the lot stay infuriatingly quiet. We dash into their midst, scanning desperately as I point and click, point and click, trying to remember where I parked the goddamn—

Right on cue, my car skids up to us. *"Get in!"* Alijyar SyCajister is behind the wheel, waving urgently.

Erany shoves me inside, then follows behind in a full-body dive. As we peel out of the lot, an irrational part of me worries about losing her clothes, but then I realize they're scattered across the seats. Some even managed to make it up front.

"Hey!" Alijyar meets my eyes in the rearview mirror. "Buckle up!"

We burst into laughter—hold your belly, crazy-in-the-head laughter. Buckle up? Buckle *up?* We just got *shot* at!

"Just my luck," Alijyar mutters. "Stuck with the Traveler and a crazy-ass White girl."

Erany explodes with raucous guffaws. For no other reason than hilarity is contagious, it makes me laugh all the harder.

"You done?" Alijyar tries to sound gruff, but a bit of mirth creeps into his voice.

"Yeah." I force a nod. "We're...we're..."

"Seatbelts."

We both strap in. "Where are we going?" I manage.

"Secret hideout."

———

We park at Golden Gate Park, right across from the Hoover Redwood Grove. Erany gets out, shuts the door, and gapes up at the majestic trees.

"Shaddock's breath, these are *beautiful.*"

"I know, right?" I throw her a grin. "Believe it or not, they're kinda small compared to the ones up north."

As we enter the grove, soul-soothing silence descends upon us—a silence so thick I can feel it on my skin.

"Oh." Erany stops walking and smiles dreamily. *"Oh..."*

"This is a magical intersect," Alijyar explains. "We're not invisible, but I do enjoy a certain amount of...I guess *cloaking* would be the right word for it. If Lyderea's folk were anywhere near, they would all come down with a massive headache."

"So they wouldn't see us?" I ask.

"That's correct. Unless they were versed in subtle magics, they wouldn't be able to sense our presence."

"Jon." Erany looks around in wide-eyed wonder. "Shift your sight."

I let my gaze soften. To my surprise, I almost go into a total Shift. It's not as strong as it was on Evermoor, but still...

Faerie-light motes glide through the grove, aglow with soft, prismatic haloes. (You think redwoods are impressive? Throw in an arcane lightshow, then come talk to me.)

"Whoa. This is *amazing.*" I shake my head in disbelief. "Magic exists here on Earth. Who would've thought?"

"It always has." Alijyar responds with a good-natured scoff.

"You just have to know where to look."

———

Alijyar blows a quartet of notes: a melodic trill that would sound perfectly at home in *Legend of Zelda.* Each one shakes the core of my being, sending an intense buzz racing through me.

He purses his lips and whistles again.

This time, each note is clearly visible—they form into ribbons of vibrant color, flowing from his mouth as blue-purple waves. The otherworldly streamers snake through the air, triggering fountains of sparks when they touch the faerie-light motes.

"No way," I whisper.

"Indeed," Erany murmurs. Her lilac eyes dance and swirl, shining with pools of mirrored light.

Centered in the grove is a circle of earth, twenty feet long by twenty feet wide. As the air erupts with flashing sparkles, the circle begins to shake and rumble.

Unease ripples up my spine. "Uh...guys?"

Alijyar smiles. "Watch."

Liquid bubbles up, transforming the circle into a perfectly round pond. The water is blue—like tropical island blue. Same goes for the reflections on its surface; they're unnaturally clear.

Alijyar wades in. When he's waist-deep, he abruptly blurs and disappears.

Holy mother of—

His voice reverberates through the clearing: "You coming?"

Erany starts forward. I almost reach out and grab her shoulder—the guy *disappeared* for Christ's sakes—but then I lower my arm.

If there's one thing I've learned, it's that reality isn't at all what it seems.

So I take a breath and follow behind. As Erany vanishes, brilliance spills across my skin, infusing me with currents of supernova shine. The buzzing in my brain builds and intensifies, until visceral relief hits me over and over. When the water laps against my waist, the world dissolves into spell-woven fractals. Then I'm—

—stumbling across a marble floor, greeted by the faint strains of classical music. I almost bump into Erany's side (she's leaning against a plush ottoman) but backpedal quickly and land on my butt.

We've teleported into a spacious house. Recessed lighting, large tiles, comfy sofa...I wouldn't be surprised if there was a high-end infinity pool somewhere nearby.

"Welcome." Alijyar's voice carries from around a wall. "Please—make yourself at home."

I shuffle up to the crown-molded corner, peering around it into a kitchen. Alijyar is bent over an oven door, pulling out a tray of chocolate chip cookies.

He places them onto a tile-island counter. "Say the word and it shall be yours."

"Pizza?" I raise an eyebrow.

He walks to a stove built into the wall—sleek and glossy and super fancy—and pulls out a bubbling mushroom and olive pizza.

My jaw drops. "My favorite toppings! How did you—"

"Don't overthink it. You?" He looks at Erany.

For the first time since we've met, she seems shy and hesitant. "Mayhap...some bread and meat and a fistful of greens? Do you have popkins in this world?"

"We most certainly do," Alijyar affirms. "But people here call 'em sandwiches." He reaches in a cabinet for bread and sauce, mayo and oil. Then he opens the fridge and pulls out some wax-paper bundles of meat and cheese.

"Y'all can eat." He starts cutting into a fresh baguette. "If there's anything else, let me know."

"Mountain Dew?" I ask tentatively. I don't want to impose, but what the hell—I can't pass up a chance at the best drink ever.

"Help yourself." Alijyar nods at the fridge. "There's code red, game fuel, and of course, regula—"

"*Game fuel!*" I dart around the island and poke my head in the fridge. Stacks of refreshments greet my eyes, but I couldn't care less. I scan each level, searching for the one drink that stands head and shoulders above the re—

Through the transparent panel of the bottom cabinet, I glimpse row upon row of Mountain Dew Game Fuels.

In the mini cans, no less.

"Oh man," I breathe. "Oh *man. You got the mini cans!*" I break off two from a plastic-ringed pack.

"They're the best," Alijyar says matter-of-factly. "They don't have much soda, so it won't go flat before you're done."

"Exactly." I nod vigorously. *"Exactly!"* I hold out my fist and he gives it a bump.

"May I?" Erany asks.

"Of course." I hand her the second can. "Got this one for you."

She examines it quizzically. "How does it open?"

"Like so." I pop the seal, prompting a crisp-sounding *SPPT*. She fiddles with hers, then jerks back as it cracks and hisses.

"Bottoms up." I raise my Dew.

"What does that mean?"

"It's something we say as a casual toast."

"Ah." She raises her can and touches it to mine. "Bright skies, bonny friends."

"Jeez," I mutter. "You guys have so many cool sayings."

"In Circle SyCajister, we say 'Clear thoughts, clarion souls.' " Alijyar clinks a flask against our cans.

"Once again—far cooler than anything on Earth."

"You want some?" He offers the flask. "They're pre-realizations."

"Say *what?*" My forehead wrinkles in puzzlement.

Erany sips her Dew and makes a face. "This is *far* too sweet. It tastes...mechanical."

"Watch it," I warn. "Them's fighting words." I turn back to Alijyar. "Did you say the stuff in your flask is—"

"Just a concept. One day, it might become a fully formed idea."

I give him a skeptical look, trying to determine if he's pulling my leg. I'm pretty sure he isn't, it's just a little hard to swallow.

"Give it here."

He hands it over. Much to my disappointment, it tastes like water. "This has no flavor," I complain.

Alijyar shrugs. "Your mental palate isn't sensitized. Maybe one day."

"Mental palate," I grumble, "what a load."

"Allow me." Erany grabs the flask and takes a swig, swishing the liquid as she ponders the wall.

"It reminds me of..." she gives the flask back to Alijyar. "It reminds me of *something,* but I'm not sure what. Honeyed milk if I had to guess, with a dash of yesper and Finnarean helshy."

"The taste is specific to each individual. Those are homey, wintertime flavors—I'd say it's safe to assume you're in a good state of mind."

"Hmm...interesting."

"Aah." I wave dismissively, annoyed at my stupid Earthling senses for denying me yet another arcane experience. "Overrated. Imma try this pizza." I tear into a New York slice, flooding my mouth with the just-right balance of sauce, cheese, and crust.

Instant heaven.

"Oh man." (My mouth is full, so it comes out as "ErfMerf"). I pull the slice away, stretching the mozzarella into fine white threads. "Oh *man.*" I gather the threads onto my finger, then gobble them down with a second bite. Salty cheesy goodness explodes in my mouth, saturating my brain with Nombastic McGobberYobs.

"Keep your philosophy drink," I sigh. "Nothing beats a hot slice of pizza."

Erany takes a delicate bite. She chews slowly at first...then her eyes widen with surprise and delight. Pretty soon, we're maowing down pizza like starving dogs.

"Try some of these." Alijyar nudges the fresh-baked cookies.

I pat my belly and wave him off, about to tell him I've eaten my fill, when I suddenly realize I'm not even close. I snatch up a cookie and take a big ol' bite.

Ermagawd. So. Freakin'. *Good.* Warm sugary dough combined with cocoa-sweet Delicious!

We spend the next half hour stuffing our faces. Our adventures drained us at an animalistic level, and now we get to recharge and refuel—feast on heaps of Tastification.

Just when I think I'm close to being done, Alijyar announces the cold cuts are ready, cueing us to dive into fresh-baked bread, crisp tangy veggies, and perfectly seasoned meat and cheese—a culinary supernova of deli-borne madness. I'm lost in bliss as we stuff chips, sammitches, and melty chocolate cookies down our eager gob-holes.

"Oh man." I waddle to an easy chair, plop down, and pat my noticeably rounder belly. "Oh *man*. Let me just say—Tom Bombadil has *nothing* on you."

Alijyar laughs. "I'll pass it along. We're old buddies, he and I."

"Right. Sure." I chuckle lightly.

Something in his expression gives me pause. I grip my armrests and sit halfway up (ugh—super full tummy). "Wait—you're not serious, are you? Tom Bombadil: the guy from *The Hobbit.*"

"I know who he is."

"*The Hobbit,*" I repeat. "Which is fictional. *Fictional.*"

"One man's truth is another man's fiction." Alijyar meets my gaze. (Interesting—his eyes are the same shade of gray as Chris Atriya's, the Marine recruiter who sent me down this fantasy-world rabbit hole.)

"You're saying *The Hobbit* is real?" I raise an eyebrow.

"If existence is unlimited, it would have to be, wouldn't it? Every iteration of causality, matter, and physics would have to be expressed in some time, some place. That has to be the case, or you would inadvertently impose a limit on existence."

"Alijyar, it's a work of fiction. *FIC*-tion."

"And that makes you what—nonfiction? Answer me this: how do you know you're not just a character in someone else's book? How do you know that people aren't reading about you right at this moment?"

My mouth opens and closes. Check and mate.

Erany plunks down onto an easy chair. "This chair is real. This food is real. My enjoyment of both are indisputably, unequivocally real. Harry me not with your convoluted claims."

Alijyar raises his flask. "Well said, Princess."

I lift my hand in a *yeah-but-think-about-it* gesture. "Hold on. What if—"

Eyes closed, she raises a finger. "No."

"If we could just agree on—"

"No."

"Erany—"

"No."

"You're being—"

Finger still up, she repeats, "No."

"I didn't say anything," I mutter.

"No. Oh, and in case you were wondering—"

This time, I beat her to the punch. "No."

All three of us burst out laughing.

"Well tell Tom B he could learn a thing or two from Alijyar SyCajister." I pat my food-baby belly. "I'm sure berries and honey are pretty tasty, but they can't beat a slice of New York pizza. Throw in some cold cuts and fresh-baked cookies? *Fuhgeddaboutit.*"

"Aye." Erany issues an unrestrained belch. *BrrrRAAAPPP.* "Your fare is far and away the best I've had, and that's coming from someone who was raised as royalty. Tom Bombadil...he's a wizard like you, I assume?"

Alijyar smiles. "More or less."

"So your food is enchanted?"

His smile grows wider. "Only in the sense that it materializes in my kitchen. You don't need magic with pizza and cookies."

"Truer words." I cast a curious glance around. "Hey, what's with the windows?" They're all brimming with staticky fuzz.

"What do you see?" His voice is casual, but deliberately so. By his tone and bearing, I can tell he's paying careful attention to me.

"Each one is filled with...digital snow? Like an old TV without a signal. But there's something else..." I squint at a window, watching as shapes and outlines shift in the pane. "Something's happening, but..." I shake my head in mild frustration. "All I can say is it isn't random."

"Your description is accurate." Erany leans forward and peers at the glass. "There is something occurring within the scrabble. As to what it is, exactly..."

"Those are other dimensions." Alijyar scans them with a thoughtful gaze. "Where space and time move in different directions and come together in different ways. It's a good thing you can't see details—I know enough magic to protect you from madness, but you'd probably still get a giant headache."

"Other...dimensions?" I try not to gape.

Erany leans back and studies the ceiling. "I have heard of such things in my earlier years. According to my teachers, we weren't designed for interplanar travel."

He responds with a nod. "Our greater aspects chose these limitations, to include the worlds we were born and raised on. A few, however, are meant to cross the dimensional bleed." He waves an open hand down the front of his torso. "Me, for example."

"And Lyderea's servants," Erany adds.

"Not the same," Alijyar replies. "They don't have the training—or the capacity—to remain here for long. They need to switch out or their minds will break." A regretful sigh. "Many wizards have suffered that very fate. They made the journey before they were ready, then ended up as homeless madmen. A couple members of Circle SyCajister—"

"Wait a sec." I sit up in my chair, faintly alarmed. "Me and Erany both crossed over. Are we about to lose our marbles?"

Alijyar shakes his head. "No. It's hard to explain, but you two have journeyed for the right reasons." He looks at the ceiling. " 'Right' isn't the best way to put it, but it's as close as…" He looks at us again. "There's a certain flow to all of existence, born from a force we cannot see."

"The True?" Erany prods.

"That's one name for it. You two are in line with its mystical current, which isn't the case with Lyderea's agents. Their presence is…it's in active opposition to their natural design." His brow crinkles in frustration. "That's not right either, since everyone at heart *is* the True and can't help but be it. What I'm trying to say is—"

"Lyderea too?" I ask skeptically. "She's part of the True?"

"Yes, but not in—like I said, it's hard to explain. Unless you experience a blow-out awakening, you're not gonna get what I'm trying to say. And even if you experienced said awakening, you would understand for a day, maybe two, then it would all go back to sounding like paradox." He pats the air with both hands. "Look —do the best you can with what you have. Take it moment by moment, step by step."

"Be dust upon your breath."

"Exactly."

"So what's the next step? I'm supposed to find Ailura's other half. Do you know where it is?"

"Yep. Guy named Cal." He reaches in his pocket and withdraws a bent, coffee stained (at least I hope it's coffee and not something gross) business card.

I'M CRAZY CAL!
FIND ME IN THE BASEMENT OF THE MARKET STREET SMOKE SHOP!
<u>AND DON'T FORGET: I'M Cuh-Cuh-Cuh-CRAZY!!!</u>

"Is this a joke?" I turn the card over, but there's nothing on the back.

"No joke," Alijyar says. "He's stayed on Earth a little too long, so he's a bit...*off*. When I was younger, we used to squad up together and hunt down liches. In those days, he was known as Elgrim SyCajister."

"So he's a wizard?" I scratch my head. "And now he's a..." I search for a description, but nothing comes to mind.

"He's still a wizard," Alijyar hedges. "Just not as uh...not as reliable. He's a high-ranking SyCajister—sorry, *was* a high-ranking SyCajister—but he's gotten kind of weird."

I give him a skeptical look. "Define 'weird.' "

"Nothing dangerous," he assures.

"Bro. His name is *Crazy Cal.*"

"He's *fine,*" Alijyar says exasperatedly.

Erany and I exchange a weighted glance.

Alijyar clears his throat. "I'll take you to see him tomorrow night."

"But tomorrow's Halloween," I protest. "Traffic will be—"

"The least of our concerns," Alijyar finishes. "Like I said, there's an underlying flow to all of existence, and it doesn't slow down for San Francisco gridlock."

"Well, damn." I rub the back of my neck, chagrined. "If I knew we'd be leaving in a couple of days, I wouldn't have bought Erany a new set of clothes."

"Save your worry," she says dismissively. "I enjoyed it."

"We clear on the plan?" Alijyar asks.

"Yep." I flick the card. "Talk to Cal. Get the revolver."

"Correct. Oh—if we have to split up for whatever reason, meet me over at Crissy Field."

"Crissy Field, got it. Why there?"

"Reality is thinner beneath the Golden Gate Bridge, which makes it easier to open a portal. That wasn't always the case, but..."

He shrugs. "Arcane tides are like tectonic plates. Given time, they shift and move."

"I'll take your word for it." I glance at Erany and stifle a sigh. I thought we were going on a date, dammit. But that would be reckless—Lyderea's hench-folk are out there looking for us, disguised as cops or soldiers or some other form of stone-faced badass.

"More food?" Alijyar asks.

I shrug in defeat.

"Might as well."

31

The rest of the evening isn't a total loss. I get to spend it with Erany, guiding her through the ins and outs of social media, Youtube, and a bunch of other stuff unique to Earth. (Yeah, I know that teaching her to play Kingdom Blitz isn't exactly a night on the town, but she's super into it, and that more than makes up for any date-night shortcomings.). Due to the interdimensional static, she still has trouble reading my phone, but the colorful graphics serve as an adequate substitute.

"Ah, I see." Her brow furrows as hordes of zombies fall before her artillery. "These are markedly slower than archers or mages, but inflict far more dama—"

Before she can finish, a vampire slips through her last-stand goalposts.

"No!" She stares furiously at the screen. "NO!"

"Don't worry," I say. "You still have nineteen—"

A couple more vampires squirt past her defenses.

"Seventeen hearts," I amend. "You've still got seventeen hearts."

"Enough of your games!" She leaps up from the couch and strides back and forth. "Chylin's Cross! If I had built more archers instead of artillery, I could have—*rrrrrrRRR!*" Her hand flies to her waist, grasping for her sword. Thankfully, we left it in the car.

"Easy, Princess." Alijyar, like me, is trying not to laugh. "It's just a ga—"

She levels a finger at him. "I *KNOW it's just a game!*"

"All right, all right." He raises his palms. "Easy."

For a long moment Erany stays where she is, finger leveled...then she starts to giggle. Seconds later, we're convulsing with laughter.

Once it subsides, Alijyar says, "I'm gonna turn in. I'll leave you to it."

I freeze in place like a jacklit rabbit. So does Erany.

"Uh...right." I clear my throat. "Do we sleep out here? Or—"

Alijyar shrugs. "There's two spare bedrooms; one upstairs, one downstairs. But if you want to share, that's fine by me."

I point at my chest, then at Erany. "Oh, you think that—" I explode with high, nervous laughter. "Alijyar, do you seriously think we're—"

"Come on, guys." His tone is simultaneously patient and exasperated. "I'm not your dad and you're both of age."

Erany blushes and ducks her head. "Jon, would you like to—"

My mouth reacts before my brain: "Hell *yeah* I would like to—"

Suddenly, I'm overtaken by a violent coughing fit. Tears stream down as I pound my chest.

"Jon?" Erany rushes to my side. *"Jon?"*

"Yeah," I manage. (due to my hacking, it sounds like *yuh*). "Yeah, I'm good." I can tell by her expression that I look like hell.

"Perhaps we should dwell in separate rooms," she hedges. "We both could use a sound night of sleep."

"I'm good!" I insist. "We can still—" Warm snot runs down my lip. I push a nostril shut and sniff up mucus. "I'm fine, I just..."

She raises an eyebrow. *Seriously?*

I hang my head in surrender. "Yeah, you're right."

"Take heart—" she touches my arm, making my stomach go gooey. "Another opportunity is bound to present itself."

I force a laugh. (And when I say force I mean *force*—I want to cry, scream, and commit seppuku with a rusty spoon). "Probably for the best. Lyderea's people are hard at work, trying to kill anything fuzzy or cute. No time for us to uh...yeah."

Her smile turns quizzical. "Ah...the specifics of what you say eludes my grasp, but the gist does not. Good night, Jon." She slips into the hall and disappears up the stairs.

I palm my eyes and clench my teeth. "God *dammit.*" I drop my hands and stare at Alijyar. The mage is regarding me with an ear-to-ear grin.

"What." I snap irritably.

"Didn't say a thing."

I stomp irritably up the stairs, fully aware that I've been handed the most epic fail in my nineteen years as a human be—

"Wrong way," Alijyar calls.

"What?" I halt in place, hand on the banister.

"She's upstairs." He dips his chin at the floor. "You're in the basement. End of the hall, make a left at the corner."

I spit, "Thanks," and head down to the other bedroom.

I plop onto bed, bury my face in a pillow, and scream as loud as I can into its muffled folds. I know, I know—I could be a starving kid in a third world country, or riddled with lumps of stage 4 cancer, but I can't stop thinking about how I *blew my chance with a HALF-ELF PRINCESS!!!*

I glare at the ceiling, willing it to collapse onto my stupid face. Predictably, it stays right where it is.

Balls.

———

The next morning, I wake up tired and grumpy. If I had just played my cards a *little* better, I could have made out with Erany. Hell, maybe even more—who knows what might have happened?

Not me, because I have no game whatsoever.

I mutter discontentedly under my breath—*razzumfrazzum-idiot derp-hole*—and shrug into my clothes. As I button my jeans, a giant yawn slips from my mouth, triggering a wave of pleasant lassitude.

Not gonna lie, it was nice to sleep on a soft mattress. Before Evermoor, I took stuff like that for granted. But now that I'm back, I'm able to see Earth through a new perspective. I can appreciate the smaller things—things like pizza, sandwiches, and Taylor Swift.

Taylor Swift...looks so much like Erany...

Why did I start coughing when she all but invited me into her *BED??? AGGH!*

Thankfully, my mood improves as I walk up the stairs. Like she said, there'll be other opportunities.

"There he is." Alijyar is sitting on a right-angled couch, holding a hot cup of something.

"Jon." Erany's face lights with a smile. She's sitting on the short section, also holding a hot cup of something.

"Kepi's in the kitchen," Alijyar says. "Help yourself."

"Kepi? Like coffee?" I run a hand through my hair. (Man it's messy—probably should've combed it)

"Kind of, but better." Alijyar takes a sip.

I head into the kitchen, looking for something resembling a pot or a kett—

Whoa. Sitting on the island is an honest-to-God cauldron.

I mutter, "Double, double toil and trouble," and ladle myself a cup.

I head back to the living room, hoping that Erany will invite me to sit beside her. She doesn't disappoint—she pats a cushion and scooches over. My heart does a happy dance but I play it cool; I smile casually and ease down next to her.

"Big day today. What do you think we should—"

"Drink your kepi," Alijyar gestures at my cup. "Tell me what you think."

"All right." Momentary worry tugs at my brain; what if it lowers my stats instead of boosting them? I'd like to keep my charisma right where it is—it's low enough without a -2 penalty.

Oh well—in for a penny, in for a pound.

My first impression is that it tastes like coffee...then nuanced flavor blooms and unfurls, soaking my tongue in dulcet tangs. They gradually reach a delicious crescendo, then slowly fade into a pleasant aftertaste. Not too heavy, but thick enough to savor and appreciate.

"Wow." I examine my cup with newfound respect. "I'm used to American stuff—loads of sugar with some fake fruit flavor. This is like an Asian drink, only ten times better."

Erany asks, "What is an 'Asian drink?' "

"They're subtle," I explain. "They don't overwhelm you."

"Wait for it." Alijyar smirks.

Suddenly, I'm flooded by a sense that all is right, all is well. I'm emphatically aware that everything happens for a good reason—the *best* reason—but it's not just knowledge, it's *certainty.* The epiphany buzzes up my spine, unfurling into tingles that runs across my scalp.

"Oh," I breathe. *"Oh."* My face melts into a dreamy smile. "This is...*wow.* "

"Alijyar's kepi is a league above others," Erany says.

"You don't say," I murmur.

I close my eyes, watching glowing patterns appear on the backs of my lids. At first they look medieval and stylized, then they start morphing into robotic 1980s stuff, like something out of the original *Tron.* And then it becomes a mixture of both—a symphonic array of future-cool layouts, alien and sleek but also regal. *Dr. Strange* magic mixed with the Protoss aesthetic from the latest *Starcraft.*

"Jon."

"Huh?" I blink my eyes.

Alijyar and Erany are both staring at me. "How long was I..." I almost say *out* but I wasn't unconscious. Kinda the opposite, actually. *Superconscious* would be a better way to put it.

"You've been sitting there for over half an hour," Alijyar informs me.

"Half an—" I gape at my cup. "Holy..."

"Don't worry." Erany laughs. "Good kepi will take you for a ride. Especially if it's brewed by Alijyar SyCajister."

"Milady." He acknowledges her compliment with a dip of his chin.

"Wow..." I look around in wonderment. "I think I'm full-on Shifted."

"I wouldn't be surprised," Alijyar says. "Kepi relieves auric congestion—it's typically imbued with a bit of magic. But you're a far cry from the standard patient, so I had to brew mine extra strong. Drink up." He urges me on with a lift of his hand. "Now that you've had it, it won't hit as hard. You can also learn to graduate the experience, depending on your skill at controlling your focus."

"I'm not that skilled, so I guess what you're saying doesn't apply."

"Doesn't it?" He raises his eyebrow. "You're a writer, aren't you? What do you think that is, exactly?" I open my mouth to answer, but he cuts me off with a raised finger. "A writer is an imaginal architect, one who employs logic and dream to link concepts together. As such, controlling your focus isn't an option—it's an ironclad requirement."

"Sheesh." I give an embarrassed shrug. "I always just thought of it as an exercise in fun."

Alijyar shakes his head, smiling. "There you go. You took what I said and simplified it into something practical and—arguably— more profound. You're a writer, Jon, no two ways about it."

"Uh...okay." Not sure what to make of that, so I take another sip.

This time, instead of falling into la-la land, I ride the buzz and...it's hard to describe, but the visuals respond to how I mentally *flex*. When I close my eyes and think of love, a bunch of pink and purple hearts drift across my sight, trailed by a series of cut-along-here lines. Like something a tween might fashion out of cheap construction paper.

"His aura," Erany says excitedly, "Do you see it, Alijyar? It's *breathing.*"

Alijyar nods. "You woke it with the hexflow, but now it's starting to come into its own."

I open my eyes. "Alijyar, how do you know about the hexfl—"

They both regard me with exaggerated patience.

"Right. Stupid question."

"Hold on. Got you a gift." Alijyar walks to a cabinet, opens a drawer, and produces a satchel. It's beautifully made—not showy or flashy, but rich and earthy and pleasingly simple.

"Your carry." He lowers it into my waiting hands.

"Whoa!" I hold it up, marveling at its craftsmanship. "Thanks!"

"It has the same enchantment as everyone else's—meaning it won't store weapons or built-up dwellings—but it's got a little boost: it can tolerate stronger magic than most of its counterparts."

I sling it around my neck. "Why would it need stronger magic?"

Alijyar makes a fist, blows on his knuckles, then opens his fingers. Lying in his palm are eight shiny bullets.

"To hold these rounds. Not Ailura, though—she has to be worn on your hip. I doubt there's a carry that could handle her power."

"Whoa," I breathe.

Fancy scrollwork adorns the casings. Different for each bullet, but the overall style remains the same. They seem to be made from polished jade, but upon closer inspection, it's clear they're cut from bright green metal.

"Use them sparingly," Alijyar advises. "They're hard to come by."

I drop them into my enchanted carry, watching them vanish into its compartment. *Shloop.* Very cool.

A second later, my pleasure turns to worry. "Uh…" I root through the bag, searching for the ammo. "Guys? How do you—"

"You have to focus," Alijyar instructs. "On how they felt to you, specifically."

"Um, okay," I mutter. "Here goes…" I close my eyes and relax my hand.

How they felt to me, how they felt to me…my mind drifts back to a scene from *Star Wars:* Luke training on the *Millennium Falcon,* fending off a hover-drone's laser while fighting blind with a blast-shielded helmet.

But I recognize the thought for what it is: a distraction. Instead of trying to repel or deny it, I accept its existence and leave it be. A flash of doubt constricts my brain—*this thought isn't leaving, it's got its hooks in*—but I keep my faith and abide in stillness.

A moment later, the thought releases of its own accord, leaving behind relief and ease. Amazingly, I don't have to try and think about the bullets; they swim through my psyche in perceptual HD.

"Hey!" I open my eyes and pull out my hand. "It worked!" I uncurl my fingers, revealing the ammo.

"Nice," Alijyar says. "That's how you do it. Let resistance dissipate, then guide your attention onto whatever you need. Seek and ye shall find."

"I imagine it gets easier," I venture. "I've seen the others do it in the midst of battle."

"You imagine right," Alijyar confirms. "It works like a muscle, only in your case, the muscle is atrophied. Don't worry—you're a natural. Soon enough, you'll be able to do it without thinking."

"Awesome." I drop the bullets back in my carry.

Alijyar checks his wrist as if there's a watch on it (there isn't) and declares, "Time to go."

"What?" I sputter. "I just woke up!"

"You slept in. It's a quarter past four." He spreads his arms across the back of the couch. "You hungry?"

I can't help but laugh. "Not in the least. I'll probably be full for the next two days."

"Good. There's two canteens inside the fridge. Help yourselves—they're full of kepi."

I clap my thighs and rise to my feet. "Appreciate it."

Erany says, "Our thanks Alijyar."

The wizard responds with an affable-sounding grunt. *Don't mention it.*

As we enter the kitchen, I'm uncomfortably aware of the looming silence. It's just me and Erany. Only for a minute, but still—I should make a move.

What would Gosling say? No, poor choice of hunk. He usually gets by with a dead-eyed stare, relying on his chiseled features to do all the lifting. Hugh Jackman? No, dude, *hard* no—aside from Wolverine, he's way too beta. (Old, too.) Pattinson, mayb—

A bright spot of pain erupts on my ass, causing me to scream, "HOMINA!" at the very top of my goddamn lungs. As I scrabble for balance, I become dimly aware that Erany is cackling fit to burst.

She just goosed me with warrior-princess strength.

"Oh you think that's funny, huh?" I reach for her wrists. "You think that's *funny?* Turnabout's fair play, lady. I am gonna—"

Still laughing, she seizes my arms and spins me around in a reverse compliance hold. My eyes widen in alarm—I'm about to experience a repeat performance.

"No, *DON—*"

She gooses me again, ravaging my buttock with preposterous force. I can't help it; I honk like an outraged duck.

She lets go and sinks to the floor, laughing so damn hard that her face turns as red as a beefsteak tomato. I briefly think about taking revenge, but there's no way—I sink down beside her and give in to hilarity.

"Hey!" Alijyar calls. "Hurry up in there!"

I try to answer, but all that comes out is a hitchy gasp. It makes Erany laugh harder, which makes *me* laugh harder. She pats the air and exhales deliberately: *calm down.* I nod in agreement, concentrating on regaining my shattered composure.

You can probably guess what happens next. Our eyes meet, and despite our tear-streaked cheeks and crimson skin, the gears shift from bust-your-guts mirth into Romantic Stare. We both lean in and—

"HEY!" Alijyar shouts. "HURRY. *UP!*"

—she breaks away, yelling, "Still your tongue and give us breath! We're coming, you cranky old doddernod!"

"Could've fooled me," he grumbles.

Erany rolls her eyes and opens the fridge. With immense effort, I muzzle my rage. Alijyar SyCajister just took the prize for Worst Wingman Ever.

The canteens are sitting on the middle shelf. Oh hey—the fridge is stocked with different food. Them's the perks of being a dimension-hopping wizard.

"Here." She hands me a canteen, which I drop in my carry. "We'll finish this later."

"Payback's a bitch," I reply.

"What does that mean?"

"That I'll get my revenge."

"Ha!" She throws her head back, allowing me a heart-stopping glimpse of her graceful neck.

As she walks out the door, she shoots me a grin from over her shoulder.

"I hope that you do."

32

Alijyar asks if we're ready to leave, to which we nod our heads yes. We follow him up a set of stairs, then into a circle of gravity-defying water. As the cool liquid touches my head, the world dissolves into a fractal mess. Words and thoughts fall away, leaving behind an ancient and inexhaustible sense of delight—

—and then we're through. We slog out of the pond and onto the turf.

Alijyar slides in my car and pops the trunk. Erany grabs her rapier, shuts the trunk, and takes the back left seat. I take the right.

"Remember the plan." Alijyar shifts into drive and pulls away from the curb. "Meet Cal, complete the revolver, then head over to Crissy Field, where—"

"You send us to Evermoor," Erany finishes. "Yes. Understood."

"Good. And just so you know, Lyderea's servants are right behind us."

"What?" I turn in my seat, scanning the park-road traffic. "What are you talking about?"

"Black Suburban, tinted windows. It's taking a left, passing the baton to...see the other one, keeping pace on our right? Obvious as hell, man."

Now that he's mentioned it, I can't unsee them. "What do we do?"

"Look under your seats. Got you some goodies."

Erany withdraws a cross-sling quiver and a collapsible bow. Her mouth moves silently as she counts the arrows. "Fifteen. My thanks, Alijyar." She loops the sling around her body. "Will the bow respond to—"

"A lock-slip charm? Indeed it will. Jon, don't forget yours."

I grope beneath the seat in front of me. Out comes a bandolier, loaded with a series of gleaming knives. "Whoa." I loop it over my head and shoulder. "Looks just like Ren's." The rig feels stable: a reassuring pressure that lets me know I have options. Six of them, to be exact—a sextet of dirks runs from my left shoulder to my right hip.

"Crafted by wizards in Zitharica Chasm," Alijyar says. "Best in the biz if you want sturdy and reliable."

"Stupid question, but are they—"

"Yes, they're packing enchantments. They're not designed to kill or injure, but—"

"Come *on!*" I throw my hands up in exasperation. "Lyderea's goons have *submachine guns!*"

"Magic is trickier here," he replies. "Spell for spell, I'm sorely outmatched. I'm working with my personal reserves, whereas Lyderea controls the Velic Tessellate."

"We need to destroy it," Erany mutters. "That cursed network is an engine of misery."

"Working on it," Alijyar says. "But for the time being, we're David and they're Goliath."

I slide my knives in and out, testing the draw. "So we can't slug it out with them."

"Correct. Your weapons will provide a temporary distraction—anything from a puff of smoke to a miniature earthquake. It's ghetto magic, but it's the best I can do."

Erany peers through the back window. "I see two conveyances. There might be more."

"Don't worry. We're almost there."

We take a left onto Market Street: a hodgepodge of shops, tourists, and low-level chaos. Costumed partiers have come out in force, ready to drink themselves silly and ditch their inhibitions. Judging by their body language, I'd say the booze is already flowing.

That's going to work in our favor—we may look a bit off, but we shouldn't have a problem blending in. Unfortunately, Lyderea's goons will blend in as well.

After fifteen minutes of snail's pace progress, Alijyar announces, "We're here."

I look out the window. Sure enough, a grungy sign emblazoned with MARKET STREET SMOKESHOP greets my eyes.

I catch his gaze in the rearview mirror. "See you at Crissy?"

"Yep. Can't stay here—it's way too congested."

Erany stares at her arrows. I can tell by the stillness of her face that she's Shifted her sight.

"The sigils are fluxing..." she mutters. "I can't tell which arrow does what."

"Like I said, it's ghetto magic—you gotta work with what you have. Which would be faith, in this case."

"Good enough." She squeezes my shoulder and grips her bow. "Get ready."

"Wait." I glance at Alijyar through the rearview. "Faith? Faith in *what?*"

"That in the end, it all works out." He throws me a smile.

Erany's door clicks open. I crack mine and get ready to move.

Then she's running and so am I.

———

Lyderea's minions jump out of their cars. I count six, all of whom look like military extras from a Michael Bay movie. They've got manly beards, roided-out torsos, and an impressive set of tacti-cool clothing: cargo pants, shades, and muted jackets with lots of pockets.

"OUT OF THE WAY!" one of them snarls. *"FECKLESS PEAS-ANT!"*

I'm surprised into laughter. Their appearance, albeit a touch aggro, isn't completely out of place. Their speech, however, could definitely use work.

A pair of shots ring out, turning my amusement to icy dread. There's a scatter of hoots and questioning shouts—*were those fireworks?*—then one of the goons fires three more rounds. Screams erupt throughout the crowd.

Erany and I sprint for the shop. As we burst through the door, we're greeted by shocked, jacklit faces. One of the customers asks, "Was that gunfi—"

He's cut short by another burst, dotting the windows with cracks and holes. A follow-on salvo hits the glass, causing it to shatter and crash noisily down.

Erany grabs my sleeve and pulls me along, bending at the waist as we shuffle-run forward. Rounds snap by, forcing us to dive behind a store-wide counter.

"Basement!" she yells. *"Cal's in the basement!"* She points at a door on the opposite wall. Beyond its weathered frame, there's a dimly lit set of descending stairs.

"I know!" I yell back. *"But they've got us pinned!"* Bongs and displays explode around us.

She mutters a phrase, lighting her temples with coral runes. Her bow telescopes out, morphing from a foot-long stick into a compact weapon. *"Go!"* She nocks an arrow, pokes up to fire, then ducks back down as several rounds chew up our cover. *"No—hold!"*

I draw an enchanted knife, holding it tight against my chest. Gotta wait for a break in their rhythm so we can—

"Now!" Erany pops up and shoots.

I race past her, flinging my dagger with a backhand toss. Mid-flight, it glows searing red and—*BOOF!*—floods the store with blue-purple gas.

I crash into the door, grab the jamb, then swing around to check on Erany. She's a few yards behind me, running sideways as she draws and fires, draws and fires. Each arrow explodes with a *whoosh*, igniting the haze left by my knife. Our pursuers curse and yell, dodging multicolored fire as it rips through the store.

"Come on!" I snatch a knife out from its sheath. This time I throw it properly: cross-body, from shoulder to hip. It digs into a goon's chest-plate armor, erupting in a mess of limb-tangling vines.

We hustle down the dilapidated stairs. As soon as we reach the unfinished floor, Erany nocks an arrow and covers the steps. I draw another dagger, ready to chuck it at the first goon that tries to rush us.

"Where is he?" she screams. *"Where's Cal?"*

I look wildly around. A naked bulb hangs from the ceiling, illuminating piles of junk-filled tubs. *"Cal! We were sent by Alijyar!"*

A smoking canister clunks down the stairs. At the same time, something goes *thump* directly behind me. I spin in place and glimpse a raggedy White guy brandishing a jacket. I try and warn Erany, but the fabric covers our heads and then we're elsewhere.

———

Huh? Looks like we're inside a well-kept house...

An elevated forest house, apparently. The windows overlook an arrangement of tall, mossy trees.

I sit up in a twitch, pulling my dagger close to my chest. "What the—"

"Heya." The voice carries from another room. A second later, it's followed by the guy from the basement. He's wearing a *Big Lebowski*-style robe, balancing a tray with three steaming cups.

Erany tracks him with her bow and arrow. I rise to a crouch, keeping my dagger in partial guard.

"Are you...are you Crazy Cal?"

He sets the tray on a stump-carved table. "The one and only." He gestures at a ring of cozy chairs, equidistant from the table's edge. "Go 'head. Pop a squat."

Erany lowers her bow. "What took you?"

"I was still coming down. Had some royal gorilla and an eighth of shrooms."

I give him an incredulous stare. "You're a drug addict?"

"*Druggie,*" he snaps. "They're not all bad. Know yer substances before you judge."

"Sorry." I raise my hands in a conciliatory gesture.

"Sounds like you buy into sheeple propaganda." He eyes me skeptically. "Times are a-changing—yer should know better." He sniffs in disdain. "Then again, you're just a kid, so I guess you have a legitimate excuse."

(I'm so not a kid, but I'm not gonna argue with a fiftieth-level wizard.)

Erany sits and examines the cups. "Kepi?"

"Ayep. It's not Alijyar's, but it'll do ya fine."

Erany takes a guarded sip. A moment later, a sunny smile blooms on her face. "You say true, wizard—your brew is delectable."

"Aw shucks." Cal ducks his head, flattered. "Thank ya bigly."

I lift my cup and try my kepi. Fruit-tinged sweetness floods my palate, fading into a pleasant tang. Just like Alijyar's, it Shifts my sight, but it's a lot milder and way more graduated.

"Wow." I study the cup with newfound respect. "You should serve this at parties."

"I do!" His face lights up. "*Aya*huasca parties!"

"You're a shaman?"

"You betcher!" A proud nod. "Bonafide curandero!"

"Guess I shouldn't be surprised. Not a big leap for a SyCajister wizard."

"Where *are* we?" Erany stares out a window. "Are we still on Earth?"

"Not exactly," Cal hedges. "This here is an In-Betweener. A place between places, so to speak."

"A hidden dimension," I murmur. "Cool."

"Yep, but that isn't right either," Cal says. "An In-Betweener is also a space between ideas, if you catch my drift."

I shake my head. "I don't."

He sets his cup down and spreads his fingers, as if he's holding an invisible ball. "It's all just—" He jams them together in a quick jerk. *"Mushed..."* He sighs in defeat. "Never mind, it's hard to explain. Anyways, you came for Ailura, right? Her other half?" He reaches in his robe and produces the barrel-and-cylinder. "Here ya go."

As I take the metal into my hands, conviction and surety fill my mind—a sensation of each muscle knowing what to do and when to do it. If I had to shoot a three-pointer, I'd be able to sink it without a doubt. Hell, I could probably hit a full court shot.

I unbutton my gun-pouch and produce the grip. When I connect the halves, the weapon shines with three blue gleams. I almost ask if there's some kind of pin to hold things in place, but the halves stay connected.

"That there's a beaut." Cal leans forward, examining the revolver with dilated pupils. "Cut right through some high-demon energy."

I press the release, making the wheel drop out with a satisfying *click.* The holes are bigger than a regular pistol's. Not only that, each one's glowing with indigo light.

I flick my wrist and the wheel snaps closed.

"Oh—almost fergot." Cal slaps his armrests. "Ya need you a holster." He strides out of the room, picking up the pace as he patters up the stairs.

I grin at Erany, holding the revolver up to my face. "Just completed my second side-quest. Bad. *Ass.*"

She cocks her head, puzzled. "Side quest?"

"Oh right—there's no way you'd know." A self-conscious laugh. "They're tasks you finish on the way to your goal. Save Elerica, complete Ailura, kiss the princess..."

"Kiss the princess?" She raises an eyebrow, amused. "You're certain that qualifies?"

I give her a devilish grin. "Let's find out."

She leans toward me. We close our eyes, and—

Jump apart as Cal tromps in, brandishing the holster. "Got it! Couldn't remember if it was under the bed or in another In-Betweener! The original holster is somewhere on Evermoor, but this one'll do. It's got some solid enchantments, believe you me."

I grind my teeth, stifling the desire to scream in frustration. Am I *ever* gonna kiss her? Jesus Christ, just *one kiss!* It's not like I'm asking for lights-out sexy time! (Although yes—I would like that as well.)

But instead of griping, I manage a stilted, "Uh, yeah. Awesome. Great."

"Here!" He thrusts the holster at me. "Try it on!"

I lay the revolver onto the table-stump, resisting the urge to voice my discontent—*razzumfrazzumjusthadtointerrupt*—and accept the holster into my hands. Conveniently enough, it's sewn onto a brown leather belt, making it easy to buckle around my waist.

"Huh." I jiggle my hips, noting the perfect fit. "It feels like..."

"Like it's made for you." Cal graces me with a gap-toothed smile.

"Yeah..." I meet his eyes, unsure of how to feel. Flattered, intimidated, and if I'm being honest, a little scared as well.

When I slide Ailura into the holster, white and green runes materialize around her, spinning once, twice, then locking into place. For a brief moment, they grow deeper and richer before gradually dimming into ghost-faint traces.

"That'll do it," Cal declares. "You two are ready ta go. 'Less you wanna stay for some wormy-squirmies."

"Wormy-squirmies?" Erany asks.

"Kinda like worms, but extra squirmy. Make you feel topsy!"

Me and Erany exchange a glance.

"Uh...maybe next time." I chuckle nervously.

"Yeah, yeah." A dejected wave. "Everyone passes on 'em. Only one that didn't was a crazy cheerleader named Holly Dent. Foller me."

Cal takes us into a hall, then stops before a nondescript door. He turns the knob and pulls it back, revealing a spiraling stairwell lined with flickering torches. Every ten feet, there's a plain wooden door carved into the wall.

My unease grows as we make our way down. We must have passed over a dozen doors...how tall is this house/tree, exactly? Out of curiosity, I crane my head back and look at the ceiling.

Big mistake.

It's not just dozens—it's *hundreds.* Thousands, maybe. There's just an endless series of winding doors, stretching into a faint point of light.

And then something happens that rattles my sanity: the air above us distorts and compresses, rippling skyward in a giant wave. Some of the doors vanish but a bunch of new ones take their place. At the same time, dread and relief batter my brain, as if I jumped with a bungie and almost got smashed on the rocks below. It's not just once; the sensation hits me over and over, racking my nerves into a tailspin frenzy.

I sink to the floor, trying to articulate what I'm seeing and feeling. All that comes out is, "Doors...*doors...*"

"What the—*hey! Quit lookin'!*" Cal darts forward and covers my eyes. "

Erany says, "What are you—" but he cuts her off with, *"No!"* and reaches out for her face. *"QUIT LOOKIN'!"*

"Hands. *Off.*" She shoves him away, takes a peek, then slaps her eyes with the flats of her palms. *"Gods!"* Tears stream down her fingers and wrists.

As crazy as it seems, a deep-down part of me still wants to see, even though I know it'll drive me insane. My head drifts back all on its own, hungry for a glimpse of relentless infinity.

No—*NO*. I can't afford to look. My mind's gonna snap.

So I force my eyes down an inch at a time, clenching my jaw and grinding my teeth. My neck muscles cramp in agonizing protest. As painful as that is, it's nothing compared to the hot-flash panic in my gut and chest.

And just like that, my desire to look suddenly vanishes.

"What...what..." I breathe deep and heavy, trying to collect my scrambled thoughts. Erany stays right where she is: eyes covered, leaning against the wall.

Cal extends his arms, as if to say, *Nice and easy—don't get crazy.* "I forgot to tell you: *don't look up.* You can't process that much novelty."

"Now you tell us." I get to my feet in halting lurches. "Erany?"

"All is well," she manages. She draws a shuddering breath, then gingerly removes her hands from her face. The whites of her eyes are completely red; the skin around them is swollen and puffy.

"You look terrible," she croaks.

"Speak for yourself." I laugh shakily.

Cal gives us a cautious glance. "Keep going. And this time, keep yer eyes to yer front."

"Any other surprises?" There's unnatural tension in my face and my spine. My body is dead set on looking straight ahead—a Pavlovian response to the assault on my brain.

"Nope," Cal stops in front of a wooden door, indistinguishable from any of the others. "This here's the one."

But as he swings it wide, it becomes glaringly clear this isn't the one.

Instead of the unfinished basement of the Market Street Smoke Shop, I find myself staring at an arid desert. Twenty yards in, a mob of horse-sized spiders are charging a pack of velociraptor-riding barbarians. Two of the raptors are mounted by Asian teenagers in Earthling clothes—the boy is shooting a sci-fi ray gun, the girl is wielding a pair of scimitars.

One of the spiders comes barreling toward us. Cal shuts the door just in time—I take a giant step back as it snarls ferociously, scratching and gnashing at the portal's surface.

"Whoops! Wrong gateway!"

"The hell was *that?*" I gasp. Erany's drawn her sword and assumed a low stance, ready to impale the oncoming spider-beast.

"Place called Elithia," Cal rasps. "Yours is further down."

"Surprise number two," I mutter.

"Well ex-cuu*uuuse ME!*" Cal sneers. "I warned you, didn't I? Card says 'Crazy Cal,' doesn't it?"

"Yeah but you're not crazy," I counter.

"Yer should see me when I run outta weed!" A gleeful cackle.

"I'll take your word for it. Please—" I dip my head and extend an arm. "Lead the way."

"Right." He continues wending down the stairwell.

After several more doors, I say, "Cal."

"Yep?" He doesn't stop walking.

"Why is it that I don't get a headache if I happen to look down? I mean, it's too dark to see more than a handful of doors, but..."

"Under normal circumstances, yer would." He sighs. "But the worlds are topsy-turvy; up is down and black is white. It's not as pronounced on Earth as on Evermoor, but you can still see it manifest in society: people don't wanna talk or work things out. Most just want to condemn and attack."

"That doesn't answer my—"

Erany says, "In magical terms, he means that an organic flow exists in both concept and form, and that it naturally goes skyward. But due to the misalignment in our collective consciousness, that selfsame flow has reversed directions. Presently, the path of least resistance leads downward, so that is the direction we are pulled and drawn towards."

"Exactly!" he exclaims. "Couldn't've said it better m'self."

"Seems arbitrary," I mutter. "Up and down are just directions, but you're conflating them with—"

"They're symbols, you dundergunt!" Cal scoffs. "Everything translates into symbols and connotations—that's the only way it makes any sense! Your mind is geared for sensory input: eyes, ears, nose, tongue...the blessing and curse of being a human. Anyways, we're here." He stops at a door.

"You sure?" I ask uncertainly.

" 'Course I'm sure, you whissy-slip heeble-feeb! Quit bein' chicken!"

As he opens the door, I tense without meaning to. But much to my relief, there's no spider-beasts, velociraptors, or roided-out barbarian warriors. Just the hustle and bustle of Fisherman's Wharf: scads of people in gaudy costumes, then a backdrop of warehouses built on the bay.

"This is the closest I could get you." Cal's voice quavers with effort. For a second I'm puzzled, then I realize that holding the door open takes an immense amount of effort.

"Thank you, Cal." Erany nods as she passes him by. "May light find you in dark places."

For the first time since we've met, Cal responds in Evermoor lingo: "Aye, Princess. May it ease your eyes and guide your feet."

And then we're back in San Francisco.

33

"Cool costume! Are you a Chinese cowboy? Do you know KA-RATE?"

I find myself staring at a quintessential dudebro—drink in hand, dressed in a gladiator costume—throwing clumsy chops and spilling beer on his armor. His dudebro buddy, a guy dressed like Heath Ledger's Joker, brays out laughter.

A couple of party girls tug on the first guy's arm, trying to get him to tone it down— *"STOO-oopp...you're so BA-aad..."*—while laughing along so as not to be killjoys. They don't care if their friend is being racist; they're toeing the line between pack mentality and plausible deniability, just in case I raise a stink.

I'm thrown for a bunch of reasons (interdimensional travel ranks high on that list), the main one being I've never encountered racism in the flesh. Call me lucky or sheltered or probably both. The second thing that puzzles me is his use of the word "cowboy." I'm dressed in Earthling clothes, so why would he—

Oh yeah—the giant revolver strapped to my hip.

DudeBro makes some cartoonish martial arts noises, then pulls the skin around his eyes. "Me so *hooooor*-ny..."

I rifle through my brain, trying to come up with an appropriate reply. I don't want to fight, but at the same time, I should—

Erany grabs his finger and bends it back. A sharp *CRACK* rings through the air.

"AAAH!" He folds at the waist and hugs his hand. I catch a glimpse of his broken digit, splayed out at a cringe-inducing angle.

"What the *hell?*" one of the party girls wails. "You're going to *jail*, bitch! You can't just—"

Erany kicks her beer, flinging its contents across her face. Party Girl and her friends (minus the one with the broken finger) tromp toward Erany, cussing up a storm.

My mouth unfreezes. Gotta warn them off before they end up in casts. "Hey guys, I really don't think you should—"

Too late. DudeBro 2 grabs Erany's shoulder.

She clamps his hand with both of hers, then does something circular with her legs, torso, and arms, making him lose his balance and crash into his buddy. The girls scream in fury and reach for Erany, but she spins away and darts between them, grabbing their hair as she slips their grasp. Skip-steps forward to gain momentum—

"Let go of my hair! Let go YOU BITCH—"

—and reverses course, clotheslining their necks with her extended arms. Their legs fly up as they slam into pavement.

Erany looms over them, fists clenched, eyes narrowed. "Jon is not to be mocked. Cede your agreement."

No response. They're way too busy moaning in pain, clutching weakly at their freshly jacked throats.

Erany scoffs in disgust, then lurches toward the bro with the broken finger, immediately catching his full attention.

"I got it, *I got it!*" He makes a hasty warding gesture and scuttles away.

She turns to his buddy. "Apologize."

"We're sorry, okay?" DudeBro 2 helps the girls up, regarding Erany with genuine fear. "We're sorry!"

"Show me your heels, lest I break the legs that lie atop them."

As the chastised douchebags scurry away, Erany gives 'em the finger, yelling something she only could have learned while surfing the web. (Didn't think it was possible, but she just became ten times hotter.)

"Wow." I grin at her. "Thanks for the rescue. I owe you a save."

"As if I would ever need saving." She returns my grin. "The folk on your world have horrible taste—I like your eyes." Her gaze ticks across my face, slowing the world to a delicious crawl.

I lean in, ready to claim my long-awaited kiss. Thought I'd be nervous, but—

"There they are! Arrest them, officer!"

A beemer-driving Karen squawks and screeches, pointing us out for a mounted policeman. He clops over and gets off his horse.

"Let's see some IDs." He beckons with a hand. "Both of you."

Erany clears her throat. "You don't understand, Kai Justicer. We were simply—"

"What did you say?" He rests his hand on the butt of his gun. "Understand: I don't give a good goddamn how much you or your parents make. Give me lip and I will split your skull."

She turns to me and whispers, "I thought they were different here."

Before I can reply, she turns back to the cop in an attempt to make nice. "I meant no offense, Kai..." she squints at his nametag. "Kai...Bacon, is it?"

"*Macon,*" I hiss, nudging her hard with the point of my elbow. "*Macon,* not Bacon! Don't *ever* call a cop Bacon!"

"I'm sorry!" she hisses back. "I told you—the arcane tides distort my perception!"

The cop becomes unnaturally still. Then he draws his nightstick.

"You think I'm funny." His tone is casual, at sharp odds with his dead-eyed gaze. "You think I'm a joke."

Erany raises her hands, trying to diffuse the tension with a half-hearted smile. "No, erm..."

"Sir," I whisper. "Call him sir."

"No sir," she says. "I meant no offense."

"Shut up." He says it coolly, without emotion. "Stop resisting."

"Wait—what?" I step in front of Erany, shielding her body with mine. "We're not resisting! She's just—"

"Drop the weapon!" he shouts. *"Now!"*

The nightstick gleams as it arcs toward me. I instinctively intuit what's about to happen—that much speed plus that much malice...

Erany slaps his wrist, redirecting the baton.

The cop's features twist with hate. "Oh you are gonna *get it,* you—"

She interrupts with an elbow to his face. He lurches forward, snarling in rage, but she cuts it short with a jab to his throat. Then she darts in, clinches his waist, and rips him down with a twisting throw. In the blink of an eye she drops to the ground, takes his back, and puts him to sleep with a rear naked choke.

Holy. *Crap.* She can duel with swords, cast spells...and also fight in the UFC. I have never felt so emasculated (or turned on) in my entire life.

Up until now, I haven't been watching the people around us. I'm genuinely surprised when they break into applause. Erany acknowledges them with a dip of her chin. "Thank you. Thank you."

"Why didn't you hit him?" I ask. "You know—knock him out?"

She gives me an irritable look. "Jon. Not only is that unreliable, but when you hit someone's head with that much force, you run the risk of accidental death. Even if they live, they might suffer permanent damage. It is much easier to use a choke."

"Oh," I manage. "Right. So it's like you just—" I clinch my hands and flex my arm "—get in there and curl it tight? Or do you—"

She cuts me off with a raised hand. "Make sure they're on their side, body slanting down toward your choke-arm. Place your choke-arm's elbow beneath their chin, grab the upper half of your top arm, and snake it back over their head. And you don't apply pressure by curling your choke-arm; you squeeze your elbows together while leaving your ankles uncrossed, otherwise your opponent could break them by—" She registers my clueless stare and amends it to, "It takes time to learn. There are defensive counters for each of those steps, and a myriad of solutions for each of those counters."

"But cops have killed with that exact same hold. Are you sure that—"

"They must have lacked training. If you know what you're doing, choking your opponent is much less risky than knocking them unconscious."

"Oh. Okay. Maybe you could teach me. When we have time, that is."

She gives me a sweet, flirty smile. "I'll demonstrate on you as much as you like." Her expression turns businesslike. "How far is it from here to Alijyar?"

"A twenty-minute jog. Probably longer, given the crowds."

"Slower than I'd like." She clicks her tongue in displeasure.

I shrug in defeat. "It's our best option. We should start walking now unless..." My gaze settles on the unattended horse.

She raises an eyebrow. "Unless?" Her gaze follows mine, then her eyes light with understanding.

"Can you—"

"I was born on horseback," she states. "Here, lovely." She scoots sideways, standing at a diagonal angle from its head. "Friends?"

It studies her uncertainly, then cranes forward and sniffs her fingers. Erany whispers in what I think is Elvish—the words flow together like a rill through a forest. (I know you can't describe language with images, but that's as close as I can come to putting it into words.)

After a couple more sniffs, the horse noses her hand onto its head. She steps closer and strokes its neck. As it leans against her, she rubs its chest while continuing to murmur in that soft, beautiful language.

A couple bystanders start filming on their phones.

"I shall call you Lyra." Erany scratches her ears. "Yes—that name suits you. Let's go, Jon."

Me? Ride a horse? "Um, how do I—"

She hop-steps gracefully onto its back. "It's fine. I know what I'm doing." She reaches down and offers a hand.

"Okaaay..." I grab hold, and—*HUP*—jump and pull, scrabbling up behind her.

She continues stroking Lyra's neck, murmuring softly into her ear. The people nearby are in mild shock; they're all watching with wide-eyed stares.

Erany catches me in her peripheral vision. "You said he's twenty minutes distant?"

"Yeah, if we jog there on foot. It's a couple of miles. I mean—" I do a rough calculation. "A little more than two faires."

"A little more than two faires..." She chews her lip, then reaches in her carry and produces a two-foot long, tapered silver rod. The top is capped with a bright blue gem, lit by a spark of twinkling gold light.

A chorus of *oohs* arise from the onlookers; their eyes glaze over as they stare at the artifact.

"The arcane tides are shifting in our favor." Erany casts a brief glance around. "If this magic was muted, no one would notice."

"What does it do?"

"I don't yet know if it's going to work. If it does, you can hug my waist. For now, grip the back of my saddle."

I reach down and grip the saddle. (Whoa, I can almost touch her butt...no, Jon, *no!* Quit perving out!)

"Typically, it isn't smart to ride double." She smooths Lyra's hair with the flat of her hand. "It stresses the animal's hips and back, but this pin will ensure that doesn't happen. It's called Jynitric armor—developed for those who need to strengthen their mount."

She inserts the pin into Lyra's mane. Despite the lack of clips, it locks firmly in place. Then she kisses her index and middle finger, imbuing them with a burst of starcore glimmer, and presses their tips against the hairpin's gem.

Beams of light shoot from its center. The scatter of rays gyres and twists, evoking gasps and exclamations as they dance across the water. For a brief moment, I have to turn away and close my eyes. Seconds later, the brilliance fades.

I blink dazedly and open my eyes. "What was..."

And then I fall silent.

Lyra is clad in violet and silver, dappled with hints of gleaming sapphire. With each breath and shift of muscle, her armor glistens like liquid sunfire. Remember Shadowfax, Gandalf's mount from the *Lord of the Rings?* Remember how he was supposed to be the most badass horse in the history of horses?

Well Lyra's got him beat by a country mile.

"The enchantment will last until I remove the pin, or the moon and the sun twice switch places."

I clear my throat. "So a day and a half, two days max."

"Correct. Now hug my waist." She reaches down and pulls my arms around her middle. "Under normal circumstances, it would be bad form for the second rider to embrace the first. Jynitric armor, however, will allow us exception to the rule. Additionally, Lyra and I will enjoy enhanced communication through a crude form of mind-to-mind speech. She'll also receive a boost in speed, as well as have temporary access to—"

"Stop." I link my hands and pull her tight. "You had me at 'hug my waist.' "

She throws me a smile from over her shoulder. (*God* is she gorgeous.) "Ready?"

"Yep. Let's do this."

As we pick up speed, my sight Shifts. Whether it's due to my openness or the arcane tides, I'm not really sure and I don't really care. Because wonder upon wonders, I can *see* Erany communicating with Lyra—glyph-formed chains run from her temples to the pin, sending information one way, then the other.

She's talking with a horse using psychic computer code. Could life get any cooler?

Somehow, she senses my grin and responds in kind. "What amuses you?"

"Nothing, it's just..." I close my eyes and shake my head.

"Just what?" she presses.

"I just really, *really* want to kis—"

An astonished voice cries out from the crowd: *"Holy shit, is that Taylor Swift? Dude, she's riding a horse and she's wielding a SWORD! AWESOME!"*

Nah bruh. My grin widens. *It's the other way around.*

Taylor's got nothing on Eralindíany.

34

People cheer as we gallop past. I totally get it—Lyra is nothing short of stunning in her lavender armor. If regular life is standard HD, then Lyra's glow-up is 1028K.

"YEEEAAAH!" A partier roars. *"Those are the best costumes EVER!"*

We clear the hill at Fort Mason, then hit an expansive stretch of level green. Nice. I thought it would be crowded, but that isn't the case. Shouldn't take us long to—

"Be ready," Erany warns. "Lyderea's servants are close on our heels."

"What?" I swivel in place, searching the field. "Where?"

"Up in the sky. Look to your right."

I stare into the night as hard as I can. There's nothing there. I'm about to say as much when four twinkling dots appear on the horizon.

Holy crap—she's got hawkeye vision.

"See them?" Erany asks.

"What are they?"

"Ekotic gargoyles. If we can make it to Alijyar before they attack, we might not have to—"

Suddenly, the wizard's voice booms through our minds: *[I'm under the bridge. Stay clear for now—I'm working on the portal. I'll let you know when it's ready.]*

Erany shakes her head, grinning half in frustration, half in amusement. "Such is life. We'll have to fight them on horseback—you with your daggers and me with my bow."

A pair of wormholes open above the grass, then spit out the two Suburbans we saw from before.

"Got another problem: the human-looking goons are about to catch up."

Erany glances back, long enough to peep our pursuers. Thanks to Lyra's boosted speed, we're staying well ahead of them.

"I believe they are Mimické."

Her sweet-smelling hair grazes my face. "Care to elaborate?"

"Dyadic automata, born from the pith of murk and shadow. They can mimic appearance and vestiges of knowledge."

"Is that good or bad? I mean I know it's bad, but on a scale of one to ten, how bad, exactly?"

"Bad in the sense they can do us harm, good in the sense they're dumb and brutish. Now hush—I'm going to bite the reins so I can free my bow." She chomps the reins, draws her bow from its quiver-mounted sheath, and punches it open with a spell-powered shake.

Moments later, shots crack past. I instinctively duck and throw a dagger. It hits the ground in front of the left SUV, exploding with a loud *BANG* and carving a giant divot into the turf. The car slips in the decline and slams into a wall of solid earth—the crater is sheer enough to stop it in its tracks.

"That's one!" I shout.

Our airborne pursuers flow into a J-turn, spreading out behind us and settling into a steady rhythm. (Weird—through my unShifted sight, they look like glowing wireframes). Meanwhile, Erany's busy guiding Lyra; she can't turn around and fire her bow.

So what happens next is all on me. Time to kick some ass. (I hope.)

I chuck a knife at the second SUV. My weapon morphs into glittering lights, but the car swerves from side to side, evading the flares with frustrating ease. I reach to my chest and draw again.

Breathe, Jon—*concentrate.*

Dissociative peace unfurls in my brain. We might be fleeing gargoyles and shapeshifters, but my focus is clear; my mind is still. As the SUV closes the distance, my hand and shoulder remain perfectly coiled.

Wait for it...wait for it...

Out pokes a guy with a scoped submachine gun. The muzzle chatters and flickers, but it doesn't matter. Nothing matters except for the fixed calm spreading through my body.

Not quite yet...not quite yet...

Now.

My hand snaps down, releasing the dagger. Mid-flight, it dissolves into a cloud of yellow-brown mist, engulfing the car in corrosive rot. The effect is immediate—holes sprout along its exterior, marring the paint with swiss-cheese gaps. Its wheels shrink into tattered discs, twirling off their hubs and onto the grass.

The decaying vehicle trundles to a stop. Four Mimické tumble out, blasting away with their submachine guns. They either suck at shooting, or we're throwing them off with our breakneck speed. If I had to guess, I'd say it's our speed—Lyra is *fast.* She's probably as fast as a goddamn racecar.

"Second car's toast!"

Erany responds with a reins-muffled grunt.

Next problem: four winged monsters, still closing in. (God, they're ugly. Like constipated Gollums covered with tumors). We could evade the Mimické with maneuver and hustle, but that isn't the case with our airborne pursuers—they're way too fast, way too agile.

"What next?" I yell. *"We can't outrun them!"*

Erany shouts through the reins, but it comes out garbled.

"What?"

She shakes her head in frustration, then—

WHOA!

—we cut sharply around, ripping up turf as we charge the gargoyles.

Erany's arm works like a piston, nocking and shooting, nocking and shooting. Her arrows blossom into traps or obstructions: shining nets woven from light, blowout puffs of arcane fog, or long-winding chains made of glowing runes.

Hope surges through me. If she can take them out, then—

No dice. The gargoyles tear through the magic like it wasn't even there. The nets fall apart, the runes dissipate, and the mist does nothing.

Erany collapses her bow and slides it into her quiver. *"You still have a knife, don't you? Why didn't you throw it?"*

"Sorry!" I reply. *"I was holding on tight so I didn't fall off!"*

"Never mind! It wouldn't have done us any good!"

"What? Why?"

"High demon energies!"

I fall silent. Then it hits me:

"Oh! The bullets!"

"Uh—YEAH!" (Great—she's using Earthgirl sarcasm.)

I reach in my carry, feeling for the rounds with not just with my fingers, but also my mind. Pretty soon, I'm clutching six bullets in my left hand. With my right, I reach to my hip and draw Ailura.

"Keep her steady!" I yell. *"I'm going to load!"* (Jesus, Jon—you should've loaded earlier, when you weren't jouncing around on a spell-powered horse! *Idiot!*)

"Hurry!" she yells.

Okay, you can do this. Hold the gun, pop the cylinder...

Click.

Six empty chambers stare back up at me. I strive to balance speed and stability as I feed in bullets, one by one. After the last round finds its way home, the cylinder spins all on its own, ratcheting smoothly into the gun.

"Ready!"

Erany clucks her tongue, signaling Lyra to reverse course. Right as we turn, gold-sparkle mist materializes in front of her. Not sure what it is (think it's some sort of arcane feedback) but it's hella pretty.

When we finish about-facing, I'm greeted by an unwelcome sight: the eight Mimické have formed a line, perpendicular to our trajectory.

"Whoa!" I flinch and duck as they open fire. Some of it glances off Lyra's armor, but she takes it in stride and keeps on charging.

Erany unsheathes her sword with a cross-draw swipe. *"Vengeance is nigh, you low-shadow wretches!"* Then she utters a phrase, one that sounds like several voices whispering at once. It marks her rapier with luminous green, followed by a reflective glare that runs across its flat.

Her next move boggles my mind—she swings her sword to and fro, chopping the bullets *out of the air*. Each deflection is marked by a spark, accompanied by an indigo flare and a cluster of runes.

Lyra cuts a half-loop into their flank, making them scatter and dive in all directions. Five manage to get clear of Erany's blade, but three of them don't—their heads fly right, their bodies fall left. Before their severed parts can hit the ground, they dissipate into a mess of light.

"I'll take the Mimické!" she yells. *"Focus on the gargoyles!"*

I hug her tight, abruptly taken by a delirious thrill. Riding hell for leather with a beautiful girl, enchanted revolver ready to go...

I'm Han Solo, John Wayne, and Drizzt Do'Urden all in one.

One of the gargoyles swoops in low, triggering a surge of red-line fear. *"Down!"* Erany shouts. I duck just in time to avoid its claws, ruffling my hair as it slices past.

Erany pops up, swinging her green-glowing blade in an elegant flourish. *"Faster, Lyra! FASTER!"*

I thought we were booking it, but as Lyra kicks up into another gear, I'm forced to reconsider. Right now it's like the entire world is made of speed—I half-expect lines to streak by our sides, like anime heroes in a full-on blitz.

Up in the sky, two of the gargoyles open their mouths, releasing billowing tides of black-and-green energy. I squinch my eyes in re-flexive fear, but Erany's got it covered: she sings a high, double-toned note, surrounding us in a bubble of enchanted air—liquid shine combined with pressurized distortion—and shielding us from the necrotic deluge. The discharge spills off the curve of our forcefield, withering and charring the grass around us.

"Whoa!" I shout, half in delight, half in pee-your-pants terror. *"If you keep this up, we'll—"*

"Takes too much magic!" Erany shouts back. *"That spell was a one-off!"*

We clear the barrage in a flash of armor, right as a gargoyle dives at our heads. *"Erany—DUCK!"* I raise my gun, fanning the hammer like an old-school gunslinger. ***CHOOM CHOOM CHOOM.***

Filigreed light streaks from the barrel, weaving together into intricate twists. My first shot wrecks its bony shoulder. The second hits it square in the chest, blasting away over half of its ribcage. The third severs its head from its neck. I'm momentarily shaken by the deafening noise—my joints ache and my skull rattles—but then that cold focus descends upon me, the same one I felt when I threw my knife.

"Stay low!" I scream.

"SHOOT them already!" Erany works her sword in figure eights, cutting down bullets left and right.

As gargoyle number two closes the distance, I grab my right shoulder with my left hand, creating a bend in my left arm where I can rest Ailura. "When I tell you to, turn right." My voice remains calm, despite the incoming fire and our ungodly speed.

"Steady...*steady...*"

The gargoyle slaloms, staying close on our heels. Its chest puffs out with a telltale inhale.

"NOW!"

Lyra jerks right. The putrid blast misses our flank.

Our pursuer shrieks as it fights its momentum, failing to match the speed of our turn. For a true-blue second it hangs in the air, caught in the dregs of its leftover thrust.

Gotcha.

Just like before, bladelike twists erupt from the barrel. My first shot punches through its wing. My second cleaves its leg at the hip. The third blows off its crusty face.

"OH yeah!" I pump my fist in celebration.

"There's still two more!" Erany screams, dousing my excitement.

"Shit!" I fumble in my carry for the last two bullets. I used three apiece for the first two gargoyles, which means there's no room for error with these last two fuglies.

Open the wheel, drop the empties in my carry (magic bullet casings might be hard to come by). Okay, good. All right, Jon, same deal—steady the gun, ready the bullets. Now feed 'em into the empty chambers. That's one. And that's—

"No!" The second round tumbles from my grasp.

"What happened?"

"It fell!" A lump of emotion grows large in my throat—dread, frustration, and the maddening desire to howl in rage. *"It fell in the grass!"*

"Kill the one!" she yells. *"We'll get the other in a bit!"*

"What are you talking about? How are we supposed to—"

"Trust me! Now focus on that damned gargoyle!"

Erany goes back to work, deflecting rounds with her enchanted sword. Once again, the Mimické scatter as she rushes their flank. This time, however, Lyra zigs and zags, keeping them in range as her aura ignites with patches of fire. (Reminds me of a spacecraft re-entering the atmosphere. Only Lyra is magical, which makes it ten times cooler.) Erany chops left and right, dispatching the remaining gunmen in one fell swoop.

I look over my shoulder, watching the other two gargoyles climb high in the sky. Think they're gonna dive, but—

A burst of surety floods my mind. *"Erany, hold tight and halt us in place!"*

Erany clucks, causing Lyra to stop and rear back. I suspect the Jynitric armor is keeping us mounted, but still, Erany and I push with everything we have—thighs, hands, whatever—in an effort to stay seated.

As our pursuers soar by, cutting quick shadows against the yellow-white moon, I laser in on the rightmost gargoyle.

K'CHOOM!

Weaponized radiance weaves and spirals, marking the night with vivid color. It hits the monster at a diagonal angle, ripping the upper third of its body—arm, wing, and head—clean off its torso and legs.

Erany whoops in delight. *"Fine shooting, Jon! DAMN fine shooting!"*

We resume our gallop across the field. I want to celebrate, but it's not over yet. *"There's still one more! How do we—"*

Erany mutters a phrase, then spits out a puff of air. Sparkling gas jets from her lips, enveloping a large chunk of field in red-twinkling fog.

"I don't get it!" I shout. *"How is that going to—"*

"There!" She points at a tiny bauble of brilliant white light, high-lighted by her enchanted mist. *"The last bullet!"*

"We need to slow down!" I scream. *"We're gonna ride right past it!"*

"No we won't!" Erany jounces in time with our breakneck gallop. *"HYAH!"* The reins whip up and down as we tear across the field.

"Erany, there's no way we can get low enough to—"

"Get ready to catch it!" She threads the left half of her reins under the grooves of Lyra's armor.

What the hell? She's lost her ability to tug from the left. Even if she pulls, the tension won't transfer to Lyra's bit; it's going to be absorbed by the juts in her plating.

"What are you—"

"Shut. UP!" Erany frees her left foot and lashes the slack around her calf. She's now riding heavy on her right. Her left leg—bound in a haphazard twist of horse-rein leather—is curled across the top of the saddle.

Oh my God. I think I know what she's going to do.

"Steady, Lyra!" She draws her sword and leans to the side. *"Get ready, Jon!"*

"I'm ready, dammit, I'm ready!"

A telltale *whoomp* tickles my ears. I shout a warning but Lyra know the score—she swerves right, avoiding the gargoyle's breath by mere inches. Ironically, *I'm* the one who yelps and flinches. Erany—hanging off Lyra like a goddamn tree-branch—remains cool and calm. But even though she's extended sideways, her torso is still too high; she can't reach down and scoop the bullet with her sword.

"You're not low enough! How are you going to—"

So she kicks her right leg up and out, away from Lyra's flank. Her body follows, flipping upside down so her head is pointed directly at the ground.

"ERANY!" I lunge forward in reflexive panic, but she's stopped short by her entangled left leg.

Her legs now form an elongated V, almost into an inverted front-splits. Her left leg—lashed to the horse and resting along its back—keeps her from falling, while her outward-pointing right leg counter-balances her weight, stabilizing her body as she hangs upside down.

"I'm fine, Jon! It's called a death drag! Focus on the bullet!"

Jeezus! 'Death drag?' Couldn't they have picked a better-sounding name? Can't *believe* this woman! She's got bigger balls than—

Not important. Breathe, Jon—*breathe.*

The gargoyle behind us inhales deeply. It's going to be big—I can tell by the extra-loud *whoomp.* I try to warn her by screaming, *"ERANY!"* but she isn't listening.

"CATCH IT, JON!"

She twists a half-turn back with Legolas-worthy dexterity, then swipes the ground with her luminous blade. A high-toned *TING* rings crystal-clear, letting me know she just made contact. My arm reaches up, my thoughts fall away...

And I snatch the bullet out of the air.

Erany kicks her right leg down, turning right-side up and jacking back in the saddle. Lyra cuts left, avoiding the blast as it spills by our flank. I drop the bullet into Ailura, swinging the gun shut with a snap of my wrist.

"We're good!" I yell. *"Same as before!"*

Erany raises her sword and screams, *"Hai, Lyra! HAI!"*

Lyra rears back, kicking her feet and halting us in our tracks. Right on cue, the gargoyle shoots past our heads. As the wind from its passage ruffles my hair, I track it with a steady eye and a steadier hand.

This is it—it all comes down to this one last shot.

I pull the trigger.

And I miss.

35

The shot flies by the gargoyle's thigh, marking the night with a scrawl of energy.

"What do we do?" I scream. *"That was our last bullet! Erany, what do we—"*

"I don't know!" she screams back. *"We have to evade it until—"*

[Portal's open.] Alijyar booms into our minds. *[You ready to head back?]*

Erany blurts something in Elvish. I don't know what it means, but I get the gist: she's happy as hell we're getting out of Dodge.

[Alijyar!] I project. *[You showed up just in time!]*

[I'm gonna—hold on a second.]

A curious sensation crawls through my brain; the mental feel of him (his "Alijyar-ness" if you will) is right beside me, hand on my shoulder. My eyes move without conscious direction, and I immediately intuit he's seeing through them, assessing where we are in relation to him.

[Go past the concert but not past the dock. That's where the portal is.]

[What about Lyra?] Erany demands. *[Our horse, I mean. We can't bring her with us!]*

[Don't worry. I'll take care of her.]

The gargoyle interrupts with a brain-raking screech. Its gravel-throated breath scrapes into its lungs, then—

WHOOMP!

Lyra weaves, but not fast enough. The corrosive barrage nicks my shoulder, scalding me with a flare of white-hot pain. It quickly subsides into a stinging throb, leaving the skin around it raw and tender. No big. I'm still alive and relatively uninjured. Took a little damage, but—

My gaze settles on Erany's back. Sullen black flames are eating her hair.

"Stay still!" I shout. *"Your hair's on fire!"*

"WHAT?"

She tries to swing around, but I yell, *"STAY STILL!"* and hug her tightly, raising up so I can smother the flames against my chest. Ow—*HOT.* I can feel blisters forming beneath my collar.

"You're good!" I shout. *"It's out!"*

Our pursuer shoots by in a gray-shadow flash. This time, instead of trying to brake and cut, it banks around in a wide semicircle. It's playing it cool, making sure it doesn't expose itself to another bullet.

Won't be long before it knows I'm out.

I reach for Alijyar, infusing my telepathy with desperate panic. *[I'm out of bullets and there's one more gargoyle! It's going to kill us if we don't—]*

[Calm down. I'm right behind you.]

Erany glances over her shoulder. *[I thought you were at the portal, awaiting our—]* Her eyes widen in amazement. I turn in my seat and follow her gaze.

Holy. *Shit.*

My first impression is that Alijyar's sprinting, but it isn't really him. It's his glowing facsimile, comprised of sparkling blue dots that shape him into a glittering constellation.

I murmur, "Erany, are you seeing this?"

"I see it, Jon, I see it," she whispers.

And it's not just visual. There's a building sense of miraculous wonder, of reality bending in the best way possible.

We pivot toward the road and away from our pursuer. Don't think we'll shake it, but...

Hold on—it's homing in on Blue-dot Alijyar.

The Vagabond King (or his sparkly avatar, to be exact) accelerates into a cerulean blur, printing the night with a sapphire dazzle. As the wizard brightens and picks up the pace, the gargoyle folds its wings and prepares to dive.

And then Alijyar's climbing the air, as if he were ascending an invisible staircase. His avatar expresses a guttural roar—rrrr*rrr****RRR***—and flies straight at the gargoyle, scissoring his legs and connecting with his fist. Firecracker blasts erupt from the strike, etching fractal mosaics into the sky.

Alijyar lands with one knee down and the other knee up. A dozen yards behind him, the gargoyle's body hits the ground, shriveling into a hunk of cinder-threaded soot.

[The concert!] Alijyar's avatar waves us on. *[Ride past the concert!]*

Erany urges Lyra into a westward gallop. At the same time, sirens and shouts sound from behind us. There's the popo, coming to the rescue. Wonder what took them so lo—

Oh okay—I think I see why. Over the bay, patterned fireworks crack and pop, accompanied by a mess of drone-borne holograms. I'm guessing the cops weren't sure if we were part of the effects or an actual disturbance. (Magic everywhere, yet everyone's distracted by first-world illusions. Oh, the irony.)

Doesn't matter—we're almost there. The concert barricades come into view, linked together with chains and locks. Can't see who's singing, but...

An announcer roars, *"San Francisco, please welcome...TAYLOR SWIFT!"*

The crowd breaks out in raucous applause. The opening riff for *Style* begins playing, then its driving percussion kicks into gear.

Erany shouts, *"Ready, Lyra! Closer...closer..."*

Lyra bobs in time with her thunderous gallop. Her armored haunches coil beneath us, then—

"NOW!"

We power up and over the nearest barrier, landing amidst a handful of revelers. Lyra doesn't miss a beat; she swerves and cuts with expert precision, navigating the crowd with gymnastic ease. Forget trick-riding—this is horse parkour, boosted by magic and ignored by physics. Every so often, her hooves strike sparks off empty space, as if she was pushing off an unseen surface. Much to my delight, the crowd voices their approval.

"Yo, is that a *hologram?*"

"I can't wait for—*oh shit did you see that??? That horse just KICKED OFF THE AIR!*"

"She looks like Taylor, only with pointy ears!"

Erany draws her sword in a glittering flash. *"Wind at your back and sun on your brow! So say the Princess and the Prophesied Traveler!"*

I rack my brains, trying to think of what else I can add, but then she kisses me deeply from over her shoulder. I'm caught off guard, but the truest part of me knows exactly what to do—I close my eyes and return her kiss. As our hair flutters back in the brisk autumn wind, time slows to an exquisite crawl.

After a seeming eternity, we break our kiss and lock eyes, basking in the warmth of our heady embrace. Her perfect lips part and sigh, sending a delicious thrill coursing through me.

Apparently, my former crush is all about it. She takes a pause and shouts, *"LADIES AND GENTLEMEN, GIVE IT UP FOR MY BADASS LOOKALIKE!"*

The crowd roars, shaking my bones with deafening noise.

We kiss again, lost in a whirl of breath and heat. If you asked me right now if I wanted to marry/boyfriend/move in/whatever with Eralindíany Ailahdi, I would give you my answer without hesitation:

Yes. Yes to all of it. All I care about is being with her.

Initially, I was planning to take her for a night on the town, but I've changed my mind with an absolute vengeance. As far as date night goes, this right here is everything I wanted.

Everything I wanted and a damn sight more.

Best. First date. *Ever.*

36

The portal is right off the dock under Golden Gate Bridge, a nexus of color hanging in the air. Its center is marked by an electric blue core.

[HERE!] Alijyar is standing on the dock, a few yards back from the shimmering gateway. *[OVER HERE!]* His fingers are trembling in lurchy tics; he's keeping it open through sheer force of will.

"We're coming!" Erany shouts. *"We're coming, Alijyar!"*

[Hurry...UP...] He bows his head and clutches the air. Luminous cracks appear around him, accompanied by a series of sharp tearing sounds.

We swing around in a wide-looping left, softening into a right-hand turn before galloping onto the wooden dock. As Lyra's hooves rack the planks, I'm hit by a wave of visceral panic.

"Slow down!" I scream. *"Lyra's going in the water!"*

Alijyar shouts, *"I've got her!"* and palms Lyra's chest with both hands, like Superman halting an oncoming train.

As we fly off the saddle and into the portal, everything decelerates into soupy slow motion. I have plenty of time to gape and stare as Alijyar braces against Lyra's trunk. She's bearing down at full speed, but before she can push him into the bay, neon runes appear by his temples, and—

Holy. *Shitballs.*

—he digs his heels into the deck, shoulder-pressing several thousand pounds of charging equestrian.

For a hanging moment, they strike an iconic silhouette above the water.

Then it all comes apart at the existential seams. Details and contours waver and fragment, dissolving into a fog of sparkling motes. I can sense Alijyar beneath it all, guiding me and Erany with channeled intent. He's cupping us both in the palm of his mind, letting us shed our outward trappings.

And my God—it isn't scary or weird, it's the *exact opposite*. As I experience the epiphany that Jon is a story, a concept through which the True can flow its undying benevolence—

(we are temporary configurations of matter and light, vessels for expansion into perspective and novelty)

—I'm deluged by a storm of unchecked feeling, by countless variations of the force that forgot its omnipotence, all so it could revel in its rediscovery. *Love* is too poor a word to describe Its breadth. We try and capture It in rules or decrees, but it doesn't work, it never takes. We make ourselves fools in a no-lose game, because It can never be contained, It can never be threatened, It was in and around us *the entire time*—

—and then we're tumbling across the grass, lit by the moons of an Evermoor night. I roll several times before she ends up on top, pinning me down with her lilac eyes.

"Did you...what was..."

"I don't know." I stare back up at her, drinking in as much of her beauty as I possibly can. The memory of our crossing is starting to fade, but the mental feel of it is crystal clear. "We were riding on horseback, Taylor Swift gave you a shout-out..."

"It doesn't matter," she breathes. She takes my face in her hands and kisses me deeply.

Once again, I'm lost to the world—free of obligation and struggle and strife.

The warmth of her skin, the press of her lips, the sweet summer scent of her long blond hair...call me crazy, but kissing Erany is right on par with crossing the portal. Technically, it may not compare with folding and splitting the pillars of existence, but damned if it doesn't feel just as good, if not better.

And maybe that's the point. The True is always there, it's always present—at a concert, a wormhole, or in the sweetest embrace of your teenage life. It makes everything pointless in the best way possible.

Earth, Evermoor, the bleed between worlds...

Like she just said: it doesn't matter.

Epilogue

According to Erany, we've materialized in a place called the Aureate Pasture. Tallgrass savannah rolls in every direction, disrupted by the occasional village. Glassy blue trees line the gullies, bearing shiny red fruit that glows like rubies. Everything here is stunningly beautiful—an alien-flora remix of a Nat Geo photoshoot.

We decide to strike out for Elerica City (a two-month journey), since that's where we parted with our adventurer-friends. I ask if we can teleport, but she says that isn't an option unless you're a high-level mage. (Apparently, it was fairly common before the Fracture—the Tessellate allowed for group teleports, and even gave birth to a magical travel industry. That went away after Lyderea took power.)

I'm good with it—a two-month walk will be a welcome break.

On our third day, she brings up the topic of Laiddinic powers, but I make it clear the topic is off limits. I'm thoroughly enjoying our impromptu vacation, and I don't want to spoil it with world-changing destiny stuff.

Every so often, we come across an unarmored Knight. Their only badge of office is a sigil of the White-Veiled Queen—a crescent moon over a crossed pair of swords—sewn onto their feathered caps. They never stop to ask what we're doing; it's always a tip of a hat and a polite *May light find you in dark places*. (I get the impression they're the Evermoor equivalent of a small-town sheriff. The good kind, though—not a foul-crotched, *Deliverance*-style hillbilly from a Tarantino torture scene.)

We pass the time by chatting and laughing. Sometimes, we visit a local establishment to trade wares or dine at a tavern. Come nightfall, we settle down for fire and food, then a decent helping of wink-wink sexy time. (Don't be shocked—we're both adults).

Honestly, this is the happiest I've been since...well, ever, really.

———

Four weeks in, while we're chewing liftweed under a secluded tree, the boundless blue sky is interrupted by a dot.

"Erany." I rise slowly, keeping our visitor centered in my vision. *"Erany."* I reach out and grab her shoulder.

"Mmm?" She follows my gaze and straightens up. "What is..." She cranes forward, peering intently at it. "Some kind of bird...it appears to be made from metal and glass."

Damn—forgot all about her hawkeye vision.

"Get ready." She springs to her feet, shooing me off. "Stand apart, Jon. A pair of targets are better than one."

"Right." I scuttle away, watching nervously as she draws her sword. I grip my last enchanted dagger and get ready to throw it. (Wish she still had some arrows.)

The bird drifts close, flaring its wings to bleed off speed, then flaps twice and eases to the ground. Erany sheathes her blade and studies our guest.

"Erany?" I tense in place, ready to sprint to her rescue. (Yeah, I know—if rescues were needed, I'd be first in line and she'd be last).

Instead of answering, she runs a curled finger across its beak.

What the hell—if it was going to bite us or blast us with goo, it would have already done so. I sheathe my knife and head back over.

"Amazing," she breathes as my shadow falls across her face. "They spoke of these in Delán, but..."

"What is it?" I crouch down beside her.

Up close, it's something to behold. The wings are made from delicate sheaves; there's a granular sheen to each "feather." Its body is comprised of shiny plates, locked together through a complex arrangement of nuts and bolts. Its most stunning feature, however, are its gemstone eyes—they're lit by purple-blue magic that serve as its pupils.

My initial impression is that it belongs inside a rich person's house, but it would probably steal all the attention. A better place would be in a high-tech museum, guarded by invisible lasers and those metal slabs that slam-block the doors.

"It's an aviad," Erany murmurs. "A messenger mechanism from the Freehold Aeries. They fell out of use at the end of the Bright Age."

"A messenger mechanism?" I reach out and touch it, marveling in the feel of its clear-edged feathers. Wouldn't be surprised if they were lined with diamond.

Erany strokes the other wing. "Rimmed with a coat of icewind sable. Incredible."

"I'm guessing that's expensive?"

"Ridiculously so. This stone glaze—just the glaze, mind you—would command a year's worth of wages from the average tradesman."

"Wow." I whistle appreciatively. "Four times more than a diamond ring."

" 'Diamond?' " She gives me a quizzical look.

"An Earthling stone that signifies love. It's supposed to cost three months' salary." I laugh self-consciously. "It's kinda backwards because they don't have much inherent value. A hundred years ago, a company boosted their price with a deceptive marketing campaign, but people still buy 'em because—"

"People are people," she sighs. "Fill their bellies and woo them with riches, and they'll veer toward the easiest path, even if it leads to darkness and suffering."

"Um, yeah." I try to think of a positive response, but nothing comes to mind. "Guess it's the same on both our worlds."

She's isn't listening; she's poking and prodding our mechanical friend. "They're designed to carry missives and items, but I don't see a way to—"

Suddenly, machine-driven buzzing arises from its belly. Its beak opens and closes in repetitive flickers, then it starts talking in a rickety voice: "I am the whole of my parts, made and renewed through fracture and unity. Speak the phrase that describes my fullness."

"Some kind of riddle." Erany's forehead crinkles in puzzlement. (I stifle the random urge to kiss the hell out of her). "Whole of my parts...made and renewed through fracture and unity..."

The answer flies from my mouth without any thought. " 'Be dust upon your breath.' "

The aviad's belly sections open, splitting down the middle and splaying outward into banded strips. Inside, a roll of parchment sits on a vise, surrounded by an assortment of gears and rods.

Nice—clockwork art with a steam punk twist.

"Strange to see such Bright Age beauty...strange but welcome." She plucks the scroll from the aviad's torso. "Lean close, Jon."

I shuffle closer, pressing gently against her (I'm still teenager enough to delight in the warmth of her body), and examine the parchment. It seems to be English, only super stylized and calligraphic.

"Sorry." I shrug. "I can't read it. Well, maybe a little, but not enough to understand."

Her lips move silently as she mouths the words, tempting me again to kiss the hell out of her. (Random turn-ons are the strangest things.)

"It was written by Gyrax," she says. "He wants to meet us at Glimmersend." In response to my inquisitively raised eyebrow, she explains, "a trading hub." She continues scanning the parchment. "Lyderea declared war against the Freecast Territories. They deadlocked her Knights at Algulis Devari, where both sides entrenched their forces.

"A no-man's land."

"Aye."

"What are the Freecast Territories?"

"From the context, I'm guessing they're a modern-day version of the Juric Unity."

"That's good...I think?"

"I hope so."

"Where's Glimmersend?"

"Five days travel on a westward heading. Hold." She finishes reading the rest of the scroll.

"No," she murmurs. "Impossible."

"What? What is it?"

"The date on this missive..." She covers her mouth. "Jon, we've only been gone for *two days.* But according to this message, it's been over a *year.*"

My mind goes blank. Off in the distance, a couple of birds sing and chirp.

"But...but..." I press my palms against my forehead. "That doesn't make sense. How can...we were just..."

She regains her composure. "Travel between planes is not without consequence."

"Glimmersend." I rise to my feet, resolving to freak out later when she isn't watching. "We're going to Glimmersend. What about the aviad?" I glance uncertainly at the exquisite bird. "It feels wrong to just leave it in the open."

Erany claps her thighs and rises alongside me. "Pity. I was enjoying our stretch of peace and quiet." She puts her hands on her hips and regards the bird. "The aviad will find its way to its sender. And if it doesn't..." She shrugs in defeat. " 'Tis a hoary relic of a bygone era. Perhaps it is meant to rust and decay."

"I hope not."

"Time will tell. And Jon."

"Yes?"

"Be wary. We know little of the events that occurred in our absence. Are you ready to step off?"

"Lead the way, Princess."

She responds with a smile. We begin heading west.

Thus begins my next side quest.

Afterword

My first foray into young adult fiction!

I hope it went well (meaning I hope you enjoyed it.) If you've read my other books *(Kor'Thank* or *Echo)* you know that I litter my stories with profanity, philosophy, and a building escalation into excitement and/or absurdity. With *The Unbound Realm,* I decided to go a different route.

Much like Jon, I've completed some literary side quests of my own. In *Echo,* I wanted to write about enlightenment amidst a deluge of action and dystopian backdrop. In *Kor'Thank,* I wanted to write comedically while honoring a bevy of teenage adventure tropes: horror movie monsters, prom night shenanigans, and the predictable yet utterly welcome scene where the bullies receive their just rewards. (And yeah—if you read *Kor'Thank,* you know those are just the basic ingredients; I tried to whip them up into something altogether different.)

The Unbound Realm comes with a different set of challenges. Unlike before, when I lashed my stories together with all the logic I could possibly muster, I'm trying to write this more from the gut. Do I know how it ends? I do. But unlike my other stuff, I'm not gonna stress over every little detail out of fear I'll drop the ball. (Yep—that's how I wrote *Echo* and most of *Kor'Thank,* sad to say).

Back to my side quests. Aside from some gross-ass ads on my online blog (dirtyscifibuddha.com) I've never written from a first-person perspective. This is the first time I've done it in a novel-length manuscript.

Boom—side quest completed.

My next quest is toning down the swearing (this is a YA novel, after all). The Motion Picture Association of America has imposed some arbitrary rules concerning cusswords—rules I shall use as a rough guide. I'm going for a PG-13/TV-14, which means I can throw in the lesser offenders, but only one F-bomb, which in no way can reference sex. (Not really sure where I'm going to use it, or if I'll use it at all. That scene in season 3 of *Cobra Kai* was kind of jarring when a bullied kid yells "He kicked the f--king *shit* out of me!")

Is this a stupid set of rules? Arguably. But society's been shaped by the MPAA, so rather than rail against those finger-wagging over-lords, I'll swallow my objections and focus on writing.

There's a couple other quests, but let me get to the main one, which is to write a sprawling fantasy-world epic. (Emphasis on the word *sprawling.*) This first volume is narrower in scope than I would have liked, but I hope to remedy that in the coming books. Much like the Gunslingers from the Dark Tower saga (or Frodo and his merry band of adventurers) I want Jon and his friends to travel far and wide, to meet strange and wondrous foes and friends.

To that end, I'm evaluating a mess of ideas and notions. A friendly ogre who's a little slow because he took a dagger to the brain and it's still right there, sticking visibly out of his dome. A magic mirror that holds the key to the future. Epic battles with dragons and serpents, galleys and warships. At least one more trip back to Earth. Death, redemption, and the temptation to condemn existence and take it out on the world.

Or something along those lines. We'll see how it goes.

Instead of planning every little twist, I'm going to *feel* my way through, much like Jon is doing. Yeah, I'll have to fire up the hamster-on-a-wheel that serves as my brain when I go through my second, third, and umpteenth drafts, but unless I'm editing, I'm really gonna focus on *feeling* the story. It's the next logical step in my evolution as a writer: over the last few years, I've become something of a "pantser," (in writing circles, that's someone who writes by the seat of their pants). Without consciously intending to, I've followed in the steps of my literary spirit animal: Stephen King. He too, has a couple of scenes and concepts that hit him out of the imaginal blue, then he writes his way toward them without overthinking it.

So now you understand: my literary ideas are just random scenes that arise in my head, waiting their turn to go from dream into story.

Which is all well and good, but right now, I've gotta *edit this book.* As of yet, I haven't explained what the Unbound Realm is, or why Jon can fix Evermoor if he ever reaches it. So I have to go allllll the way back to the earlier chapters, draft that in, smooth it out, and repeat ad nauseum. I've reached the point where the real work begins—I'm gonna re-read the manuscript over and over, trying to bind it into a seamless flow.

When the dust settles, I envision three books, possibly four. (I had the same idea for *Echo*—volumes two and three were originally going to be one book—but the second took on a life of its own and became the mother of all gunfights.)

As far as what the future might hold, I believe Jon and his friends are going to acquire two more items of great power and immense consequence. I'm going to throttle down my five hundred words a day to two hundo, maybe two and a half, so I can focus on editing.

The adventure will continue in *The Unbound Realm, Volume 2: Weapons of Old.*

Stay tuned. If you're a writer, I wish you inspired drafting and insightful editing!

Kent Wayne,

January 9, 2021

A Note From The Author

At the time of this writing, I have authored a four-book science fiction series called *Echo,* as well as a high school absurdical (yes—that's a made-up word) called *Kor'Thank: Barbarian Valley Girl.* If you like pew-pew warrior stuff with cybernetics, psychic powers, and existential spiritual implications, check out *Echo.* If you like an R-rated version of Calvin and Hobbes where a psychotic cheerleader and a barbarian king switch bodies, all while an angry teen-genius and his master strategist friend race to save the world from an extra-dimensional horror, check out *Kor'Thank.*

My website is dirtyscifibuddha.com.

Thanks for reading!

www.ingramcontent.com/pod-product-compliance
Lightning Source LLC
Chambersburg PA
CBHW070721010826
48977CB00006B/164